The three pe
to kiss or bite
against his featu
vitreous humour spattered into his gaping mouth.

He woke up choking, sweating, staring at the daylight.

'*Faugus, massius, in vos cavaribus laudec . . .*'

Only as he made the effort and swung his feet out of bed did he realise that the chant was lingering, echoing, still calling from his nightmare in the dawn.

Also by Bernard King from Sphere:

WITCH BEAST
THE DESTROYING ANGEL
TIME-FIGHTERS
SKYFIRE

Blood Circle

BERNARD KING

SPHERE BOOKS LIMITED

A SPHERE Book

First published in Great Britain by Sphere in 1990

Typeset by Selectmove Ltd, London
Reproduced, printed and bound in Great Britain by
Cox & Wyman Ltd, Reading

ISBN 0 7474 0416 X

Sphere Books Ltd
A Division of
Macdonald & Co (Publishers) Ltd
Orbit House
1 New Fetter Lane
London EC4A 1AR

A member of Maxwell Macmillan Pergamon Publishing Corporation

To H. with love and gratitude
for secrets kept and pieces picked up.

Many thanks to Aubrey Melech for access to much unpublished research material, and to himself and his publisher, Sut Anubis Books, for permission to quote from *Missa Niger: La Messe Noire*.

Although this is a work of fiction many of the events described in its progress, and several of the procedures attributed to the Sons of Samael, are based on actual fact. The characters, however, are all fictitious, as are the companies. This is not a true story so far as I know, but things very like it could be happening right now.

There can be little doubt that the dark spirit of Satanism is with us today as strongly as it has ever been in the past. Indeed, we must not doubt that this is so. Whilst it has never again reached the peak of organized criminality that it enjoyed in Guibourg's time, at least not openly, who is to say that there is not some dreadful Satanic underground which plays its part in controlling the lives and beliefs of the creatures trapped within its coils?

Aubrey Melech, *Missa Niger: La Messe Noire*

Time was

1

SHE CAME HERE quite often. That old book of grandma's that she'd found on the shelf called for all manner of flowers and herbs, and this was one of the best places around for finding them. They grew wild between the forgotten gravestones and table tombs, twining in with the ivy which had spread itself across the remaining stonework of the ruined church.

The ache of her father's death had subsided since they came to live with her grandfather. The change of surroundings had done her good, and the old herbal beauty book of grandma's had given her an interest she'd never had before. Little by little she was learning to know the different plants by their leaves as well as their fruits and flowers, to know which did what when, and how to conserve what she wanted from them in between.

It was already the end of April and she had to remember to say 'White Rabbits' before she said anything else to anybody in the morning. You always said 'White Rabbits' on the first of the month. It gave you some of their luck. Even granpa said rabbits were lucky.' That there mixymertosie should ha' wiped they out, bhuy.'

So she should have been in bed. She'd done this lots of times, creeping out when the rest of the house was asleep to gather what she wanted. Somehow there was never time on the way to or from school, not with helping her mother and talking to her grandfather about the lavender and the other things he grew. That was why she crept out in her night-dress and cut through the wood from the farmhouse, her special plastic bag in her hand.

The old church and the sleeping, forgotten dead which surrounded it, held no terrors for her. It was too much of a place of wonder, a special place, to be frightening. And on nights like tonight, when the moon was close around full, though it was actually past full and waning at present, the herbs and flowers, their petals closed up for the night, were fresh with night-dew and, in their resting, immune to the pain which picking them in daylight would have caused. You had to thank them for being there, and respect them even as you took their lives away. That much was only right. They'd work the better for you if you did things properly.

Her mother encouraged her interest in natural cosmetics. It kept her interested in things around the farm instead of off in the village, doing Christ knew what with the local boys. Rough farmers' sons and labouring types. Not right for her daughter. Not at all. Besides, she was still only fifteen, and fifteen was too young to be doing things like that. Mother had been pregnant too early, even though she was over thirty at the time. Her child had kept her from the heady pleasures of the sixties, the joys of flowers in your hair and dope-smoke in your lungs. Yes, her little daughter had cheated her of that last chance to be young, and it was only right that she should

4

finish growing up before those rams got at her, wasn't it?

Oh, they talked about it at school. They whispered about what Merrill and Pete did in the back of Pete's old van. And about Georgina. And Pauline, who always had those funny bruises on her neck and once, changing for gym, had shown off the one beside her left nipple as well. But this one didn't know *all* about it yet. The flowers of the field had seen to that.

Tonight she was after Sweet Cicely. She'd spotted it last time, small white tufts of flowers growing almost a yard high in that far corner by the broken wall, divided leaves and reddish stalks. Her bag had been full, then, and she hadn't been entirely certain what it was, so she'd only picked a flower and a leaf to take home and identify. Now she knew what it was for certain. *Chaerophyllum Sativum* was the proper name, but they liked to call it Chervil and Sweet Cicely as well. People knew what you were talking about if you used the common names. They didn't think you were a stuck-up little bitch like Mary Corder was. Nobody liked Mary Corder.

She already knew what she was going to use it for. It would steep in oil for a while, then reduce into an ointment for Pauline's birthday in July. It worked wonders with bruises if you did that with it, and Pauline was always saying how she didn't like her gran to see her bruises because she got into trouble with the old lady if she did.

Pauline was a big girl. She laughed when you mentioned her bruises. 'Yeah,' she'd say, winking to her friend Georgina. ''Ass ruyt, *bruises*.' Then she'd laugh some more.

If she'd gone round by the road she might have seen the car parked by the entrance to the churchyard. As it was it was shielded by the hedgerow, so she didn't know it was there until afterwards.

Coming from the woods she crossed over the southern side of the churchyard and picked her way through the ruin, holding her long night-dress up above her knees to stop it tearing on anything, her calves and feet protected by rubber boots. The night was warm and she'd not bothered to put anything else on. Nobody was going to see her and she wasn't going to be cold. Even if she lost some heat while she was filling her plastic bag she could easily make it up again by running home through the wood. As she passed the broken chancel arch she thought she heard something. It sounded like a hymn without music, though she couldn't make out the words. They sounded foreign.

By the time she'd stopped to listen she could already see where the sound was coming from. A hooded figure, its body wrapped in a long garment like a monk's robe, was holding a burning torch aloft and chanting softly to the night. In the light from the torch she thought she could see bone in the depths of its cowl.

A phantom? A demon?

Her heart pounded with the recollection of Christmas ghost stories, recounted by candlelight in her grandfather's most sinister voice. If the figure was truly skull-faced then it couldn't be alive. Yet its hand, the hand on the end of the arm which held the torch aloft, was human and ordinary enough. That meant it was either a trick of the wavering light or the person under the hood was wearing a mask. Maybe that was why the chanting was so muted and she couldn't make the words out.

The reasoning, though, came later. Too much was happening all at once for her to sort out the various elements at the time. The robed figure wasn't alone. On the fringe of the circle of torchlight, wavering about it, was a table tomb, its flat surface obscured by the wriggling, gasping, intertwined shapes above it.

6

Two people with no clothes on. A man and a woman. No, a boy and a girl. Or a young man and a girl, anyway a familiar girl with distorted features.

Locked together. *Doing it.*

That had to be the explanation. This was what Pete and Merrill did in the van. *This.* Slamming their crotches together like *this.* And his bigness going in and out, making her groan, making him cry out as she groaned. And the figure with the torch still chanting, not even bothering to watch.

That was probably the most unnatural thing about it.

Fifteen-year-old Andrea, however, had to watch. She might never see anything like this again in her entire life. It shocked her, frightened her, but it fascinated her as well. The hand holding up her night-dress moved higher of its own volition. It began to stroke, to penetrate.

Andrea began to moan as well.

The chanting continued, but the hand holding the torch moved its revealing light towards her. The woman on the tombstone didn't notice, but the man did. Still pumping, still pounding towards his climax, he turned to face her where she stood, mouth slack with her own growing, consuming pleasure, eyes glazing, beyond noticing the tableau before her.

Slowly she noticed him looking at her. He had a young face, a handsome face with blue eyes and a frame of long fair hair. Yet there was a quality in his features Andrea didn't like, a quality which, though indefinable, brought her back to consciousness of where she was and what she was watching.

And what she was doing. To herself.

With a final, exaggerated thrust Ennio Zabetti spurted his seed into his partner's waiting womb. She had been chosen to be fertile, to be ready to receive it and conceive from it, and she would. But standing there, suddenly panic-stricken, on that particular May-Eve in her life, Andrea Duncan didn't know that. It would be almost her lifetime round again before she did.

The plastic bag floated down into the grass, forgotten. The Sweet Cicely remained on the other side of the table tomb, untouched. Ennio's eyes continued to stare at her, only slightly glazed by his exertions. They were hard, and cruel, and inviting.

She dropped her night-dress. It settled back about her legs. Then stretched and folded and creased as she began to run.

She ran for the road. Its metalled surface was hard beneath the rubber soles of her boots but familiar and normal and comforting. She took some perverse pleasure in the movement of her thighs as she ran past the parked car, big car, expensive car on the roadside. Suddenly the wild places she'd always loved, the wood and the overgrown churchyard, were alien and hostile. Their charm had vanished with her childhood.

But they would continue to haunt her, just the same. As the dreams were to haunt her for the rest of her life.

To begin with the dreams were merely confusing and unpleasant, jumbled memories of that night mixed with a young girl's fantasies of ways in which it might have developed, had she stayed, had she been seen earlier, had she been the one upon the altar. And guilt rode with them through the hours of darkness, guilt at the way she had behaved, the way she'd touched herself, become involved with whatever foulness was being enacted before her. It had all been too easy, too shameful, and Andrea was fully aware, from her experiments since, that she must have been very ready for what she'd done.

Those, however, were merely the first of Andrea's dreams. As the months went by others began to creep past them, others that were just as chilling, as shameful, yet less defined. Babies wailed. Friends disappeared. Robed figures chanted in her night by the light of flickering torches. Once the head of the young man she would one day know as Ennio burst from the belly of a pregnant friend and laughed at her. She woke up screaming that time, knowing her hands were red and sticky and wondering how they came to be that way.

She plunged herself determinedly into life, into her interests and schoolwork and mother and grandfather and the farm. But that night in the churchyard evil had crept into her experience. Not the simple rivalries and jealousies of young girls with their friends, the meanness and spite and petty hatreds of growing up, but something more tangible. Something that had crept past the flowers of the fields and the herbs of the hedgerow. Something that was not to come full circle for many years to come.

2

Daily Telegraph, Friday 7th January 1977. Page 3.
MUTILATED GIRL FOUND IN HEDGEROW.
POLICE IN KING'S Lynn disclosed today that the body of a teenaged girl has been discovered concealed in a hedgerow near the village of East Bilney.

The body was discovered by retired resident Mr Eric Penrose whilst he was walking his labrador on Wednesday evening. 'You can imagine what a shock it was,' he said. 'Judy is always going off and exploring things, but this time her behaviour called me over to take a look as well.'

The body, which was naked, proved to be that of a girl of sixteen or seventeen who had been seriously mutilated about the head and neck. A preliminary forensic examination showed that she had recently given birth. No clue as to her identity has so far been forthcoming and police are checking lists of missing persons and conducting local enquiries in an effort to establish her identity. Other lines of investigation are being pursued in an effort to establish her attacker, who must be regarded as both armed and dangerous.

Time is

3

THE FIRST TIME Andrea saw Ringley Abbey she was
almost overwhelmed by its sheer presence. Josh had
dropped hints, of course. He'd always been good at dropping
hints, few of which were ever subtle. Come to that there was
very little that could be described as subtle about Josh.

He was a big man, almost a foot taller than Andrea's
five feet five, and heavy boned. His physical presence,
now approaching grossness in middle-age, seemed to lend
strength to his will, and there was very little in either his
private or business life that Josh failed to achieve.

'Think it'll do the job?' he asked her, grinning.

She reached out a gloved hand and gently touched the
walnut of the dash in front of her. Beside her, behind
the wheel, looking enormous in his heavy Burberry, her
husband was expecting an answer, and he wasn't going to
wait for ever.

'I . . . I don't know what to say,' Andrea told him,
ambiguously. Then: 'Won't you keep knocking your head
on the beams?'

If she'd opened almost any work on English medieval architecture Andrea would most certainly have seen a picture of Ringley Abbey. The bulk of the house was covered with early sixteenth-century features, including an oriel window extending up to roof level above the semi-circular entrance porch with its twin arches. Some parts looked even earlier, including two or three of the turret chimneys which broke up the irregular roofline still further. One wall appeared to have been created from a series of bricked-up cloister-arches, and was the only real indication on the outside that the house had ever served any ecclesiastical purpose.

Josh shook his head. 'One or two of the back stairs and galleries are quite low, but they're the Tudor additions. The Abbots built for space, so's they could impress the peasants in the hovels round about.'

'It would certainly do that.'

They were approaching the Abbey from the east, and the low morning sun of a frosty February day was staining ancient stone and brickwork an almost uniform orange-yellow, reflecting off the irregular glazing of the windows in bursts of erratic dazzle.

So far they had viewed it only from the road, through the screen of rimed and leafless aspens which normally concealed it throughout the spring and summer months. Now Josh swung the wheel, turning the BMW into the long gravel drive. A small sign which simply stated PRIVATE was attached to one of the fence-posts, but there were no gates at the entrance. The drive had been cut lower than the level of the grounds to either side, and its edges banked up, grey-green with brittle grass, to the stark, bare tangle of the shrubs which lined it above. At the first turn, set in the bank, a green-painted wooden upright failed to blend with its more wintery surroundings.

14

'Electric eye,' Josh explained. 'Anyone coming ʌ, far sets off an alarm in the house. Better than gates.'

Andrea wasn't sure about that. Wandering sheep or cattle could trip the alarm any time of day or night. Even a large dog at four in the morning could have been kept out by a gate and left her in peace.

With her nightmares.

At the very least, she decided, the exterior of Ringley Abbey gave it a presence in the landscape which was impossible for her mother's mock-Georgian house in Slough, or even Josh's present St John's Wood address, to achieve. Its isolation seemed to parallel, perhaps even to mirror, her own private estrangement from the rest of humanity. Even from Josh.

He'd be away most of the time, she told herself. She'd be mistress here, controlling everything like Vathek's mother in the Gothic novel. Brooding and feeding off her inner darkness in a personal Castle of Otranto.

She reached over and touched his arm as the car reached level ground and the Abbey came into sight again, closer and more desirable, even with its range of stockbroker-Tudor outbuildings huddled to one side like architectural carbuncles. 'It's lovely, Josh,' she whispered.

'Your personal Strawberry Hill, eh?'

She wondered if his pleasure was derived from her own, or if it was merely the vindication of his will triumphant yet again. Maybe that was why he still attracted her, because there was a dark need to dominate which matched something she felt within herself.

He parked the car some yards from the main entrance beneath the oriel window and walked round to open her door. 'Come on,' he instructed, 'we'll walk up to the house. I want you to take in the feel of it.'

Andrea was already beginning to do that for herself. Not unfriendly, yet too forbidding to be exactly welcoming, Ringley Abbey had squatted on its site, a monster waiting to be fed with its inhabitants, for six hundred years. The impressions it gave to those who approached it varied with their personalities. For Josh it was a final mark of status, the country pile. For Andrea it could be either island or tomb, a place of sanctuary or the entrance to a mental vault from which she might never emerge. Here she could be either happy or destroyed.

Or destroying.

He walked her, slowly, his arm through hers, with the frosted gravel complaining underfoot. The world was February-cold and their breath steamed. The Abbey looked February-cold, its welcome as chilling as a corpse-embrace. Beside her, Josh's free hand, still sheathed in a driving glove, fumbled against the heavy material of his pocket for the keys. To one side of the oriel a demonic corbel leered down at their approach, licking its devilish graven lips in unholy anticipation. Andrea caught its weathered eye and licked her own lips back at it, unsmiling, deadly serious, then pouted as the corbel seemed to turn its glance away.

No house was going to master Andrea Buchanan. Not even Ringley Abbey.

Josh found the keys, tied to their paper tag, and fitted one into a black iron mortice lock in the glazed, arched door. He turned it, withdrew it, then repeated the operation with a Yale higher up. Before he opened the door he sorted out a small, white metal key and held it ready.

Grasping the handle of the mortice lock he pushed the door inwards and strode into the hall, crossing it with rapid strides. His leather soles echoed as they slapped down onto the flagstones. Andrea followed, more slowly, her eyes drawn upwards to the timbered

16

roof two storeys above. No wonder that hall echoed so much.

Then she felt the warmth.

Opening another door at the far end of the hall Josh disappeared briefly, then re-emerged. 'Twenty seconds to shut the alarm off,' he said flatly. 'It can take a bit of doing until you get used to it.'

Andrea wasn't listening. Instead she was pulling off her thick Jaeger beret and letting her hair fall free. The long bob she wore it in wasn't particularly fashionable, as she was in a better position than most to know, but it suited her features so she kept it. Not quite to her shoulders, the strands bent haphazardly against the collar of her sheepskin overcoat, coppery-brown against the creaminess of the fleece. Her face remained immobile but her eyes, never quite as large as she would have liked them to be without make-up, widened a little in surprise.

Ringley Abbey was warm. Welcomingly warm. Not at all the cold, forbidding, long-socks-and-Iceland-slippers temperature she had expected.

'Andy? You listening to me?'

Take no notice, the beamed roof whispered down to her. It's of little consequence to us.

'Sorry. Josh?'

'I was telling you about the alarm.'

He reiterated and she appeared to be listening, trying hard to keep her gaze from wandering up away from his face, away from that inspection of his deepening wrinkles she always undertook when she wanted to appear attentive. Andrea didn't hear him the second time either. She was listening to that other voice, that whispering from overhead.

Take no notice, Andrea. He'll pass.

Welcome home.

Her husband took her hand as she loosened her coat, surrendering herself to the warmth of the Abbey's welcome. 'Upstairs first,' he told her. 'I'm going to save the best for last.'

'Josh, why is it so warm? It ought to be freezing in an old place like this. 'Specially in February with it standing empty for months.'

'Oh, that. There's an old boy in the village who used to work here. I laid in some fuel and dropped him a few quid to keep the boiler going. He's been cooking the walls ever since Christmas for me.'

He led her across to the wide Jacobean staircase, its dark oak almost black against the pale distemper of the walls. The boards creaked and rose unevenly beneath her feet. On the half-landing she paused, holding him back while she looked up to the beams and then down to the flagged floor of the hall some twelve feet below her.

'Come along,' Josh insisted.

They toured the first floor rooms, then made their way up to the attics to the north of the entrance hall, chill little rooms with exposed roof-timbers in place of ceilings. Bare of furniture as they were it was almost impossible to visualise what any of the rooms would look like once they were inhabited. Of what she saw only the bedroom to the left of the main staircase took Andrea's attention, with its arched window and linen-fold wainscoting. And on the outside, to the oriel side of that arch, Andrea realised, that leering corbel was by now wondering what to expect from her presence.

'My room,' she told Josh, determinedly.

They didn't sleep together any more. Not from lack of passion, but because Josh found his wife to be a noisy sleeper, talking and calling out from the depths of her vivid dreams. At least she'd sold her chain of beauty salons shortly after they'd got together. But he still had enough interests to need all the sleep he could get if he was going to maintain his extra-curricular activities as well. Whilst he was in love with and proud of his wife it was not in Josh Buchanan's nature to be monogamous. Besides, what Andrea didn't know wasn't going to hurt her. Or him, for that matter.

'We could do with at least one extra bathroom up there,' she told him as they came back down the main staircase.

Josh nodded. 'One at the end of the first floor corridor. And I'll have two fitted en suite in the larger guest rooms.'

'Do I get the impression you intend to do more entertaining than we've been doing in the past?'

'Not so much that, Andy. More that we're far enough from town for dinner guests to want to stay over. We might have the odd weekend party, though. There's some shooting rights go with the property.

'Now,' he continued, steering her towards the inner end of the entrance hall, 'see what you think of this.'

He opened a comparatively modest door and ushered her through. The leather heels of her boots clicked and worried at the tiled floor. Several paces in she stopped and turned slowly round.

'My god,' she whispered.

'Interesting little room, isn't it?' Josh remarked.

To call it a room was rather like comparing the Empire State Building to a terraced cottage. Once the refectory of Ringley Abbey, the main hall rose through two storeys before a heavily beamed ceiling blocked off the slope of the roof towards its apex. Above were the attics. The west wall consisted of a series of arches glazed into windows running from just above floor level to the height of the hall. Along these, as along the two end walls, a minstrel gallery bisected their height. Beneath this at either end sat tall fireplaces set flush into the thickness of the walls, each headed with a lintel worked with quatrefoil tracery. Only the floor, a geometric Victorian design of red and ochre quarry tiles, marred the general medieval appearance of the massive chamber. Even the carved wainscoting, though obviously a later addition, was entirely in keeping with the overall effect.

Her eyes swept up to the distant corners, tracing its lines. It felt cooler than the other parts of the house she'd seen so far, but not unwelcoming.

'Make a lounge–diner, d'you reckon?'

At the very least, Andrea thought. You could hold a fair-sized dance in here. With a small orchestra providing the music.

'Need a couple of fair-sized pictures here and there,' Josh continued, joining her in the centre of the hall and gesturing. 'Battle of Begorrah, that sort of thing. I'll have a word with Tony Fluter.'

'Forget the pictures, Josh. How the hell are we going to furnish it? The whole house, I mean? Even if we emptied our old place and my mother's it'd still look like a half-finished museum.'

'Leave the worrying to me,' he smirked, annoyingly. 'I promise you won't be disappointed.'

Oh god, she thought. He's got something up his sleeve again. Another bloody surprise I'll have to look grateful for.

To be fair, she conceded, she usually approved of Josh's surprises. He worked hard to make sure that she would. Keep the little woman happy, he believed, and she won't start asking too many awkward questions about those nights in town. And nothing kept Andrea happy like style and status.

Like Ringley Abbey was going to.

* * *

They'd been married nearly three years now. Josh was still delighted with his ornament and Andrea, somehow never able to give herself entirely, had settled for displays of affection which her husband read as something deeper. It wasn't her fault, she kept reminding herself. It was all down to that bastard she'd had an affair with before Josh came on the scene. She'd been financially comfortable long before that, with the days of shampoo-wet hands well and truly behind her. Smart guesses and common sense had made her specialise her beauty salons towards the older clients, picking her staff to suit them and running a home-visit service as well. The young took care of their looks themselves. It wasn't until they passed thirty that they considered the luxury of having it done for them. And when they did there was an Andrea Duncan Salon waiting just for them, be it high street frontage or in-store concession.

She and Josh Buchanan were only recently married when the offer for her chain had come from a leading cosmetics manufacturer. Her solicitor managed to build in a deal licensing her name, making sure of a generous royalty on each new product. At twenty-nine Andrea Buchanan née Duncan was a very wealthy woman in her own right, though she was careful to conceal the true extent of her wealth, even from her husband.

He can do the providing, she considered. He can afford it. I'll settle for the role of a dutiful wife. For now.

The only permanence in Andrea's life was what she'd made for herself. Her father had died on her twelfth birthday, drenching her presents with tears and rendering the cake inedible. Her mother, deprived of his income, had sold their comfortable home in Woodbridge and taken Andrea to live on her grandfather's farm near King's Lynn, where the summer fields were mauve and purple with Norfolk lavender. She could still remember his dry old voice telling her that it took nearly a hundred pounds of lavender to still out an ounce of strong-smelling essential oil.

Her interest in beauty treatments and cosmetics had grown out of those days. Though not a beautiful child she quickly learned how to make the most of herself, and how to improve the appearance of those around her. She left school at sixteen and worked in a salon in Hunstanton, before borrowing enough money for a small third-hand hatchback and the equipment to offer a freelance home service. By the time she could afford to open her first salon her reputation was already established and there was sufficient work and profit to risk a second. She spread down the Norfolk coast, catering for holidaymakers by taking on extra staff in the summer months, and by twenty-four her first London salon, off Kentish Town Road, was open and Andrea Duncan Salons were creeping down through Camden Town towards the West End.

Then she met Tim Garfield.

The break into the West End was going to be the biggest gamble of her business career. Whilst there was no shortage of smart money prepared to back her she also knew that word of mouth, her chief source of customers so far, wasn't going to be good enough in the heart of the forbidding and impersonal metropolis. Of the agencies bidding for her account Quinton Benson Burrell came out on top. Smart, sharp and deadly in the marketplace, QBB hacked out a campaign aimed at Andrea's ideal clientele which worked to perfection. Their most telling stroke, however, was to assign Tim Garfield as Account Executive.

Tall. Blond. Elegant. Just enough little boy in his features to prevent him being a Clint Eastwood clone. Impeccable Oxford accent which complemented, rather

than contrasted with, Andrea's remaining trace of East
Anglian drawl. And sufficient charm to have kept the
Titanic afloat after the iceberg.

Yuppie didn't fit. Neither did whizz-kid. The thing was,
Tim Garfield had real ability, not just agency hype, behind
him. He was bloody good, Andrea conceded. And she was
too busy being successful to realise how lonely she was. Up
until then.

It was the sort of situation of which old Frank, her
grandfather, would have said: 'It'll aynd en teers, bhuy.'
He called everone *bhuy*, including his patently female
granddaughter. And had he still been alive he'd have
shaken his head sadly to be proved right.

They genuinely liked one another, and they were both
hard-headed enough to keep their personal feelings out
of their business relationship for several months. Several
months, though, wasn't long enough. The attraction was
too mutual, too compelling, to keep them out of bed any
longer. Both soon realised that they were becoming friends
as well as lovers. For Andrea, unwilling to commit herself
before her ambitions were fully realised, it was too much.

She always told herself that the break-up was Tim's fault,
that he tried to pressure her into something she wasn't
ready for. That came close to the truth, but it wasn't all
of it. In her heart she knew that she needn't have turned
down his proposal, that she was already on the threshold
of the success the little girl from Woodbridge had craved
since her father's death. Yet she couldn't say yes, and
deep inside she wasn't adult enough to simply maintain
the relationship until she could. She had to kill her love
with a torrent of insults and abuse which came from her
head, not from her heart.

Within days Tim Garfield allowed himself to be head-
hunted by one of QBB's most persistent rivals. Andrea

still glimpsed him occasionally, across Stringfellows or on the other side of the upper room in L'Escargot. Sometimes their eyes spoke together, but their voices never did.

From then on her social life was full but not fulfilling. Her West End gamble paid off and the salons spread to Kensington and Knightsbridge, attracting more and more attention from manufacturers eager to have an Andrea Duncan endorsement. She held off, determined to go for the package that would set her up comfortably for the rest of her life. When she finally knew it was on the way she said yes to Josh. So he wasn't Tim Garfield. He was comfortable, instead, and he appreciated her without ever being too demanding. It was good enough.

Another bloody surprise to be grateful for.

He led her into the other rooms on the ground floor, all humble by comparison with the main hall. She nodded and ooed in appropriate places. They ended up in the kitchen, which was adequate but would need completely refitting, then went down to the cellars, probably the oldest parts of the ancient Abbey, where wine-snob Josh was going to store and age his treasures in temperature-controlled surroundings.

'This is the best, Josh?' she asked him.

'Hmm?'

'You said you were saving the best until last.'

'Oh, you mean the bit I didn't pay for.'

He was grinning broadly as he walked across to an ancient set of wooden shelves, the only piece of furniture in the cellar, set against an inner wall. He grasped one side of the fixture firmly and pulled. It swung towards him, exposing a doorway that it had covered completely. Turning towards Andrea he beckoned for her to follow as he stepped over the threshold.

Beyond the concealed door the passageway widened out before bending at right angles to its previous course. A heavy oak door blocked the further end. As Andrea followed Josh, a little uncertainly, he took a separate key from his pocket and unlocked the gleaming new fitting he'd installed. Then he waited for his wife to catch up.

'*Et voilà!*' he announced, straining slightly to swing the heavy door open one-handed. His other arm, in the small of her back, pushed her gently forward.

Andrea looked from flagged floor to vaulted ceiling, her eyes following the lines of the stone ribs to the columns supporting them. A small undercroft was the most she'd expected, but instead the vault extended before her like a cathedral crypt. Six arched double bays, springing from the walls and supported centrally by a row of columns came dimly into view when Josh switched on the engineering light he'd run through. Suggestions of carving appeared on the capitals and the roof-bosses, but Andrea was too bewildered by the extent of the hidden chamber to take significant notice of them. Why, she thought, this is almost the size of . . .

'Where are we, Josh? In relation to the rest of the house?'

'Under the main hall,' he grinned. 'Like it?'

'It's magnificent. But what did you mean when you said you didn't pay for it?'

'Just that it's not on the plans. Somehow the last set that were drawn up ignore it. Even the agent doesn't know it's here. If he'd known, he'd have shown it to me.'

'You mean we're the only ones who know anything about it? What about the lock and the light?'

25

'Temporary jobs. Did 'em myself. Yes, we're the only two that know it's here. And it could be rather fun to keep it that way.'

A secret. A real secret, she thought to herself. A dark and mysterious hidden chamber in her Gothic castle. Somewhere to be alone with her fantasies.

Except for Josh.

They returned to the known cellar and Josh pushed the shelves back into place. 'How did you find out about it?' Andrea asked him.

'One of those silly little accidents. The estate agent was going back upstairs and I needed to blow my nose. As I pulled out my kerchief a coin came out with it and rolled under the shelves. It shouldn't have done that if they'd been sitting on the floor. But they're not. They're fixed to the wall and slightly off the floor. That's why there're no marks on the stone in front of them.

'When we got back to the car I told him I'd left my gloves, which I had. He waited while I came back to get them. That was when I moved the shelves and saw the corridor. I kept him waiting while I checked out the hidden vault. He didn't mind. Not with the prospect of the commission he's earned on this place.'

Andrea was about to ask him what he intended to do with the vault, then changed her mind. She had a few ideas of her own bubbling, and right now wasn't the time to discuss them. They could do that later, when she'd had a chance to work out how best to get her own way. That would mean mellowing Josh down a little, and she knew exactly how to do that.

Andrea hooked her arm through his. 'Let's go and get a drink,' she told him. 'I spotted an interesting little pub as we drove through Abbots Ringley. And as we're going to be living here it won't hurt to check out our new local.'

She waited outside, studying the front of the house, whilst ⟨…⟩ re-set the alarm and locked up. As the BMW swept Electr⟨…⟩rds the road she realised that the electric eye in ⟨…⟩ be turned off. Well, it could stay that way.

Just so long ⟨…⟩d do a much better job.

That would be unfor⟨…⟩idn't have his initials set in them.

Later on.

4

DURING THE NEXT few weeks men swarmed all over Ringley Abbey, preparing it for habitation. The large kitchen was gutted and refitted, the walk-in pantry being plumbed as a utility room. A succession of vans passed the electric eye in the drive, bringing carpets and household goods, together with Josh's surprise.

Andrea hardly saw Josh whilst this was going on. Neither did anybody else. He spent his evenings in the cellars, preparing shelving and checking the thermostatically-controlled heating in readiness for installing his wine. In addition he broke into the ring-main and ran a loop off to light the hidden corridor and the vault under the main hall. If his wife wanted to indulge her Gothic fantasies that was all right with him, just so long as they stayed together. That was what the Abbey was really about, as far as Josh Buchanan was concerned.

The work went well and, despite Andrea's impatience, quite quickly. Several times she wondered about driving down to see how things were going, but she restrained herself, knowing that her husband only wanted her to see the results of the transformation he was making, not the work which was going into it.

She waited alone except for the daily, now under notice, in the house in St John's Wood. Occasionally a neighbour would drop round for coffee and gossip, but Andrea had never cultivated friends outside her business, and with that sold she saw fewer and fewer people. 'Every wood should have its hermit,' she joked to her husband. 'Why should St John's Wood be any different?'

He'd been worried in the early days of their marriage about his wife's introspective nature. 'Outgoing,' he once told a friend, 'she ain't. But she still has the three most important qualifications for marriage as far as I'm concerned. Good in bed. Rises to the odd social occasion when she has to. And most important she keeps her nose out of my *affairs*.' He stressed the ambiguity of the final word to the point where it was no longer ambiguous.

He could have added that Andrea was worth enough millions to provide a very comfortable life-belt, if he ever needed to be thrown one, but he didn't. He wasn't talking to that kind of friend.

So her behaviour and chosen lifestyle wasn't exactly normal. So what? Normality was determined by general consensus, all said and done. A taste for horror stories and videos didn't make her a freak. Kids that pulled the back legs off grasshoppers didn't grow up to be perverts.

Did they?

She could have the vault at Ringley Abbey as a sort of adult playroom. He'd fit it out for her himself so that it remained a secret. She had a right to a secret. Everyone had. She could fill it with high-backed carved oak chairs and red twisty candles. Watch *The Exorcist* and *Dracula Sucks* (he'd had trouble getting that one) whenever she wanted on

29

a thirty-six-inch Sony, sipping blood-red wine. Something cheap like Vranac would do. Andrea had never become a connoisseur, no matter how hard he'd tried to help her appreciate fine vintages.

She could even have it off with a broomstick if she wanted, so long as she kept him happy when he was home.

Yeah. Pentagrams and panty-hose.

The one thing which somehow never became clear to Josh Buchanan was exactly who the country pile was for. Sure, he wanted it for status. But Andrea, who never seemed to worry about that sort of thing (*nobody* who drove a Ford through choice could possibly be worried about that sort of thing, Josh believed) was just as keen as he was himself. Okay, maybe her reasons were different. But they added up to the same thing in the long run, and that was what counted.

So long as she stays in line we'll all do all right, he believed. And we'll need a good address after I get my K for services to industry, and strategically timed donations to Tory party funds. Sir Joshua and Lady Buchanan. Perhaps even Lord Buchanan of Ringley?

Give it time, boy. Don't rush the fences. Just keep on clearing them comfortably.

The BMW crunched into the St John's Wood drive just after noon on a chill and foggy March day. Josh was grinning as he stepped out of the car and still grinning when he let himself into the house. The daily, Mrs Coombs, scuttled out of the kitchen at the sound of his entrance, wiping her hands on her apron and mentally cursing the lack of notice she'd been given of Mr B being home for lunch.

Andrea, ever alive for any indication that her privacy was about to be violated, had also noticed his return. Curious, not to mention mildly pleased that her husband had finally decided to make personal contact again, she swept down the stairs in a flowing day-robe to greet him.

Josh kissed her warmly, ignoring Mrs Coombs as he usually did.

'You should have let me know you'd be here for lunch,' Andrea admonished him gently.

'I'm not,' Josh smirked back. 'And neither are you.' Then, looking past her: 'Sorry, Mrs Coombs. We'll both be going out, as soon as Mrs Buchanan is ready.'

With a grunt the daily disappeared back into the kitchen.

Andrea pushed back from him and looked up into his face. 'Out? Where, Josh? You should have given me some notice.'

'You've had nearly three weeks' already. C'mon, Andy. The Abbey's finished enough for you to have a look at it.'

'You mean we're going down to Abbots Ringley? Now? But what about lunch?'

'No problem. I'm clear for the rest of the day so we'll stop off at The Bell And Horns on the way. And after that I'm going to take you *home*.'

5

ENNIO ZABETTI PERMITTED himself the same self-indulgent smile that he always wore whenever he passed the occult shop in Coptic Street. He never went in, though sometimes he would stop and look in the window, shaking his head in mild amusement at the sight of the various goodies on display.

Despite his name Ennio had been born to immigrant parents, actually within the sound of Bow bells, and was technically a Cockney. Neither his speech, which bore only the slightest trace of an East End accent, nor his fair appearance betrayed any hint of his Italian background. With his light hair and a hint of olive in his skin which passed for a good tan he could have easily claimed a Scandinavian background, and been believed.

The window display was the usual collection of charms, trinkets and books on mysterious subjects, with a few packs of sun-faded tarot cards scattered about for effect. Pairs of Chinese dogs vied for the remaining space with fresh brass incense burners. But what had actually caught his eye, he eventually realised, wasn't in the window at all. It was on a shelf to one side, just inside the shop.

For a moment or so Ennio hesitated. Then, breaking the habit of several years, if not a lifetime, he stepped inside, a string of Indian bells jingling as he passed through the door.

The interior smelled of stale tobacco and joss. The shopkeeper, an open packet of Marlboro on the counter beside a crowded ash-tray, accounted for the former. Two smouldering sticks of bayberry, their light brown ash not quite landing on the burner they were set in, provided the incense smell. Ennio walked over to the shelf and took a closer look at the carving, noting the small amount of the stuck-on price tag with surprise.

The two girls further up the shop were giggling over *The Modern Witch's Spellbook*. Ennio looked towards them, then back down the shop with its rows of bookshelves and display cases, past the dummy female modelling a witchy robe, plaster nipples projecting through the thin fabric, which was being groped by a life-size paper skeleton, assembly numbers showing on every folded-card bone.

The carving was cheap. Too cheap for what it was.

He hung back whilst the girls bought their book, then made his way up the shop towards the counter as they passed him and went out. The proprietor lit another cigarette and scruffled at his ginger beard as Ennio approached.

'Interested in the goat, are you?' The question was punctuated with a cough.

Ennio nodded. 'Yeah. It's cheap, isn't it? I mean, it's one of Bel Bucca's.'

The proprietor grinned. 'It was, before some idiot took the finish off and stained it black. The whole point of

Bucca's work is that you can see the wood, not paint over it with Finnegan's Hammerite or whatever.'

He dropped the cigarette onto the ash-tray and indulged his lungs with a brief, if hectic, spasm. Then he asked: 'What made you come in this time?'

'Hm? Oh, you've seen me looking in the window before.'

'Several times. And if you know Bel Bucca's work then you're into the sort of things we sell.'

'Not exactly.' Ennio waved an arm around the shop. 'Most of this is kids' and tourist shit. Even that,' he added, pointing towards several copies of LaVey's *Satanic Bible*.

The proprietor laughed and coughed again. 'Try telling that to the Jesus freaks that picket me every so often. But you're right. The real stuff doesn't get published. The odd manuscript comes along, though. I had a copy of the Order of Satanic Templars' work book for years. Wouldn't shift at thirty quid. Then there was that scandal about Ramon in the papers. I stuck a sixty tag on it and it went next day. You want the goat?'

'At fifteen I'd be silly not to. You can't even get a resin cast at that price any more.'

The shopkeeper nodded and got up off his stool, picking up his cigarette for company on the walk down to the front of the shop. The carving, traces of the grain still showing through the heavy, patently artificial black finish, squatted on goat-like haunches, penis erect, wings outstretched. The horned goat-head watched their approach through slitted eyes.

'The Baphomet of Mendes,' the proprietor announced. 'Older and less innocuous than the Eliphas Levi engraving it's been based on. But I suspect you know that already?'

Ennio said nothing.

Right hand raised in benediction. SOLVÉ.

'Anything else catch your eye? Ever actually read LaVey? Surprisingly common-sense philosophy, considering the title.'

Left hand lowered in the sign of the horns. COAGULA.

'Pallid pap from a crap-merchant showman,' Ennio dismissed the suggestion.

The shopkeeper picked up the carving and started back towards the counter. 'Man, that makes you sound heavy,' he muttered over his shoulder. 'Brethren of Asmodeus?'

'Not this side of Brum, as you well know.'

'Okay. Just fishing.'

'Wrong bait. Besides, you couldn't handle a bite if you got one.'

'Whew. Heavier and heavier, O Son of Samael.'

He didn't see Ennio, behind him, hesitate and reach into his pocket for the butterfly knife he always carried. Respectably dressed, past thirty, he stood little chance of being stopped on sus. Not with his WASP appearance to back it up. Then he changed his mind.

'Brethren of the Peacock Angel,' he said quietly.

'Ah. West Sussex Satanist-Yezidi cross. That explains it,' the proprietor nodded, satisfied. 'If you want to leave your address I sometimes get some interesting items in.'

Ennio shook his head. 'Just the goat,' he instructed.

Something in his tone told the shopkeeper not to press his luck. Some of these guys could get nasty if you backed them into a corner. Yet there was a strong smell of brimstone coming past the bayberry. It didn't make sense for a Brother of the Peacock Angel to want a Goat of Mendes carving. The two traditions were sufficiently different for the one thing to be anomalous to the other.

He crushed out his cigarette and lit the next one to keep his hands steady. Let's get this guy out of the shop, he told himself. He's no more one of the Horsham Arabs than I am.

35

He slipped the goat into a brown paper bag and taped it closed. 'How d'you want to pay?' he asked through a cloud of exhaled smoke.

'Cash,' Ennio answered, laying three fivers on the counter.

'That'll do nicely,' the man said, handing over the package.

Ennio left the shop, fully aware of the proprietor's sigh of relief behind him. He continued down Coptic Street and into New Oxford Street, then past Centrepoint into Charing Cross Road. From there he cut off into Soho.

One more look. Maybe this time he'd remember.

To the casual observer there was only a fair-haired man, reasonably good-looking, in a business suit to be seen entering Meard Street. Nobody would have thought twice about their passing glimpse of Ennio Zabetti, except perhaps for a prowling, hungry office girl in search of adventure. It was an image he had worked long and hard to cultivate, sufficiently on the distinctive side of anonymous to be just another face, individual but not conspicuous. The circles he moved in required that of him.

Meard Street was drab, forgotten. It consisted mostly of uninteresting doorways leading to offices and small workshops. On a foggy day Sherlock Holmes would not have looked out of place prowling its narrow confines. For Ennio Zabetti, though, it held a mystery.

One of the few shop-fronts in Meard Street was that of the Andrea Duncan Salon. Until that one time he'd needed to cut through to Greek Street in a hurry Ennio hadn't even known it was there. There was no reason why he should, being neither female nor given to excessive vanity about his appearance. Yet on that one occasion, hurried though he'd been, the portrait-sized photo of Andrea Duncan in the window had caught his eye. And held it.

There was something terribly familiar about that woman. Whether it was the eyes, slightly too small, which followed you around as you passed, or the straight nose or full mouth Ennio didn't know. But he did know he'd seen Andrea Duncan somewhere before. Or she'd seen him. Or both.

It had become a ritual, whenever time permitted, that he studied that photograph. Sooner or later, he knew, he'd remember where he'd seen her before. Sooner or later the photo would give up its secret and satisfy him. Or leave him even hungrier than before.

A carefully presented woman in . . . what? Late twenties? Early thirties? Probably the former. Darkish hair. Familiar face.

Where familiar? How familiar?

The goat began to feel heavy in its paper wrapping. Take me away or set me down, it ordered imperiously like the figure of a deity that it was.

Ennio set it down.

Familiar. Yet different, he told himself. How different? Fatter? Thinner? Younger? Older?

Older . . .

That was it. Yes, he'd seen that face before. Years before. All he had to do was to decide how many years before. Five? Ten? Fifteen . . .

Fifteen.

And now it was beginning to come back. Now at last he was beginning to remember. Even fifteen years ago, at the age of nineteen, he'd been a member of the Sons of Samael. And at last he remembered where he'd seen Andrea Duncan before.

Ennio Zabetti was whistling happily as he picked up the goat again and headed towards Tottenham Court Road tube station. The mystery was solved, and with its solution a new chapter in his life was already beginning.

Andrea Duncan, startled young girl, eyes wider than in the photograph, mouth gaping, lurked in his memory of the distant past, almost half his lifetime away. Now there was another Andrea, a present Andrea. And there was going to be a future Andrea, one which could be used to fulfil his commitment to the Sons of Samael.

The circle was coming round. He'd make sure of that.

Quite when, or how, had yet to be determined, but the circle would come round once more. It had to, for the glory of the Black Angel to be fulfilled.

He walked on into Greek Street, with its pubs and bistros and delicatessens. There was nothing Greek about it. Neither was there anything Greek about either Andrea or Duncan. *Duncan* was a Celtic name, frequently Scots, that meant *brown warrior*. *Andrea* could have been simply the female of *Andrew*, but it wasn't. That was Andrina. *Andrea* was closer to that traditional witch-name for the mother goddess, *Andred*. Only one letter different in over a thousand years.

Ennio Zabetti, Cockney, and something more, walked down Greek Street whistling the *Horst Wessel lied*, the anthem of the Nazi Party.

Andrea Duncan, wherever, whoever, she might be now, was already his.

6

SHE COULDN'T REMEMBER who he was. Neither could she see the remains of his features through her tears.

But she had to stop them.

His identity, if he had ever truly had one, didn't really matter. He was simply another that she had loved.

'You can't,' she whimpered. 'You can't. I won't let you.'

They tore her away from him roughly, throwing her down and slapping her as she began to scream hysterically.

'Stay there,' one of them told her firmly. 'Don't interfere any more. It has to be done and that's an end of it.'

Their clothes weren't right. Laced-neck shirts worn with breeches and stockings. Big buckle shoes of scuffed and muddied leather. One wore his hair long, falling over his pock-marked face, straggling down in front of his good eye and the empty socket behind the eye-patch. He was the one doing most of their gruesome work, the one with the long, dull, rusty knife with the jagged edge. The other was fractionally cleaner and better-dressed, his hair kept back with a greasy ribbon. The ancient attic room, bare of furniture, leaped and shuddered fitfully in the guttering candle-light.

She began to crawl back towards the coffin, sobbing. Hair-tied-back stood deliberately on one of her hands, pinning her in place. She howled and writhed, the single long white garment she wore falling open, exposing her body to them.

Eye-patch turned and waved the knife at her. The blood on his hand was already beginning to crust and flake off, striping his knuckles. 'Maybe later,' he sneered.

'A bit more,' Hair-tied-back instructed coldly. 'He doesn't fit properly yet. Cut a bit more off.'

'But he isn't dead!' she screamed. 'He isn't dead! He isn't!'

'Don't worry about that,' Eye-patch smirked. 'He will be when we get the lid on.'

'And we can't get the lid on 'til he fits, now, can we?' his companion added.

Ropes stretched across the top of the coffin were holding her lover down. As Eye-patch worked to saw off a protruding knee-cap her lover strained to rise through the rope across his neck. Choking with effort his tongue protruded. Eye-patch seized it with his free hand and drew the dull edge of the knife backwards and forwards across it. Blood welled and dribbled down the sides of the tortured creature's face. As the tongue, half-cut, half-torn, came away the torturer sliced off the end of the nose above it.

Her lover sank back, gurgling and coughing.

'Save us a bit of time later,' Eye-patch grinned, showing bad teeth and canines elongated to the point of deformity.

40

Then he returned to the knee-cap, hacking it free and dropping it back into the coffin at the head end.

'Right. Try it now,' Hair-tied-back instructed.

Eye-patch stood up and dropped the knife on to the bloodstained floorboards. He crossed to the open doorway, darkness beyond it, and carried back the coffin lid which was lying there, a rough shape of battened planks. A hand clawed up at the edge of the coffin as the lid was thrown down with bone-crushing force. The protruding fingers trembled, accompanied by a frothing moan. Eye-patch took up his knife again and cut them off, one by one.

The last inch of lid thumped dully down into place.

'That's it,' Hair-tied-back announced to her. 'He's dead now.'

The creature in the coffin began to shuffle, still straining to breathe through its blood. The lid bumped, then moved, then flew off as the restraining ropes snapped free. It stood.

Through her tears she saw what they had done to him. The damaged eye and burnt hair had happened long before they tied him into the coffin, but the loss of his nose and tongue had ruined what remained of his once handsome features. He stood at an awkward angle, swaying to keep his balance, his body striped with flowing blood and panic sweat. The arms jerked and flapped like shattered wings, the remaining fingers struggling to reach out to his tormentors in a last gesture of defence or supplication.

The remaining good eye focused on her and his mouth sprayed flecks of crimson foam as he tried to speak. She tried to wriggle towards him but Hair-tied-back twisted his heel as he moved to stand on her other hand as well.

'Finish it,' he hissed.

Eye-patch moved round behind the dying creature and wrapped his left arm across its forehead, forcing the head back and the throat forward. With the knife clasped firmly in his right hand he began to saw at the neck, a series of rough, shallow cuts eventually penetrating through the windpipe and jugular. Blood sprayed from the wound in a horizontal fan and the figure went suddenly limp in his grasp. He continued to hack as the angle of the jetting blood slowly changed, spurting upwards, spattering further, raining across on to prisoner and captor watching together.

Eye-patch kept cutting until the head came off and the body crumpled untidily back into the coffin. 'Lots more room now,' he muttered, breathing slightly heavily. Then he tossed the severed head down to lie between the mutilated feet and heaved the lid back into place.

'There,' he beamed, sitting down to rest on top of the coffin. 'That's that for him. What about her?' He gestured the knife towards her as he asked the question.

'I've been giving that some thought,' Hair-tied-back replied. 'Why don't you go downstairs and bring that other coffin up here?'

7

ANDREA WAS SITTING bolt upright before she realised she was awake. Her chest was heaving with massive gasps and chill sweat trickled from her hairline and armpits, sticking her nightdress to her like a damp shroud. Hairtied-back's final leer persisted in the darkness, stamped on her memory, refusing to fade.

She stared sightlessly at the curtained window, lips trembling, hands clawed into the bedclothes. Slowly, very slowly, the faint light from outside began to superimpose the shape of the arch upon her tormentor.

How could I have seen his face when he was above me, standing on my hands? she asked herself.

It didn't matter. The strange logic of dreams was such that the dreamer could view their progress from outside as well as within. You always realised that when you woke up, though, never at the time, no matter how hard you might be trying.

Hair-tied-back began to recede, taking his leer with him. Gradually he returned his borrowed features to the stone corbel outside on the Abbey wall.

Did you like it, Andrea? the Abbey asked her.

She didn't notice so much when it spoke to her now. During the few months she and Josh had been living there she'd got used to the strange promptings, the questions and offered conversations, which came unbidden at odd moments. On the whole she enjoyed her life there, making the most of her feast of solitude, surrounded by the little strangenesses which made up her normality. Her nightmares persisted, sometimes, as tonight, with terrifying force, but were more welcome than she would ever have thought they could be. Watching her horror videos was one thing. Actually participating, *being there*, was quite different. Even if she did want to seek Josh out and climb into his bed for comfort after them.

He didn't mind her waking him up and getting in beside him. Once the thrashing about and the muttering, sometimes the screaming, of her participation was over she became a welcome visitor. Then she was child and lover. Child to be soothed and comforted, lover to be consoled by his attentions. The father she had lost as a child and the lover she had denied as an adult.

It made sense to both of them. When Josh was there.

Tonight, though, she realised as she wiped the sweat from her neck with a tissue from beside the bed, Josh wasn't there.

It happened occasionally, though more frequently since they'd moved to Ringley Abbey. Sometimes once, sometimes twice a week Josh would have dinner with a client and stay over for an early meeting the following morning. It really wasn't fair to expect him to drive the M25 and the M4 home with a drink-for-drink volume of alcohol in his system. His large frame gave him an advantage over anyone smaller when it came to coping with booze. Two bottles of claret or even the better part of a bottle of gin hardly seemed to touch him, but a breathalyser test might not agree.

Yes, he could afford a chauffeur, but the luxury was also an inconvenience. Especially for someone who might want to keep certain of his movements quiet. So he stayed in town, always ringing in like a dutiful husband. Always reassuring her that he was all right and, subtly, on his own.

Andrea, wrapped in herself, unsuspecting, usually didn't mind. It only worried her on nights like this. Nights when the little girl had to try to be a woman.

She reached across to the chair on the other side of her bed and pulled a robe around her shaking shoulders. A drink would help, so she'd slip down to the main hall and pour herself a stiff vodka from the Chinese laquered cabinet. Sliding across the sheets she pulled back the covers and slipped her feet into the waiting slippers.

No matter how many times she had seen the heroine wander alone through the old house towards whatever horror lurked within it never applied to her. The Abbey was too communicative, too friendly, to hold any horrors that were not of her own making and controlling, with the exception of the dreams she'd always had. And you had to be asleep to be dreaming. Not listening to the creak of the ancient boards and the clicking of light switches as you made your way around. Besides, dreams never took account of the sounds of settlement as old houses cooled and contracted for the night, even when you dreamed of old and mysterious places.

Andrea made her way down the main staircase, her slippers flopping on the old oak treads, then on to the Persian rug in the entrance hall and through to the tiles and carpets of the main hall. It was the way she'd always gone, spurning the cast-iron spiral staircase Josh had installed which communicated with the minstrel gallery. She poured herself a vodka and, as an afterthought, shot a measure of dry Martini into it, drinking the mixture without ice. She mixed another and wondered about watching a video for company. Something trivial and therapeutic like *The Sound Of Music*.

Outside the birds were beginning to sing, waking up before the sun did.

She checked the grandfather clock, ponderously and dependably ticking away her life. It was nearly six o'clock on an early April morning. Josh would be getting up soon.

Maybe I could wake him up anyway, Andrea thought. I'll give it another half hour or so.

She walked over to her writing desk, sipping her second drink as she went. Her Filofax lay there open and she flipped through to the address pages. Josh was usually consistent in his habits so it was probably the Cumberland Hotel number that she wanted. Her fingers, no longer trembling, found it easily.

The dream was fading. Hair-tied-back and Eye-patch were returning to her tortured subconscious and to history. Only the memory of an encoffined and mutilated lover threatened to persist.

The dot glowing on the console told her the TV was still on stand-by from the night before. Andrea found the remote control and pressed the red button. The world news on Thames was just ending, fading through the credits into commercials, so she hopped across the channels. BBC 1 and 2 were still out. So was Channel 4. The satellite channels gave her a choice of breakfast shows, including one in Swedish or Dutch. Eventually she found a Daffy Duck cartoon and settled down to watch.

In the corner by the door she'd come in through the Grandfather continued its monotonous measuring of mortality.

The screen narrowed to a central circle of Daffy's grinning features. She'd known a girl with lips like a duck's bill once. Quite pretty in an off-beat kind of way. And popular. The men seemed to take one look at her mouth and she'd be fighting off the dates she didn't want.

Bugs Bunny followed Daffy. Andrea had always had a sneaking admiration for the cartoon rabbit. He could turn any situation to his advantage, no matter what the odds. His *nous* (she'd never liked the expression until she learned it was Greek for *mind*) was getting on for infinite, confused only on occasions by his pursuit of the demonically tempting carrot. Right now he was running literal rings around Elmer Fudd.

Eight minutes past six.

She finished her second drink. It was too near morning for a third. The only way to prove to herself she wasn't an alcoholic was to avoid drinking in daylight before noon, and even then there were exceptions. She remembered the story she'd once been told by an osteopath.

'I was called out to a lady from Fort Lauderdale staying at Claridge's early one morning,' he'd said. 'She'd done herself a mischief with a toy boy and it was my job to sort it out. Well, I got her on her feet and she was immensely grateful, even offering me a drink before I left. I declined on the grounds that I never touched alcohol before twelve mid-day.

"'Hell, honey," she said. "Somewhere in the world it's twelve o'clock right now."'

Andrea wondered and was tempted. Then Bugs ended and a real kids' cartoon came on. Not adult watching by any excuse. She got up and went into the kitchen to make herself a jug of coffee. Being awake early didn't matter. She could sleep through the afternoon, providing she was up to welcome Josh back.

47

Josh. She was going to ring him.

The filter machine hissed and bubbled. The jug filled with dark brown liquid. Pouring herself a cup of bitter blackness she returned to the television.

Oh shit! she thought. Of the whole range of merchandising toy cartoons she found *My Little Pony* the least digestible. Too much carcinogenic saccharin. All light and love and impotence, even in the villains. At least Bugs Bunny had his macho moments. Even Tom and Jerry had an (implied) sex life.

Like Josh and herself?

The early morning was passing. The Grandfather clock now read six twenty-two.

Soon be time to make that call.

Andrea tried to remember what she was calling Josh about. 'Hi, Josh,' she rehearsed. 'Sorry to wake you but I had this dream about a lover who was cut up in a coffin.'

'A lover?' he demanded. 'Not even me? Just a lover?'

Oh, Christ. That wasn't good enough. She needed an alternative. She sipped her coffee.

Six twenty-seven.

Andrea went back to her desk and picked up her Filofax to have the number with her. One of the main hall's two phones was on a low table beside the sofa she was sitting on.

'Hi, Josh. Just thought I'd say good morning, and I love you.'

That was better. Much better. That was the line to use, she decided.

Why bother him with a dream she could only half remember anyway?

It was time. She dialled the number and waited for it to connect.

'Cumberland Hotel,' said a man's voice. 'How may I help you?'

'Will you connect me with Mr Buchanan's room?' Andrea asked. Then, to forstall the question: 'This is his wife calling.'

'Just a moment, Mrs Buchanan.'

The click followed on with a ringing tone, which persisted for a few long seconds. Then a voice grunted: 'Yes? What is it?'

A woman's voice. A young and probably pretty woman's voice. In her husband's bed.

She hesitated. This couldn't be right. 'Is this a joke?' the woman asked.

'I . . . think it's a mistake,' Andrea ventured. 'I asked for Mr Buchanan's room.'

'Oh.' A pause. The unmistakable sound of a hand sliding over the mouthpiece. Then: 'I'll try to get you back to the switchboard.'

'Don't bother,' Andrea snapped, hanging up.

She finished her coffee and sat there, brooding. The Grandfather clock chimed half six.

Andrea dialled again.

The same male voice answered from the Cumberland's switchboard, polite and, she felt, restrained. The ringing tone sounded once more, going on for the better part of a minute. Finally Josh's voice answered.

'Yeah?' he demanded.

'Josh? Are you alone?'

He recognised his wife's voice. 'Well,' he responded, 'good early morning to you too.'

'Is there anyone with you?'

'At this time? You must be joking. My alarm call isn't for a half hour yet. Still,' he yawned, 'it's nice to hear you. All the same,' he added.

Andrea hesitated. 'I . . . called before. A woman's voice answered.'

'Must have been a mistake on the switchboard,' Josh told her. 'Even the night staff get sleepy round about now.'

Was he more awake than he sounded? She couldn't be sure if it was herself or the house asking the question. 'I just thought I'd ring and say have a good day,' she told him.

'That's very nice of you, darling,' he grunted through another yawn.

8

HE PUT THE phone down gently, killing his yawn the moment the handset touched the rest, and looked across at the buxom woman snuggled into the bedclothes.

'That was a fucking stupid thing to do, Steffi,' he snapped.

'Sorry, Josh. I wasn't thinking.' She tried a pout, all wide eyes and tangled blond curls. It was the wrong thing to do but it would take her a couple of days to find that out.

Josh Buchanan appeared to relax. 'Ah, what the hell,' he smiled. 'Looks like we've got away with it, this time. But never again. Understand me?'

She understood, nodding slowly then looking down to where a scarlet-varnished nail was tracing rings round a hardening nipple. Make amends, she thought. Keep the brute happy. She could always find another way to tip his wife off and force the divorce. Her other hand slid the covers down leaving nothing to the imagination.

'Want some breakfast?' Steffi asked him, archly.

He moved closer across the bed and reached out to draw her to him. 'What's on the menu?' he enquired, biting gently at the side of her neck.

'Nothing you haven't enjoyed before. Oh yeah, Josh. C'mon. Don't hang about . . .'

He had no intention of hanging about. His alarm call would be through in just over a quarter of an hour and his mind was already busy with the extra wheels to be set in motion with Personnel. One way or another Steffi Holt had become a liability. Whether she was dangerous or simply careless didn't matter. She knew never to answer the phone when they were together in a hotel, in exactly the same way that he knew never to answer it when he was in her flat. For her to have done so this morning meant one of two things.

Either she wanted to tip Andrea off and make him leave her, or she was getting careless after the several months they'd been sleeping together. No matter which it was, Steffi had just said goodbye.

He'd keep things amicable, he decided. An upgraded salary and a transfer to the Manchester office should do it. It could also set him up for a little diversion when he went up there himself. After all, Andrea wouldn't automatically know which hotel to ring if she woke up with one of her bloody nightmares.

The alarm call rang through and he disengaged himself from Steffi and ran a shower, the water washing her away even while she dressed. J B Enterprises plc was sailing rather close to the wind at present. All it would take would be a medium shift in the market and Josh's empire would be in serious trouble. He'd need Andrea's money to bail him out. And that meant Andrea was the perfect and indispensable wife, no matter what her shortcomings might be.

9

THE ROBED FIGURES moved aside, breaking the circle, to permit the Magister Inferi to enter. Unlike the others present, who were garbed in purple, dark blue or crimson, their faces covered with skull masks beneath their cowls, he wore a long, flowing garment of black and a goat's-head mask completely covered his features. The front of the gown, which was obviously intended to open, was embroidered with an inverted pentagram with a stylised goat superimposed, the whole enclosed by a serpent biting its own tail.

A gong sounded once, its note echoing discordantly around the converted cellar. Behind the goat-masked dignitary walked his Madonna, breasts and genitals exposed and oiled, body encased in studded and spiked black leather, legs booted to the knee, fringed black armlets dangling to her wrists. Unlike the Magister, who was empty-handed, she carried a cat o' nine tails in her right hand and a wickedly-gleaming *kris* in the other.

Magister and Madonna took their places. The circle reformed around the figure squatting nervously on its haunches at the centre. The Magister spoke.

'I, Magister Inferi of the Sons of Samael, make ready to welcome a new daughter to our numbers. Let us declare ourselves. I am Astaroth.'

'Blessed be Astaroth,' the circle chorused.

'I am Lilith,' the Madonna, her beauty contorted as she spoke the name, proclaimed.

'Blessed be Lilith.'

'I am Ball-Phegor.'

The naming and blessing continued around the circle. At last it returned to the Magister, who bent his goat's head towards the squatting Postulant in their midst. Under the blindfold she was probably on the desirable side of pretty. Under the thin white robe, its fabric little more than curtain netting, her small breasts and slight outline were still maturing. Under her haunches, glimmering whenever the fitful candle-light penetrated past the surrounding robed figures, was a gem-encrusted crucifix.

'Declare yourself,' the Magister instructed, his voice harsh and angry as if she were guilty of some heinous omission.

'I . . . have yet to be Sataned, Magister,' she whispered hesitantly.

'That will pass, as other things will pass,' came the reply, the Magister's tones now sounding amused. The circle around him sniggered. He continued: 'Daughter, you have chosen to enter the Porta Inferi Coven of the Sons of Samael. You have passed many trials and your sponsors speak well of you. Yet tonight the false Jehovah and his pallid spawn will seek to bar you from your chosen company. You must cast them out of your path with a bodily token of abnegation.'

54

As he spo... Madonna left the circle and ignited the
charcoal in a bla... censer set upon the altar in the west
of the cellar. Behi... against the wall, a stuffed alsatian
dog, penis prominent, ...s screwed into its dead skull,
reared above an inverted c... Black candles in Georgian
silver candelabra burned to eit... side.

The charcoal caught. The Mado... fed it with a mixture
of myrrh and hashish.

'God is dog is dog is god,' she intoned.

'Dog is god,' the circle responded.

'Bring the cauldron,' the Magister instructed.

A purple-robed Priestess left the circle and returned with
an iron cauldron which had been standing against the north
wall. She kicked the Postulant roughly to one side and
positioned it in the centre of the circle, the arms of the
crucifix resting on the rim. Two other worshippers helped
the startled girl to her feet and sat her above the crucifix.

'You were fed from the paps of the Enemy in your
childhood,' the Magister told her. 'Long has that food
remained to poison your body and mind. Yet our Master
Satan is merciful . . .'

'Satan is merciful . . .'

'. . . and knows the fault was not your own. Are you ready
to accept His mercy?'

'I am,' the Postulant said faintly.

A Priest slapped her face. 'Louder!' he commanded.

'I am!'

'Then let His will be done.'

The two priests who had positioned her now ripped the
thin robe away from the lower half of her body. 'Void the
poison of the despot,' the Magister commanded.

The circle took up his words. It began to chant, softly and
slowly at first then increasing in speed and volume. 'Void,
void, void, void, void . . .'

'Hail, Master of the Void!'
'Hail, Master of the Void!'
'In rioting and drunkenness I ... again. Fulfil the needs of the flesh.'
'Fulfil the needs of the fl...'
'Void!'
'Void!'

The circle squatted, inhaling the fumes from the censer, eyes peering through their skull masks as the girl's naked buttocks strained and clenched and unclenched. She jiggled desperately around on the rim of the cauldron and the crucifix whilst they chanted.

'Void. Void. Void!'

With a low moan the postulant relaxed. The unmistakable sounds of her compliance trickled up from the cauldron. Before she had completely finished the same two Priests dragged her away and the Magister Inferi knocked the crucifix into the soiled vessel before raising the cauldron above his head.

'Behold the symbol of the Enemy, degraded with his own body and blood,' he proclaimed. '*Ave Satanas*!'

'*Ave Satanas*. Hail Satan,' the worshippers responded.

Through the slits in a skull mask cold blue eyes regarded the proceedings with gathering ennui. Surely the others must be becoming as bored as he was with these pantomime blasphemies?

'*Akhera goity, akhera beiti*!'

'The He-goat on high! The He-goat below!'

Couldn't they even sort out their symbolism into a coherent whole? Let alone the liturgy? Snatches of Latin. Snatches of Basque. Dog is God/Devil. Goat is God/Devil. All this shitting and pissing around. There was only one way to worship, and that was to get out there amongst Satan's subjects and *do it*. There were plenty of little girls

56

out there willing to be debauched, even slaughtered if you
got them jacked up enough, without bothering with these
charades.

'*Vide Satanas!*'

They disrobed, retaining their masks. The Magister
Inferi retained his gown, which the Madonna opened and
tucked to either side below the waist. His penis, ringed by
dark fur and studs, stood stiffly out, oversize and glistening
artificially.

If he didn't keep his robe on we'd all see the straps, Ennio
Zambetti thought beneath his skull mask, one hand gently
massaging his own accomplished member.

'We stand before you naked, Lord. As our bodies are
unclad so are our minds free of the guile of the Enemy. We
are yours!'

'We are yours!'

(Yawn.) We are yours.

The assembled worshippers adopted the Stance of the
Demon in turn, according to their proclaimed identity.
When it came to the Postulant, still blindfold in the centre of
the circle, the Magister grabbed her by her hair and pulled
her across to the altar.

'Adopt the Stance of Lachienne!' he commanded.

She fell to her knees, then dropped further forward onto
her hands as well. The two Priests ripped the rest of her
soiled and torn robe away, then one held her frightened face
up towards the rearing horned alsatian. As the blindfold
was torn away from her eyes, as they widened, the pupils
dilating with the light and with the first full knowledge of
her surroundings, Magister took her from behind, forcing
the full length of his artificial penis into her. A squirt of
blood began to mingle with the dampness lingering on her
thighs.

Her scream was drowned out by the chanting of the

circle, a chanting timed to the Magister's slow, deliberate, brutal strokes: 'Ride the bitch. Ride the bitch. Ride the bitch . . .'

The chant maintained as male and female worshippers came in turn, posturing, to present the appropriate part of their anatomy to her captive mouth. She moaned and slobbered and cried as the Magister slammed on.

'. . . Ride the bitch . . .'

As the last of the worshippers moved away the Magister reached into the small of his back and squeezed hard. A jet of cold goat urine surged through the tube in the artificial penis and drenched the girl when he withdrew.

They held her upright again, mumbling, wild-eyed, legs refusing to obey properly. The Magister stood before her.

He reached down and collected some of her dribbling juices on his fingers, then signed an inverted cross upon her forehead. 'I Satanise thee, *Pravus*,' he informed her. 'What is your name?'

'P . . . Pravus,' she whispered.

He struck her hard across the face, droplets flying from his hand. Replenishing his ink he drew another inverted cross on her belly. 'What is your name?'

More boldly: 'Pravus.'

He struck her again, less viciously, then drew a third cross between her breasts. A stain of pinkish fluid began to trickle down towards her navel. 'A third time. What is your name?'

Her features contorted defiantly and tears started anew from the corners of her eyes. 'Pravus!' she spat. 'My name is Pravus!'

The goat-mask nodded. 'Excellent, my child,' the Magister soothed, kissing her lightly on the lips and touching the artificial penis to her body once more. Then he turned away and strode to the centre of the circle to close the gathering.

Ennio stifled another yawn. Then his brow began to furrow beneath the rubber skull. Pravus didn't sound like any demon-name he'd heard before. The ending wasn't right. No EL, like Samael or Barachiel or Hagiel.

Okay, so it wasn't Hebrew and it wasn't traditional. But the Magister never did anything without a reason, and that especially included naming Postulants.

He'd look it up later, after he'd had some fun.

10

THE POWERFUL SOUND of Magnum's *Vigilante* album surged through the flat above the little shop in Coptic Street. Slumped across a worn chesterfield, a can of Special Brew open and half-drunk on the floor beside him, the remains of sweet and sour king prawns clinging to the plate on the carpet, Johnny Howard was at peace with the world.

'. . . Smoking in a room in Lebanon, Hotel's serving but the hospital's gone . . .' the lyrics pounded, fighting through the beer.

Good strong music. Good strong beer. When you sold spiritualist crap and crystal balls all day you needed some strength in the evening.

He half sat up to light another Marlboro, then flopped back again, exhaling noisily, his eyes wandering across to the Giger poster, its edges tattered, taped to the wall above the fireplace. Both the Sabbatic goat and the Lilith figure riding its horns leered disgustingly back at him.

Johnny had done quite well out of people's gullibility, all said and done. He only camped in this so-called flat, part bed-sit, part storeroom, during the week. Weekends he put a mate in to cover the shop (one of only two he could guarantee wouldn't rip him off) and headed for his cottage just north of Gerrard's Cross. That was where he really came alive.

'. . . Midnight you won't be sleeping . . .'

He never was. Somehow sleep never happened until about two o'clock. The rumpled cot on the other side of the room was about as appealing as a dead cat. Johnny kept meaning to smarten the place up, maybe get rid of the bug-eaten furnishings and rig a partition, curtain or something to hide the stacks of books and boxes of stock that blocked off the further end, but he never got round to it. One day, maybe. Then he could take advantage of some of those inviting looks he got in the shop from time to time. Not with that shitty little cot, though. He could hardly bear to get into it himself.

His eyes followed Giger's intricate, mechanistic nightmare whilst the music and the beer swept through him, turning off the present. It took several moments for him to realise the familiar track wasn't right, that there was something extra he'd not heard in it before. A ringing that wasn't in time with the insistent beat. With a groan that doubled for an inarticulate curse he hauled himself to his feet, turned down the stereo and picked up the door-phone.

'The Howard residence,' he announced, facetiously.

'Yeah,' came the reply through the handset. 'Look, you keep the shop downstairs, right?'

'So? What's on your mind?'

'I bought that Bel Bucca goat off you a while back, remember? There's something I'd like to talk to you about. It's important.'

61

Johnny sighed and looked at his watch. The time was just on eleven, so the guy wasn't pissed up from *all* night in the pub. He thought back, remembering the so-called Brother of the Peacock Angel. Well, it never hurt to be well-informed about what was going on, and this particular Nick-head had felt weirder, and better informed, than most.

'Okay,' Johnny said, pressing the electric lock control. 'C'mon up. Just you, mind,' he added, cautiously.

'I'm on my own.'

He put the handset back and picked the plate up off the carpet in a token show of tidying up for his visitor. And yes, there was a spare beer he could offer, if he could find a clean glass.

Ennio Zabetti knocked on the door at the end of the narrow hall (kitchen one side, bathroom the other) and Johnny shuffled down to open it. Only when he recognised his fair-haired guest did he recall the feeling of unease that his presence in the shop had generated. He both recalled it and felt it again. By that time, however, Ennio was inside the flat.

Johnny waved him to a seat and poured the spare beer out. Ennio took it with a nod and tasted it before settng it down beside his feet. The shopkeeper returned to the chesterfield and lit another cigarette without offering one.

'So what do you want to talk to me about? Come to that I don't even know your name.'

'Ennio Zabetti. And you?'

'Johnny Howard.' Then: 'You don't look Italian,' he added, accusingly.

'My parents were. I'm a Cockney.'

'You don't sound Cockney, either. So what's the problem?'

Ennio sighed, hesitantly, wearing his best little-boy-lost expression, the one that told people what an innocent

62

abroad in a hostile world he really was. Then he said: 'You mentioned the Sons of Samael when I was in the shop. I was wondering if you could tell me any more about them.'

'Did I? Maybe I did. Suppose you tell me what *you* know about the Sons of Samael?'

'Oh, not much, really,' Ennio lied. 'I think they're quite a recent order. At least, I've only heard the name once or twice.' From people outside the Sons, he added mentally.

'That doesn't surprise me. They keep bloody quiet about their activities, which is probably just as well. I don't think they'd want the pigs sniffing too close. Christ knows I get enough hassle just through selling Tarot cards. You'd think I was unloading Nepalese Temple Balls as well.'

'Yeah. I can guess. So where does the name come from? Samael, I mean?'

Johnny shrugged. 'Two theories. Explanations, if you prefer. And they could both be right. The first is the good old occult one. Samael was the angel of death and head honcho of the Satans in the Rabbinical writings. *Sam* means poison, and *el* is the standard angel ending. So the Sons of Samael would be the sons of the angel of death. Make sense?'

'Could be.' Ennio picked up his beer and took a good swallow before setting the glass down again. 'And the other?'

'You remember the Son of Sam killings in the States some years back?'

'Can't say's I do.'

'Well, some nut called Berkowitz kept blowing people, mostly girls, away with a .44. Just another only-in-America, on the surface.'

'And beneath it?'

'Some guy called Maury Terry wrote a book titled *The Ultimate Evil*. It linked Berkowitz to Manson, and both of them to a satanic cult that stretched from New York to California, right across the whole bloody continent of North America. And you know what they say. We get it over here five years after the US dreams it up.'

'You mean the Sons of Samael are going round killing people?'

'Bit up-market from Malek Taos, the Peacock Angel, as demonic creator of the world dispensing blessings to his servants, isn't it? Uh huh. Could be. Whether it's true or not I've heard enough about the Sons of Samael to know they're *nasty fuckers*. And I do mean nasty.'

'But . . . how do you find out about them?'

Johnny shrugged. 'Odd hints picked up in the shop. Whispers from wiccans. The traditional satanists don't like them because they're supposed to have perverted the Black Mass. Can you believe it?'

Ennio shook his head and looked bemused. 'You can't do that without denying Satan, and that'd mean they're not satanists.'

'Depends.'

'On what?'

'Your point of view, and whether or not you have to believe in Satan to be a satanist. After all, LaVey doesn't. Not as a physical reality, anyway. It all comes down to a word-trick in the end.'

'I don't follow you.'

'Satanism is Christianity backwards, right? The Sons of Samael celebrate the Mass of the Dog. Dog is God backwards.'

Ennio made no reply to this, simply sitting there with his mouth open, his features thunderstruck. This character actually knew what he was talking about.

Too much of what he was talking about.

His foot moved, knocking over the glass of . . . he mumbled an apology and Johnny, scowling, went out to the kitchen to fetch a cloth. In one of the moments he was gone Ennio took the butterfly knife from his pocket and flipped it open, concealing it behind him in the chair. When the shopkeeper returned and bent over to mop at the frothing stain Ennio drew the wickedly sharp blade across the back of Johnny's knee. Hamstrung, he flopped over like a doll collapsing, his light trousers quickly darkening with escaping blood. He'd hit the floor before the pain struck and he began to howl.

Ennio walked over to the stereo and turned it up. Behind him on the floor Johnny Howard was writhing and clutching at his useless leg, unconcerned at the prospect of clearing up the new and larger stain which was spreading across the threadbare carpeting.

The album was *Wings of Heaven*. The track was *Days of no Trust*. Ennio returned to his struggling victim. Johnny glared up at him through pain-filled eyes, spittle accumulating on his beard. Ennio sat down again.

'You know far too much, Mr Howard. Now I want you to tell me more precisely how you know it.' A sudden thought clouded his features. 'Are you the Magister Inferi?' he demanded.

'The . . . what?'

Ennio sprang on to his chest and inserted the point of the knife into his right nostril, pulling it outwards and up. Blood spattered over Johnny's face, dying his ginger beard crimson.

'Aagh! Jesus!'

'Wrong deity. I ask you again. Are you the Magister?'

'Shit, man! I'm just a fucking shopkeeper!'

'Who told you about the Mass of the Dog?'

'Fuck that. I'm bleeding to death!'

'So you are.' Ennio took the loosely-knotted tie from Johnny's neck and improvised a tourniquet with the spoon from the dirty plate. 'Hold that,' he ordered.

The moment the command was obeyed he grabbed Johnny's free hand and severed the index finger at the first knuckle. Johnny screamed again.

'Talk to me, Mr Howard. Do try to be coherent or I shall have to hurt you even more. Who told you?'

'Some . . . girl at a . . . party . . .'

'Name?'

'I can't remember! Get me a fucking quack, will you?'

'Time for everything. Keep that tourniquet tight, now.'

The album stormed on. 'We hold the keys, we are the caretakers of insanity . . .'

Ennio's knife took off another joint. The insistent throbs from his hand, face and leg were tearing Johnny's head off.

'Name?'

'Steffi! Steffi Holt. But she's not here. She's moved!'

'Where?'

'Man . . . Manchester!'

'Not good enough.' The knife poised to cut again.

'Wait. Wait! Christ, wait!'

His mind was spinning. Pain lanced into it from every conceivable direction. His world was a flagrant agony, sticky with cold panic sweat and sour with the bitter taste of adrenalin.

'I'm waiting.' Ennio's voice was calm, almost reassuring. The efficient tones of the instructor, not the gloating sneer of the torture-master.

'She works for JB Enterprises up there. It's a big firm. You'll track her down from that!'

Ennio released the injured hand. 'That wasn't so hard, was it?' he asked. Then, slowly and calmly, with infinite care and patience, he began to flay Johnny's face.

66

11

ANDREA HAD FIRST discovered the other kind of privacy some days after the opening of the Meard Street salon. The girl from East Anglia, accustomed during her youth to the genteel bustle of King's Lynn, a bustle which offered frequent glimpses of friendly or familiar faces, in antique but comfortable surroundings, had been too busy building up her business to discover it before. The constant round of premises, accountants, financiers and, not least, her visits to QBB, together with the interviewing and selection of staff compatible with the Andrea Duncan Salons philosophy, hadn't left her time to wander the impersonal, crowded streets of England's first city.

She'd know soon enough if the West End gamble was going to pay off. QBB's campaign was in full swing and, so far, the new salon was doing steady business. A few weeks would show if the repeat bookings were coming in and there was little point in making firm plans until then. Thus it was that Andrea decided to take a few days out of her crowded schedule and explore this new world she was now endeavouring to conquer.

Besides, she needed some time to herself for another reason as well. A reason that marred the satisfaction she should have felt every time she glimpsed one of QBB's ads in the tube. A reason called Tim Garfield.

They had broken up, bitterly, less than three weeks before, and despite her active role in their parting Andrea was left with a sense of loss only slightly less than the death of her father had caused her. She tried to compensate by only remembering the pleasant moments, knowing as she did that it was both foolish and impossible to try and forget completely, but that last argument, all her own work, she chided herself, kept returning to haunt her thoughts at unexpected moments.

She mingled with the crowds of shoppers in Regent Street and Oxford Street, women laden with carrier bags, girls in Next Directory dresses, businessmen with a window in their diary buying shoes and shirts, mothers being dragged, mentally screaming, towards Hamleys. Surrounded by people and alone, except for her memories.

Even after her marriage to Josh she took pleasure in these solitary sorties. The others were there for the shopping, or snatching lunch, or hurrying to and from appointments. But Andrea was there to be alone in the crowd, to find a species of anonymity in its amorphous mass.

Occasionally, especially after the move to Ringley Abbey, when it was so much more difficult to just happen to be in town, she would find some excuse for the indulgence. A rare ingredient for a culinary confection, though she hardly ever cooked. A haunting of the Bond Street galleries for a macabre print, or a search of the antique shops for a demonic Victorian figurine. On this particular day, though, she had a purpose that was to be more far-reaching than was usual for her. It was also taking far more courage than she had needed to show for several years to follow through.

Andrea cut away from Oxford Street towards Soho Square. Once past the corner windows the bright gaudiness of the shops vanished behind her, replaced with stepped doorways and a general impression of urban darkness. Glass windows appeared dim where they weren't actually dirty and company signs were small, modest affairs, like the one she eventually stopped and stared at. The gilded letters were chiselled into marbled perspex and it was held in place with dome-head screws.

FACTFINDERS it said. Then, smaller, SECOND FLOOR.

She mounted the steps and tried the door, which opened rather stiffly. Her dress, for the occasion, was deliberately anonymous and her hair was gathered up beneath her hat. As she stepped into the narrow hallway, stairs ahead of her with worn lino treads, blank door to the ground floor offices to her right, she felt that prickling in her bladder which always worried her before any kind of meeting. Today, out of practice, it worried her even more.

Still, they must have a loo up there, if she really needed it.

Outside, the taxis and despatch bikes struggled not to dent each other. Inside, mounting the creaking stairs, only the seediness was left to remind her she was in the city. That and the air of darkness which the light in this sort of building always seemed to generate as a protesting paradox.

The stairs turned and she turned with them, her hesitancy forgotten before an onslaught of inevitability. She passed a door on the first floor landing without looking at its grime-brown sign and continued upwards. The colour

69

of the lino changed, but that was all. Diffused light from the cloudy day outside entered through a high window in the stairwell, serving only to deepen the shadows surrounding her ascent.

The door on the second floor landing bore a smaller, dirtier version of the sign at the street entrance. Taped beneath it was a Letraset card that said PLEASE ENTER. She took it at its word and pushed through the door.

Glaring electric light surrounded her with its artificial summer. Andrea blinked, then focused on a small office with a door at the further end and seats to one side. On the other side was a desk with typewriter, telephone and too many stacks of paper. Behind it sat a woman with greying brown hair who might once, Andrea decided, have been described as pretty. The bone-structure was still good, but the flesh above it had sagged and begun to wrinkle like a neglected chamois leather.

Muddy eyes looked up at her. 'Can I help?' the painted mouth enquired.

'I have an appointment to see Mr Gaunt,' Andrea replied, her old assurance returning before this prime candidate for the Andrea Duncan Salons treatment.

'Can I have your name, please?'

Pure ritual if she was on time, which she was. Still, the niceties had to be observed. Even Josh realised that from time to time.

'Mrs Buchanan.'

The woman checked a diary. 'Of course,' she smiled. 'I'll just tell Mr Gaunt you're here.'

She stood up and walked to the inner door. Her clothes had once been as good as her features. Some lived in life. Others, like this one, died in it. A manicured hand tapped the glass, then twisted the handle carefully, as if afraid it would come away. The head vanished briefly.

'Mrs Buchanan is here,' filtered around the half-open door. A mumble from inside followed and the head reappeared.

'Please go in,' it said, the body opening the door wider. Andrea complied.

The inner office was larger than that outside, but just as clogged with paper. Obviously Gaunt needed a few good clients in order to afford a few more filing cabinets. His own desk, though, was relatively clear, centred by a leather-cornered blotting pad and with an ageing trimphone on one corner.

His appearance belied his name, Andrea immediately decided. Gaunt was a small man, about five six or seven, with no hair and only half an eyebrow. Yet despite his lack of height and relatively slim features he must have been a forty-eight or fifty chest. In his suit, the jacket obstinately refusing to button, he looked as if someone had plugged an air-line to his big toe and blown him up several sizes too big. As he came around the desk and extended his hand, however, his speed of movement belied his size. His handshake was firm, not flabby, and he smelled of an expensive aftershave.

'Do sit down, Mrs Buchanan,' he gestured to the only available chair on the other side of the desk. Then he seated himself.

'How may I help you?' he enquired, solicitously. His voice was deep, with the matured edge of a pipe-smoker, though there was nothing in the office to confirm he was.

Andrea hesitated.

'Be assured that everything you tell me will remain in the strictest confidence,' Gaunt told her. 'Believe me, I wouldn't still be in business if that wasn't the case.'

This was being in business? Andrea asked herself. Oh, what the hell.

71

'I have reason to believe my husband is being unfaithful,' she stated flatly.

'I'm so sorry.' The voice was sympathetic and the expression matched it. Somewhere behind the eyes the mind was saying: Not another fucking divorce snoop! 'Would you care to give me some details?'

A sheet of paper appeared on the blotter and a pen slid out between the pudgy fingers, waiting mutely.

A prompt seemed to be needed. 'Your husband is?' Gaunt enquired.

Joshua Buchanan, she thought. My husband is Joshua Buchanan of JB Enterprises plc, and in my own way I love him too much to be doing this. That was what she thought, but her mouth gave Gaunt the details just the same.

'And what is the basis of your belief?' came the next question, still oozing sympathy and understanding instead of boredom.

Andrea dragged it out of herself, suspicion by painful suspicion. As she listened to her words she had to admit it wasn't much. It was enough for Gaunt, though. His pen scrabbled over the paper like a demented electro-cardiograph.

'That would seem to indicate some basis for your misgivings,' Gaunt muttered, peering up at her through slightly rheumed dark eyes. 'Do you have any idea as to when he might next have the opportunity to provide concern?'

Andrea found herself hoping that Gaunt's reports would be easier to read than the man was to listen to. Too much of his cut-price Civil Servantese would set her teeth firmly on edge and keep them there. Still, if he could do the job . . .

'I know he'll be in Manchester this evening. He usually goes up for two or three days every month.'

'Excellent, Mrs Buchanan. Well now, I think that you may safely permit me to expedite enquiries from this point on. Are you acquainted with my charges for this type of work?'

'I think I'll be able to afford you, Mr Gaunt.'

'Quite so. Well then,' he continued, standing up, 'I may only add that my pleasure in meeting you has been sadly marred by the circumstances promoting our meeting. Be assured that I will do all in my power to assist you in settling this matter, one way or the other.'

The interview was obviously over and Andrea stood up and took her leave. In the outer office the secretary handed her a folder (marbled finish, gold lettering) containing some background information on Factfinders and a charge sheet.

She made her way back down to the street and wandered aimlessly towards Soho Square. Then, missing the crowds, she cut across to Charing Cross Road, intending to head for the impersonal sterility of the British Museum. As she turned from New Oxford Street into Coptic Street she found the road blocked to traffic by several parked police vehicles, lights flashing, and an ambulance with open doors. A crowd had gathered on both pavements and whilst she was pushing her way through a stretcher bearing a zipped body bag was brought out from a doorway beside a bookshop, uniformed figures clearing a path for it.

A police radio crackled somewhere. An officer bent to the transceiver clipped to his tunic. 'Not yet, sarge,' he said quietly. 'Need a dental check for confirmation. Poor bastard had all the skin peeled off his face.'

Andrea shuddered briefly to herself, then carried on by. When she reached the British Museum and began to climb the steps outside, she was smiling, lost in her own inner world once again. The body in the bag had nothing to do

73

with her. It was as separate, as remote, as one of George Romero's celluloid walking dead, face or no face.

Would the muscles keep their shape without the ectodermic layer? she wondered. Would they stay firm enough for a death mask to reveal the person's features, only a millimetre or so smaller all round? Or would they relax and collapse, distorting the face, making it unrecognisable, a shapeless mush with glaring, lidless, poached-egg eyes?

She passed through the swing door, with its obligatory security guard, and made her way towards the replica shop in the entrance hall. Andrea was level with the corridor leading to the Reading Room, thinking about the predynastic mummy, curled up and shrivelled like an outsize foetus, in one of the galleries upstairs, when the figure, hunched over as it walked, returning the ubiquitous Filofax to its Samsonite briefcase, slammed into her.

Her thoughts collapsed. Her arm throbbed briefly with the impact. Her balance faltered, but held. The briefcase slammed to the polished floor and lay there, echoing.

'I'm so sorry,' said a voice. 'Are you all right?'

Andrea froze. Only her eyes moved, swiveling to stare at the figure, its fallen briefcase forgotten for the moment. She knew that voice. Well. Too well.

'Andrea? It *is* you, isn't it?'

Slowly she began to function again. She forced her frozen muscles to relax, as if the constricting skin had been flayed from them. Here and there people were still looking at them, their eyes drawn by the sudden noise. Security guards seemed to have appeared from every entrance and exit, watching, speaking briefly and quietly into hand-held transceivers before melting quietly away.

She touched a hand to her hair and then faced him, unsmiling. Here and there the suspicion of a line had been added, but they'd suit his features as they deepened and multiplied with age. His blue eyes twinkled, despite their obvious concern, and his hand gripped her arm firmly but gently, instinctively steadying her against a fall. Andrea looked down at that hand and waited for the fingers to uncurl and release her.

'Hello, Tim,' she said flatly. Too flatly. He'd never believe her show of indifference if she couldn't even convince herself of it. 'What are you doing here?'

He shrugged. 'Oh, you know. Just the usual research.'

'I'd have thought Company House would have been your most likely stamping ground. This place caters for dons and boffins, not ad men.'

Stay cold. Anchor an iceberg and tow it in between.

He bent to retrieve his briefcase, which had miraculously closed in falling instead of spilling its contents by landing butter-side-up.

'You are still an ad man, aren't you?' Andrea asked, reproving herself immediately for showing any kind of interest. It would probably take the rest of the day and several drinks to get her heart back under control without prolonging the chance meeting.

He grinned. Same old Tim Garfield grin. 'Sure am. Got my own firm now. Here.' He set the briefcase down between his legs, handle up, and pulled a card from his pocket.

PHANTASTICADS
Tim Garfield
Managing Director

'Well, well. Very up and coming.'

'You look well, Andy. Things going okay with Mr Buchanan?'

'Yes. Thank you.' Don't quibble about him calling you Andy. Just find a way out of here. Now. 'I ought to be going.'

Her feet stayed put. She told them to move again. They took no notice.

'So soon? We could have a cup of coffee . . .'

'No. I must be on my way. Well, goodbye.'

'Okay. Hey, you're looking great. Let's have a drink sometime,' he called after her, her feet finally doing what she told them to, trying not to quicken up on their own in their enthusiasm to make amends.

He stood there, watching her push out through the swing door and vanish from the feet up down the steps. Same pretty Andy he'd first fallen for on the outside. Still trying to pretend indifference and not doing it particularly well. But inside there was a change going on. It wasn't the same old Andy looking out of her eyes. There was a fear, almost a desperation, in them that had never been there before. Not just the alarm of their sudden and unexpected meeting but something hungry and unhealthy as well.

He'd known her too well for Andrea to ever really be a stranger to him again, no matter how much she might pretend to be, or want to be. Did she really want to, though? It felt like an act, and with Andy Duncan that usually meant it was an act. He reached down and picked up his briefcase, patting it affectionately with his other hand. It had played its part well, better than either of the two humans had done. Now all that remained was to wait and see if she called him.

Even if she didn't, Andrea Duncan wasn't going to be too hard to find.

Suddenly Tim Garfield shuddered and looked around him. The last echo of the falling briefcase was long gone now and people had stopped looking. A school party was heading up the main staircase, an adult at either end. There was a small queue at the hand-luggage office and the usual one or two people checking the museum plan.

Apart from that a variety of miscellaneous men, women, children and races were crossing and recrossing the hall, on their way to or coming from.

Both the shudder and his thought about finding Andy had arrived together. The more he thought about it, his eyes darting from stranger face to stranger face, the more Tim Garfield became convinced that the thought hadn't been entirely his own. For the first time in his life he was ready to credit telepathy, ready to believe that he had picked up another's thoughts. And the shudder was because he didn't like it. There was a particular nastiness about a stranger getting inside his head like that.

He looked over at the swing doors. Two children and a woman coming in. A fair-haired man in a business suit going out. Three Japanese standing examining a camera. All strangers.

Tim forced himself to dismiss the thought and began to leave. Metaphysical speculations were okay in their place, he decided. And that place wasn't out winning new accounts. Or mooning about Andy Duncan, who probably wouldn't call him anyway.

On impulse he stopped at a phone box outside the railings and riffled through the battered directories. Eventually he found Josh Buchanan's St John's Wood address and ran his finger across to the number. Keeping it there he fed in his phonecard, hooked the receiver between neck and shoulder, and dialled.

The steady, unbroken unobtainable tone whined in his ear. He replaced the receiver and punched in Directory Enquiries.

'Directory. Which town, please?'

He read Josh's entry in the book and asked them to check it. The pleasant, impersonal voice kept him holding a few moments, then came back: 'I'm sorry, that number has been disconnected. I'll try New Numbers for you.'

New Numbers, eventually, didn't have anything either. He hung up and pocketed his phonecard again. So much for Andy being easy to find, he chided as he continued along Great Russell Street to his next appointment.

12

SHE SAT ALONE in the black room most of the time. There was a strong light in one corner and a shelf of books behind it, and there was a desk where she did the writing they required of her. There was also a plain black carpet on the floor which showed up anything she dropped, any scrap of paper or fingernail clipping. These she picked up almost before they'd fallen and carefully placed them in the small black cauldron in the corner which served for a waste bin.

In addition she had a high backed chair, elaborately carved and stained ebony, with a velvet-covered seat. Black, naturally.

Of course there were other colours in the world besides black. The light wasn't black. Neither were the illustrations in some of the books, though the print was. The brightest, most colourful books were the ones she'd had from the very beginning, the ones with the photographs of men and women and children and animals and the objects they used. Like the great fat imitation man-bits that the women put up themselves, and the hollow tubes the little white mice ran along, and the douches and masks and whips and dog-collars and shackles. Every so often the man would come in and give her a new one. Nuns torturing men's privates with canes and cigarette-ends. Priests doing painful-looking things to children. All so realistic you could even count the hairs.

When the woman came to give her her lessons they read from some of the other books, the older ones with dark blocks of print and no pictures. Many had strange diagrams which gradually became familiar. Some had funny writing where the letters weren't quite right, where the S was written as an F and the pages crumbled if you handled them roughly. Not that she ever did. She knew much better than to do that.

Sometimes they didn't come to give her things, but to see how well she remembered what she'd learned about drawing the diagrams or saying the words. The words had to be said properly or there would be anger. Not from the man or the woman, but from the one outside, the one they told her about but whom she never saw. Usually about once a day they'd test her on the sucking and stroking and rubbing actions she'd mastered, and if she was very good they'd do it back to her as a reward.

She didn't know the words *mother* and *father* except as the designated terms for two people making a baby. Somehow she knew that the man and the woman hadn't made her, that she was different sperm and egg to theirs, but she couldn't have explained just how she knew. A sort of instinct, she supposed. Perhaps a manifestation of one of those extra senses they kept telling her about.

The room was warm and comfortable and she didn't bother to wear clothes inside it, only dressing from the rail in the ante-room when she was allowed into the rest

80

of the house. This happened twice a day for meals, late morning and early evening, plates of fruit and bread and thinly-sliced raw meat, washed down with water or wine. Sometimes in the evening she'd be allowed to stay down and watch one of the films they'd made of her with the strangers they brought to the ritual room, praising the whiteness of her skin or the size of her nipples on the still-developing breasts, or the capacity she afforded to even the largest of her partners. She took delight in this, and in hearing about how she was finally going to be initiated shortly.

Initiation was everything. After initiation she'd have a name of her own, instead of just being *girl*. Although she wasn't sure exactly why she knew that having a name was going to make her important in some way. Neither man nor woman had a name. Not one she'd heard, at least. But *she* would.

Now initiation had come and gone. Pravus stood in front of the long mirror in the black room and examined herself to see if her name had made any difference that she could see. The reflection disappointingly showed her the same thing that it always did, an unclothed girl not quite half-way through her teens, still developing, her blond hair cut just above the shoulder, framing an attractive if slightly sharp-featured face with a wide mouth and large eyes.

No change.

Of course the initiation had hurt at times, but there had to be pain in order for her to enjoy pleasure to the full. Sometimes the two mingled in a most remarkable way, and that was what Pravus sought the most. It happened on the bed in the ritual room sometimes. And the toys that the man and woman had given her, like the ones in her picture-books, could often help her to do it to herself.

One of the most amazing things about the initiation had been the number of people she'd seen there. They had to be people behind those skull masks because of what she'd had to do to them. Only people responded as they had when she performed those rituals. But so *many* of them. To a girl brought up alone in seclusion it was all very bewildering.

Still, they had names. She'd heard them call them out. And now she had a name as well it meant that she must be one of them. That had to be a good thing, didn't it?

Woman told her that the Magister Inferi would be coming to see her soon. Pravus wasn't frightened at the thought of the goat-headed figure, though she worried about his artificial penis and told woman that she didn't like it very much. Woman stroked her hair and told her not to be such a silly girl. The Magister was only coming to talk to her. Soon now she'd be taking a more active part in the workings of the brotherhood, and the only reason for the Magister's visit was to explain what he expected of her. And if he did anything else he'd do it with his real penis, not the one he wore for initiations, and that wasn't going to be anything to worry about.

So there, Pravus dear. Don't worry your pretty head.

She felt calmer after that. Or not so concerned about the impending visit, anyway. In fact Pravus began to become quite excited at the prospect. She'd always suspected that there was more to her life than just the black room and Man and Woman, and now the Magister was coming to prove her right. If he was taking this special interest in her then she was bound to rise through the ranks of the coven and become important in her own right. One day she might even be the Madonna.

So why hasn't he come already, Woman? Why is he taking so long?

Hush, little Pravus. Don't pester. The Magister is a very busy man. He has other things to do first. More important things.

That crushed her a little. If the Magister had more important things than coming to see her she wasn't as important herself as she'd begun to believe. But that he was coming at all, no matter when, meant that she was at least a little bit important.

And that would have to be good enough for now.

13

ANDREA'S HEART WAS still pounding when she unlocked the door of her Escort Ghia, in an underground
car-park off Russell Square, and slid in behind the steering-
wheel. As she reversed out of her space and started up the
spiral exit ramp she began a vain attempt to sort through
the sheer range of emotions that her casual encounter with
Tim Garfield had generated.

Anger, yes. There was definitely anger. He'd been
banished from her life, albeit never terribly successfully,
and he had no right at all to come blundering back into it. It
was neither fair nor just of him to revive those old memories
which she'd painted over with Josh. Especially now, when
good old Josh himself was showing signs of decay.

If she was honest with herself there was also a trace
of their former love for one another, still glimmering
faintly like an ember that could be fanned back into
life. That caused more anger, though this time tainted
with despair. Supposing she wanted that to happen, but
he didn't? Supposing she left Josh to his infidelities and

started her own with Tim again, only to fail a second time? Thoughts previously unthinkable began to circle in a carousel, riderless horses harnessed to impossible possibilities.

What had she done with his card? She'd only glanced at it in the BM, not taking in the phone number. She slowed, near the car-park exit, ready to brake and check her bag. A Datsun Bluebird behind flashed its lights and shattered her wondering with a brief blast on its horn. She speeded up again.

When she reached the barrier she opened her bag for her purse and glimpsed the card lying beside it. Good, it was there if it was wanted, just like Tim had always been.

Andrea paid at the booth and swung out into the traffic without any clear idea of the direction she was taking. Behind her the blue Fiesta slipped off its hazard lights and drew away from the kerb, following her up to Euston Road, then across towards Hackney as her memories took over the wheel. She turned north through Islington, heading for Green Lanes and the A10, driving back towards the familiar country of her childhood. When she reached the outskirts of Greater London at Ponders End the Fiesta dropped back, its blond driver smiling to himself as he maintained a discreet distance.

After all, this was as good a way to Manchester as any. And it wasn't as if he couldn't guess where Andrea was going. The only puzzle was why she had taken his road, through nothing little villages, instead of speeding up to Cambridge on the M11. Nostalgia, perhaps. The sort of sentiment that Ennio had rooted out of his life for ever. Like conscience and compassion.

She took the by-pass around Cambridge and was through Ely shortly after one in the afternoon. She'd skipped breakfast that morning and lunch was beginning to beckon strongly. There'd be a little pub somewhere offering vodka and sandwiches. Plenty of time. She could even be through Downham Market and into King's Lynn before the pink-washed Duke's Head Hotel on the Market Square had finished serving lunch.

Sunshine burst sporadically through the clouds to her left, threatening to end the day's dullness as she abandoned her car in the Market Square a little after two and entered the Duke's Head. Instead of pausing in the bar she went straight into the green decorated dining room and ordered a bourgeois cru claret from the wine list. Home territory always helped her to relax, to bathe herself in a world that was somehow surreal because it didn't emerge from a video screen.

The Fiesta parked a little way away from her Escort. Once Andrea was safely out of sight Ennio got out and stretched himself, languidly, indulging in a yawn as the cramps vanished from his knees and elbows. There had been times on the drive that he'd thought she'd never stop. For anything. A Flying Dutchman of the highways and byways, leading him ever on without a pause to satisfy his desires. Thinking of which . . .

He checked that she was in the dining room before he found the Gents and returned to the bar. A sandwich would hold him and he could watch for Andrea to leave without being seen himself. It was important she didn't see him. Not yet awhile. Premature recognition could be dangerous for both of them.

That was, of course, assuming she remembered. But she'd remember, Ennio reassured himself. Oh yes, she'd remember. There was no way she could have forgotten. Especially if this little pilgrimage of self-indulgence was leading her to where he believed it would.

He replaced his first gin and tonic with a second and finished his ham sandwich. Probably Andrea would drive out and look at her grandfather's farm before she went on to her final destination, but Ennio wasn't to know that. He'd follow her, puzzled at first, then reassured as she drove on without getting out. Since the old man's death his son Martin had been running things, and Uncle Martin had been one of the few adults Andrea hadn't felt secure with during her childhood. He had a way of looking, a way of touching her, that wasn't altogether the same as her other relations.

She'd park and look down the lane: fields of lavender to either side, the plants dull and scrubby still at this time of year, house behind red brick against the sheltering woodland, then continue on her way towards the other place. It was near enough to walk to from the farm, as indeed she had done, often, in her childhood. Not any more, though. The place was sinister enough without the walk to bring back the full flood of her nightmare memories.

The claret went well with Andrea's steak and kidney pie, roast potatoes, brussels and carrots, and she finished the bottle almost without noticing. After coffee she checked her watch and discovered that it was gone three o'clock. Sunset would be about seven, and she wanted to be back at Ringley Abbey by then. The drive wasn't exactly easy as it meant cutting west and south across country from Cambridge, though she'd start making time once she picked up the M1 south of Milton Keynes. Her leisurely sit-down lunch had cost her more time than she'd bargained for, and she paid and left the Duke's Head with unceremonious haste, unwittingly tearing Ennio away from his next gin and tonic.

He followed her out of Lynn on the A47, hanging back just as far as he dared and taking the turn past West Bilney after slowing almost to a halt to give her time on the country lane. When her brake lights showed on the next corner he drove up to it and parked, skirting the hedgerow on foot to make sure she was parked beside the lane leading down to the farm.

She wasn't.

Running late, she'd decided not to stop at the farm but to carry on to her ultimate destination. Cursing to himself Ennio sprinted back to his car and twisted the key in the ignition. Foot down, his back wheels tore up the grass verge as the Fiesta ripped away in smoking pursuit. He almost missed the tiny right turn which led down beside the lavender field towards the woodland that sheltered the farmhouse, braking hard and squealing around it, tread-marks on the road recording his passage. As soon as he drew level with the woodland he abandoned the vehicle and began to run through the trees, the bracken clawing and whipping at his trousers. Cutting through this way he could still be there, even if Andrea chose only to remain for a few fleeting minutes.

Where the trees ahead began to thin out he saw the broken chancel-arch stabbing upwards like a gigantic open crab-claw. The sun had finally decided to shine for the last few hours of the day and the ancient stonework, threaded with ivy and splotched with lichens, showed stark and bright in the afternoon. Apart from a few low, overgrown walls it was all that remained of East Bilney church. Indeed, it was all that remained of East Bilney, except for the mouldering bones of centuried inhabitants in the surrounding abandoned churchyard. The village itself had perished as a result of land enclosures during the seventeenth century, together with so many others. The houses and other buildings, as well as much of the church itself, had been robbed for their stone by local builders in later times, eventually disappearing altogether.

He slowed down as he reached the bushes adjoining the overgrown churchyard. It wasn't part of his plan to rush out and confront Andrea. He intended to be much more subtle than that. A mere glimpse of him would be quite enough for now.

Ennio's eyes surveyed the overgrown desolation of the scene. He knew that Andrea wasn't going to be on this side of the church. She'd be across the ruined nave, staring at the table tomb that was burned into her memory, and into her dreams as well. She'd be wrapped in her nightmares, her arms folded across her breasts as her hands clasped her shoulders, alone with only herself to hug for comfort. It might not be the most grotesque of her sleeping memories, but it was by far the most recurrent.

He crossed beside the chancel arch. The floor of the church had long ago been replaced with a carpet of grass, cropped close and spotted with sheep droppings, and his progress was virtually silent. Only the occasional upward flutter of a bird betrayed his advance, and Andrea would be too drawn in to notice that. By the time she eventually saw him his appearance would be as effective as that of a stage magician catapulted upwards through a smoke-bomb shrouded trap.

She was there, sure enough, her car behind her on the road, on the other side of a distant fence standing defiantly above the encroaching vegetation. Her hat was gone and her hair hung down loose, as it had done all those years ago, and she had her arms about herself in exactly the way that Ennio had envisaged.

Or remembered.

He was forced to admit, watching her, that the exact details had become blurred in his own mind. But at least he had an excuse for that. He'd been preoccupied as Andrea advanced, not quite a woman but too old to be just a little girl. Preoccupied with his duty to those who had nurtured him from birth. Those who now called themselves the Sons of Samael.

Names didn't matter that much. He took pride in knowing the meanings of names. He'd felt a thrill of achievement when he'd finally tracked *Pravus* down in a Latin dictionary. It meant *crooked, deformed, perverted,* and he could have kicked himself for not having recognised the root of one of his favourite words. *Depraved.*

No, names didn't matter that much, but they usually had something to tell you. Like Andrea's relation to Andred, witch-goddess, bitch-goddess. Even demoness, from a Christian point of view. Not that Ennio was a Christian, but he'd learned enough of polemics to be able to think like the enemy when he had to.

One thing at a time, though. He could track the Magister Inferi's thinking on dirty little Pravus later. Right now there was an impression to be made. Or, rather, *another* impression to be made. On the mind of a fifteen-year-old girl who was now both a woman and a millionairess. The latter fact was hard to believe watching her drive that Escort, but Andrea had come up from nothing, guarding her copper coins, from a background that would have taught her modest tastes. She'd worked hard to build it and it could still vanish in a fraction of the time it had taken to accumulate. So she remained modest in her wants, indulging herself in clothes only to make Josh happy and to keep up the Andrea Duncan image.

So she was Andrea Buchanan now. She'd never been Andrea Buchanan to Ennio. Neither when he first saw her through ecstatic eyes, nor at this moment whilst she stared, remote and lost, at the table-tomb, decayed but still standing, that she had discovered habited in her youth.

He trod carefully, approaching with the stealth of the hunter, the violence-concealing grace of the killer. She remained within her memories, unseeing, unknowing, standing at one end of the raised and desecrated tombstone, her eyes riveted to the decayed inscription.

SACRED TO THE MEMORY OF JOSHUA SAMSON OF EAST BILNEYE . . .

Ennio stood at the other end of the tomb, willing her to raise her eyes and look at him. Gradually Andrea began to sense the presence of the intruder, to feel that she was no longer alone with her nightmare. Slowly she looked up, not knowing whether she was to find confirmation or solace, seeing at first nothing beyond the tall man, fair-haired, still good-looking, in the worsted business suit.

The executive in the graveyard. Was there really such a distance between executive and executioner? Even the distance of a slab of rotting tombstone?

'Hello, little girl,' said Ennio Zabetti. 'What are you doing here?'

When nightmare becomes reality, when Freddy Krueger chases you out of your dreams into the reality of Elm Street, there is only one reaction left.

Andrea screamed.

Then Andrea screamed again. And again. And Ennio watched and nodded to himself as her screams continued.

She was still screaming as she fled down the overgrown path and through the broken gate. As she fumbled with the ignition and stabbed the accelerator with her foot and roared off towards the insane and distant sanctuary of Ringley Abbey.

14

'DIVISIONAL CHIEF EXECUTIVE'S office? Hello, this is Mr Grimley in London. Look, I have a slight problem. Mr Buchanan's already left, you see.'

The woman's voice at the other end of the telephone responded sympathetically. 'Well, Mr Grimley, is there anything we can do to help?'

It's only a little thing, but I promised Mr Buchanan I'd let him have some figures tonight. His secretary's gone, you see, and his diary isn't available. I wonder if you know which hotel he'll be using?'

'Let me see if I can help you, Mr Grimley. I'm sure I have a note of the usual arrangements somewhere.' A pause. 'Yes, here we are. Mr Buchanan will be staying at the Picadilly Plaza Hotel.'

'Is that one C or two?'

'Just the one. I have a phone number here for it as well if you'd like it.'

'That's very helpful. Yes, I would.'

'Here you are then. It's 061–234 7313.'

That's marvellous. Many thanks.'

Leonard Gaunt put the grimy trimphone receiver back on its clear plastic rest and stood up. Walking around his desk he crossed over to the door and stuck his head into the outer office.

'See if you can find me a room for tonight at the Picadilly Plaza Hotel will you?' he asked his secretary. 'And find me train times. Probably from Euston. Oh, and Margot?'

'Yes, Len?'

'Make sure Mrs Buchanan's advance cheque goes into the night safe tonight. I don't want to bounce the tab after breakfast tomorrow.'

He returned to his desk and waited for Margot to get the train times. No point in packing anything. There probably wasn't anything clean at home to pack, even assuming he had the time or the inclination to bother to call in and look.

All that was going to change, though. Josh Buchanan's wayward prick was going to set Leonard Gaunt back on his feet.

Or take him off his feet. For ever.

15

ENNIO ZABETTI HAD stopped chuckling when he picked up the A17 outside King's Lynn, though he was still grinning broadly with the memory of Andrea's reaction to his appearance in the churchyard. He'd begun to sober to the work in hand by the time he reached Newark and connected with the Chesterfield road.

Dusk was falling as he passed south of Sheffield on his way to Stockport and, eventually, the centre of Manchester. He had the address of a woman who ran a bed and breakfast place off Moseley Street who could be counted on to keep her mouth shut if she had to. That was close enough to the regional office of JB Enterprises to be convenient for his purpose.

He thought about his purpose again. He also thought about the call he'd made earlier in the day, the one to Directory Enquiries to pick up the new number for a woman called Steffi Holt. That in itself had been fruitless because she'd not been up in the city long enough to have her number assigned. But the call to JB Enterprises, to the personnel office, having made sure that Steffi wasn't in the building, had reaped the harvest of her home address. It was amazing what people would volunteer if they thought you were somebody's brother.

While Leonard Gaunt smoked his pipe in the limbo of a second-class carriage between Crewe and Altrincham, Ennio was finding a parking space off Compton Road, where Mary Jordan's modest guest-house was. The streetlights were making the city centre look darker than it actually was, but Ennio didn't mind that at all. The dark was something he thought of as his natural habitat.

One phone call based on lies was going to discover Josh Buchanan's marital infidelity. Another call, also based on lies, was going to set Ennio Zabetti further along his chosen and committed path within the brethren of the Sons of Samael.

He greeted Mary Jordan in the prescribed manner and she responded appropriately. It was all very Masonic and theatrical, but worked. Doubtless at the end of the world they'd also shake hands with the devil in exactly the same way, then go off and collect their pitchforks.

She showed him to a comfortable room, the largest and best appointed in the entire dump, he decided, and offered him a meal. He accepted and they made small talk before they made love. Mary knew enough not to ask him why he was there. And by the time he'd finished in her bed he knew she also knew enough not to check with his Magister Inferi.

Ennio watched television (a re-run of *The Fury*) and drank several cans of beer before he went off to his own bed. He set the alarm Mary gave him for half five and settled down to a dreamless four hours' sleep. In the pocket of his suit jacket the butterfly knife slumbered as well, unaware of its owner's hunger for Steffi Holt's young flesh.

16

IT WAS ALMOST ten in the evening when the shabby figure of Leonard Gaunt checked into the Picadilly Plaza Hotel. His room was far from being the best of the singles and all he had to help him find his quarry was a magazine photo of Josh Buchanan from the pages of *Chief Executive*. Even so, it didn't take him long to discover the original of the likeness waiting (obviously) in the hotel's Starlight Bar.

He sat himself down with the *Evening Standard* he'd bought for the train and a half of bitter, at a table which gave him a clear view of both the bar and the doorway. The paper was already well-read, but it at least gave him a palpable excuse for being there, half watching Josh, half reflecting on his own situation.

So he wasn't Sam Spade. At forty-nine, privately dreading fifty next year, he was never going to be. He wasn't even a retired policeman. Leonard Alfred Gaunt was simply a lad from Croydon who'd grown up on a diet of Raymond Chandler and Dashiell Hammett. His education had been basic, stopping at fifteen when he'd been apprenticed as a tool-maker. From then on for the next twenty-seven years his outer world consisted of heavy plant, the smell of hot oil, the sound of grinding metal (every steel had its own note on the key-scale, depending upon the operation it was being subjected to), power lines and glass-panelled engineering workshops. Inwardly though he was investigating sordid mysteries in the grimy surroundings of tenement blocks and LA back alleys, his 1911 Government Colt .45 in its shoulder holster, one round already in the breech so he didn't have to give away his position by pulling the slide back when he needed to use it. Various medical problems reduced his fitness, piling weight on and stealing his hair, but Len Gaunt PI knew it was all in the mind really, and dreamed determinedly on.

Then, as his dreams were beginning to fade, as life was souring back into the dull, omnipresent grind of reality, the impossible had happened. A £100 000 Premium Bond win had broken the machine-shop shackles for ever, freeing him to do whatever he wanted. And naturally there was only one thing he'd ever wanted.

Thus FACTFINDERS was born. Gaunt leased his grubby office, not quite in Soho but probably a little safer for that, converted his wife Margot into his secretary on the advice of his accountant, and ran modest newspaper and Yellow Pages ads to let the world know there was a new Private Enquiry Agent ready to do battle with the forces of evil. The only problem was that the forces of evil never quite lived up to his fantasies, and the income only occasionally matched up to the expenditure. Instead of tracking down drug smugglers and the murderers of beautiful, semi-clad victims he spent his time following errant husbands or wives, compact camera in his pocket, or posing as a shop-floor worker to discover who was pilfering the stock. Even the Firearms Act conspired against him, stopping him from even carrying the replica government Colt that reposed in a drawer of his desk. The British police didn't like private citizens running round with shooters, especially as they didn't do it themselves all that often.

And so he sat behind his paper in the Picadilly Plaza Hotel, eyes half-focused just above the headlines, not exactly watching but certainly aware of the presence of Josh Buchanan. Gaunt was going to get a good fee for this, regardless of results. Margot knew enough to make sure Mrs Buchanan was on the upper scale of charges when she handed that folder over and extracted the retainer. One way or another Buchanan was going to pay off a few debts, Len smiled to himself behind the football features.

Josh checked his Rolex and hefted another handful of dry-roast peanuts past his whisky and water. He was too much of an old hand to show the nervousness he felt, sitting waiting for his company to arrive. This was the first time he'd have seen Steffi since her transfer north, and although he'd put a fair amount of personal effort into finding her an excellent position and a flat to go with it he wasn't sure exactly how she had reacted to the move. What made it even worse was that her reaction when he'd proposed their meeting on the phone had been completely unreadable. That was one reason why he'd taken the chance of suggesting that they meet here at the hotel. Steffi's acceptance had been as non-commital as the rest of their conversation, and he wasn't certain that they'd eventually be going upstairs together. Not by a long shot.

See how it goes, he told himself. Feel it through. Then, if this is 'Fuck off, Josh,' I can call it quits and walk away. I can do without some action for one night, he added mentally, surveying the lone females in skimpy evening wear scattered around the bar area. Most of them looked as if you could catch something nasty off them. And these days there were several very nasty somethings just waiting to be caught.

Len Gaunt was also aware of the working girls setting themselves up with a drink before starting the night shift, but for a very different reason. He wanted pictures of Josh and whoever Josh met, male or female, innocent or guilty. That way he'd have demonstrable proof for Andrea of her husband's activities. The main problem was that the film in his camera was only 400 ASA, and he doubted that there'd be enough light in the Starlight Bar, winkies twinkling from the ceiling and bar area backlit, for his compact to provide clear results. Still, Sam Spade would have found a way round it, and Lenny Gaunt was going to as well.

One of the girls (definitely a euphemism, Gaunt decided) was looking over towards him. He lowered his paper slightly and raised his glass in salute. Dyed blonde, her hefty bustline looking like a prosthesis, she had the one thing the investigator was looking for.

No glasses.

She smiled and teetered over on five-inch heels that only served to emphasise her short, fat legs. Between the tightness of her skirt and the careful balance of her feet the movement reminded Gaunt of pistons rotating on a cam-shaft. Even so, he closed his paper and stood up as she reached his table, motioning for her to sit down out of courtesy, as well as not liking having to look up at a woman while he was talking to her. She smiled again, bathing him in breath flavoured with onions and dental chewing-gum, then sat.

'Woss your name then, luv?' she asked him in broad Lancashire.

'Len,' he told her. 'Want to earn twenty quid?'

'I'm worth a bit more than that, dearie . . .'

'Not for two minutes' work, my sweet.'

Her mascara-clad eyes narrowed, the flagrantly false lashes threatening to embrace in an unholy and permanent union. 'You some kind of pervert?' she demanded.

'Only with my clothes off, and we both keep them firmly on. What I want is simple enough. And the only time we have to touch is when I pay you.'

The eyes remained narrowed but attentive. At one point, early on in his explanation, Gaunt asked her to widen them. Two minutes after that she returned to the bar and bought herself another drink while Gaunt returned to the *Evening Standard*, now more dog-eared than ever.

Twenty quid, Monica thought. Well, if nothing else came along in the next few minutes, it'd be better than nothing. In fact she could almost make a living out of doing this one small thing twice a night instead of bedding and spreading.

Gaunt propped the paper up and slipped the camera out of his pocket. The ideal, as far as the client was concerned, though no longer as far as the law was, had to be an *in flagrante delicto* shot. An on-the-job snap. That took more time and effort and bribery than he wanted to put into the job, though, unless he was extremely lucky. And while there were people around who regularly committed adultery with the lights on, few of them ever left the hotel bedroom door open for a photographer to sneak in and snap them. So, Gaunt reasoned, down here would do. And if he got away with that without being noticed he could always *try* the bedroom later. Just in case.

Monica was about to give up on the easy cash and take a turn down Picadilly when Steffi arrived at the entrance to the Starlight Bar. Real blond hair, big eyes, big tits, easy walk, she was everything that Monica pretended to be and wasn't. That made her a hate-object. It also made earning her twenty quid much more of a pleasure.

She watched Steffi walk past her and stand beside the big man with the whisky and water, listening carefully. For a few moments they just looked at one another, Josh hangdog, Steffi faintly smouldering. Only when Steffi's features began to relax did Monica begin to earn her cash.

'Hey, Nick,' she beckoned the barman. Then, more quietly: 'I've dropped a contact lens. Can you put the main lights on a sec?'

'Yeah, okay,' Nick grinned.

Three things connected almost together. The first was Nick's hand with the lighting panel behind the bar. The second was Steffi's lips with Josh's. The third was Gaunt's finger on the shutter-button of his compact. Rapidly he wound on and clicked again, but the moment was past and Josh and Steffi had separated in surprise.

Monica made a show of groping around the carpet. 'Here it is,' she announced. Then she trotted unsteadily off to the Ladies to replace the imaginary object.

Gaunt slipped the camera back into his pocket, refusing to allow himself to grin until his paper was firmly back in place. By the time Monica returned the lighting was back to the subdued usual, and nobody noticed the bald little fat man in the corner slipping her a couple of tenners. Least of all, he was delighted to observe, Steffi Holt and Josh Buchanan. They were too involved with making up.

Shortly afterwards a waiter brought menus through and Josh and Steffi settled to the serious business of selecting the evening's culinary delights. Gaunt was delighted to notice that they both drank as if neither one of them was going anywhere that evening. While they swilled it down he stuck to his original glass of bitter. You couldn't be Sam Spade if your head was swimming the channel.

Eventually they surrendered the menus and ordered another round, Nick the barman replacing the bowl of dry-roast nuts in front of Josh. Shortly afterwards they were politely summoned to the dining room. Gaunt followed them far enough to see them seated, then treated himself to another half.

The evening dragged. Ennio Zabetti was watching Kirk Douglas looking for his son, the CIA hot on his tail, when Josh and Steffi eventually left the dining room and moved towards the lifts. Taken slightly by surprise Gaunt had to fight his way through the late evening drinking throng and almost missed riding up to their floor with them. He left the lift just as the doors were beginning to close again and hung back, retying the shoelace on his elastic-sided boot as the lovers paused and Josh dug out his key. Within half a second of the door swinging closed Gaunt was outside it, listening for the click of the lock.

It didn't come.

Great. There was a chance for an on-the-jobber later. All he had to do was keep an ear to the door and listen for the sound of the bed creaking. Meanwhile he found out where the stairs to his own floor were and worked out how to reach them while appearing to bolt in the opposite direction if he had to. Not that there was much chance of being pursued through hotel corridors by a man with no clothes on, but he had to be sure. Fat men don't run very fast. Neither are they much good on stairs. They get out of breath and their hearts start pounding if they're summoned to unwonted exertion.

Fortunately Josh's room was within sight of the lift doors, so that whenever they opened Gaunt could be bending over, picking up a dropped glove or credit card, something that would give him a reason for being stationary when whoever it was got out and went towards their room. Not that they particularly noticed him at that late hour. Either they were too tired or too drunk, or both, to care about his presence.

He checked the door-handle to be certain. It turned. He pushed against it slightly to make sure it wasn't chained or snubbed from the inside. It wasn't. Finally he pushed it open and stood in the doorway. The lounge was in darkness, but a glimmer showed through the bedroom door. Good. He could get his on-the-jobber and be away before they realised what was happening. In fact, he told himself, if they're as involved as they could be, they won't even notice me.

Eat your heart out, Sam Spade.

For a heavy man he made surprisingly little noise as he crept across the lounge, light from the open outer door aiding his passage, and approached the bedroom. One thing he was going to do after this was get himself a camera with motor-wind so that he could manage two or three shots in this sort of situation without having to wind on by hand. *And* a dedicated flash that would take the speed of the motor. With a 1600 ASA film he'd never have to worry about low light again. The gear would soon pay for itself if he worked out the cost in terms of Monicas.

He heard the big man grunting with effort. The blonde bird was starting to make noises as well. Just a few little squeaks to begin with, but she sounded as if they were just the prelude to a very noisy climax. She was putting more and more voice into them, matching their rhythm to her partner's thrusts. With the light they'd left on he'd probably manage a good shot. Maybe two if he hung back until they were well and truly there.

Josh and Steffi grew louder. Her grunts had become moans and there was a questioning note in Josh's exhalations that told everyone he was hanging on for grim bloody death until she came. And from the increasing volume she was belting out that wasn't going to be too long at all. The moans became gasps, at first timed to Josh's thrusts then taking on a separate rhythm of their own, breathless and, in their way, quite as urgent.

The end is coming, Gaunt told himself. Then he suppressed a giggle as he noticed his own pun.

How dare you accuse me of being a peeping-Tom, he told an imaginary watcher. I'm doing this to perform a valuable service to a distressed lady, not for any personal gratification. That's purely a fringe benefit.

After all, when was the last time I had a woman like that? Maybe in a previous life, if I was into reincarnation.

His reverie shattered as Steffi voiced the first of several breathless screams. Josh responded with cries of 'Yeah. Yeah!' which almost drowned out his partner's shrieking. Gaunt edged closer, mentally egging the lovers on, then pushed the bedroom door further ajar.

The view was of tangled legs and bedclothes and a great hairy arse going up and down. He snapped it, then wound on and moved around, snapping again. A little further and he could get both their faces, suffused with pleasure at the merciful relief, eyes glazed, brows sweaty, mouths howling.

Click.

He was out of there before the moment passed. As Josh bellowed and flopped to one side Steffi wondered if the bedroom door had been that far ajar when they began. She tried to calm herself and listen, but Josh was still making too much noise, albeit contentedly. Steffi gave up and stroked his forehead. Later she'd stroke lower down and see if he was good for another bout.

Gaunt closed the outer door silently. Once back in the corridor he pocketed his camera and congratulated himself on his good luck. With two or three on-the-jobbers, at least one of which showed a face or two, and what he'd got in the bar earlier, Andrea Buchanan was going to have the answer she didn't really want. But by Christ she was going to pay for that answer, Gaunt decided.

He decided to take the lift back to his room. Maybe it wasn't the way an old hand like Sam Spade would have done it, but it was close enough. And much more comfortable for his bulk than all those stairs.

17

ANDREA WAS STILL running, her feet and legs entangled with the bedclothes, when she awoke. Her journey home had been uneventful enough, except for the two near-accidents her initial panic had generated at rural road junctions.

She'd arrived home shortly after seven and found Ringley Abbey deserted. In itself that wasn't surprising, as their help came up from Abbots Ringley and didn't live in. But the way the old house tried to sooth her with its creaking timbers and whispering galleries only served to put her nerves more on edge, sending her down to the silent stone comfort of the hidden vault, where every comfort she might require had been installed by her cheating husband.

Her hands were shaking as she slammed *A Nightmare On Elm Street* into the video and poured herself a glass of Bulgarian Cabernet Sauvignon (1982). *Nightmare* was always a good defence because the basic idea was so clever. If she was going to dream, if her past was going to reach out to haunt her in the shape of Ennio Zabetti, though she still didn't know his name, the character of Fred Krueger was a marvellous antidote. Someone who could follow you out of your dreams to kill you was preferable, in Andrea's eyes, to someone who remained inside them to haunt your sleep.

She watched the film to its conclusion, Freddy's razor-gloved hand smashing through the little window in the front door and wreaking its ghastly havoc, then opened a second bottle and carried it up to bed. Somehow, whenever she awoke, she felt that grinning corbel outside the arched window of her bedroom leering at her, so she set down her glass and bottle and went downstairs. Opening the front door she stepped outside and peered up at the stone face, then shuddered as the renewed familiarity of Ennio Zabetti stared back, the weathered sandstone blowing her an unwelcome kiss.

As she slammed the door and fled upstairs without bothering to set the alarm she knew that Freddy Krueger was a pussy-cat compared to the man she'd seen again today.

'Here's Freddy,' sneered the voice in her dreams. But it wasn't coming from Freddy's burned and blistered face. It was coming from somewhere behind those cold blue eyes, from the depths of that fair-haired skull. And that wasn't Freddy's glove slashing towards her. It was some sort of folding knife that was going to take her face off, slice by painful slice. And in the background was a robed, skull-masked figure, torch upraised, revealing the body of a mutilated female stretched across a table tomb. Her legs were parted, too parted, and her face was missing.

She tossed and turned, but remained asleep.

'Come to me?' the gargoyle asked. 'Visit me in the void?'

The skull-masked figure chanted. 'Void . . . void . . . void . . .'

'Who . . .are you?' Andrea asked hesitantly.

'I am your last and greatest love,' came Ennio's reply, the knife still glistening wickedly in the torchlight.

'Void . . . void . . . void . . .'

He began to chase her. She ran, stumbling through the treacle of her sleeping world towards dementia. Her screams rang out as he gained on her, coming ever nearer, the knife growing ever sharper, figures bursting from their coffins and groping blindly to pull her down. She aimed a kick at one and the wrist-bones shatterd, the gaunt hand flying off into forgetfulness until she realised that it was Josh's hand, and it had been trying to aid her in her terror. With a howl she fled on.

'Come to me?' the gargoyle that was Ennio asked again.

She glanced back at it. Suddenly it was as handsome and compelling as she had always wanted it to be. The Adonis on the gravestone was calling out to her, tempting her, impelling her. The knife was gone and there was only the growing bond of desire, drawing them together. He took her gently in his arms and bent his face towards her, his breath sweet and his body warm and wonderful.

Then he bit her lips off and she screamed again. And again. There was nothing to keep it in now and it rattled agonisingly past her exposed and bloodied teeth.

It was still rattling when she woke up.

Both her body and the bed were wet with sweat. The sheets clung to her like the sexy draperies she'd never quite managed to wear. Her legs ached with her dreaming flight and she wanted Josh, strong Josh, to comfort her. And knew that Josh wasn't there, and might never be there again.

Her head fell back onto the pillows, those not-quite-large-enough eyes full of tears, some of them gritty and congealed. She wiped a hand across them and felt its fingers caressed by the figure beside her. Tim lay there, smiling, his other hand massaging her breasts. With a sob she pushed herself into his arms and took what pleasure she could from his embrace.

Until he became the other one and bit her lips off once again.

Andrea threw herself out of bed and onto the floor. She hadn't meant to do it but the hard boards beneath the carpet pushed its pile into her soft flesh and woke her properly.

No, Josh wasn't there. He was in Manchester sleeping the sleep of the just-after. The day after tomorrow Leonard Gaunt would be along to show her the photographs which proved it beyond dispute. She'd hate Gaunt and pay him well.

And then she'd take her revenge, when he came back.

Not right away. There'd be some planning to go through first. But she'd be avenged. There could be no doubt about that.

And then she'd find the fair man with the blue eyes, the man she'd only seen twice in fifteen years. And she'd have revenge on him.

For haunting her. For invading her dreams with his threats. For wanting her.

And for her wanting him as well.

18

STEFFI LEFT THE heavily sleeping Josh to take up most of the double bed all by himself. The time was nearly half-five and the sparrows were singing their hearts out on the masonry ledge beneath the window.

It was all right for him, Steffi mused. He could lie there until his alarm call came through. Then he'd order a leisurely breakfast and dress in his own time before getting someone to find him a cab to the regional office. But she had to go back to her flat, change, then grab a cup of filter coffee before finding a bus. The buses were so much easier than driving to work and then struggling for a parking space.

She blew him a kiss as she finished dressing and picked up her bag. In many ways Steffi was genuinely attached to the big man, though she knew only too well that he'd never leave his wife for her, for purely financial reasons. He was an able lover and generous with his gifts. Old-fashioned in many ways, and Steffi liked old-fashioned men. They were more comfortable, more romantic. And there was also that hidden side to his nature, the side she doubted that even his wife had seen. The side that made him even more exciting in a bizarre sort of way.

Steffi carried her shoes until she was through the outer door and standing in the brightly-lit hotel corridor. Then she slipped them on and headed for the lift, attending to a last few details as she rode down to the ground floor. The night clerk on the desk looked up from his book at her as she passed. No luggage. Slightly rumpled. Just another whore going home in the dawn after a hard night's fucking. Steffi felt the thought behind his look and coloured slightly.

As she walked back down Moseley Street towards her flat, heels clattering outrageously in the faint, mostly distant sounds of the city dawn, she remembered that brief feeling of being watched that had slightly marred the first climax of the night. It persisted even now, though only vaguely, making her glance up at the tall buildings with their age-grimed windows which were keeping the light away from her. *Had* there been somebody? One of Josh's people perhaps?

She shuddered at the thought, then pulled herself together and clattered on.

The flat Josh had found her was in a tall Victorian terrace close by. Once the houses had all been town residences for businessmen, made prosperous by the mill trade and, later, with the completion of the Manchester Ship Canal in 1894, the export/import business. Now they were mostly commercial offices, but one remained as a hotel and another two had been converted into expensive apartments. Parking on the street was free at night but restricted during the day, and the nearest garaging for rent being several minutes' walk away was another reason for not bothering with a car of her own. After all, it wasn't as if she didn't earn enough to be able to hire one if she needed it, and her escorts had a duty to provide transport for evenings and weekends.

As she turned the corner and began walking along towards her door the street was fully parked on both sides. Occasionally a vehicle threaded its way along and the milk-bottles on the step were enough to tell Steffi that the passing cars wouldn't have to worry about getting stuck behind a slow-moving float. A cyclist passed her, head down, pedalling determinedly. Somewhere in the distance a police siren sounded briefly.

In the few trees left jutting through the pavement, their branches past budding but not yet into leaf, the birds chirped their song into the burgeoning morning. Except as Steffi clattered past.

She turned off the path and walked up the steps to the front door, tall and wide with a brass knocker that was bolted closed and a row of bell-pushes and name plates to one side. She fitted her key into the lock and turned it, opening the door. Her flat was on the first floor and, as the house faced north–south and the hall and stairs were still comparatively dark, she felt for the timed light switch and pressed it.

Nothing happened.

Something to tell the agents when she sent her next cheque from Josh off to them, she decided. Still, there was just enough light for her to make her way upstairs without having to grope through total darkness.

Steffi hadn't bothered to shower at the hotel, deciding it would disturb Josh and could just as easily wait until she got home. Now, as she fitted the apartment key into the lock and opened her door she was looking forward to sluicing away the dried sweat of their exertions. Her legs and armpits felt sticky and her hair could do with a quick shampoo. *And*, she'd noticed with disgust, there was a ladder in that brand-new pair of tights.

She was half-way through the door when the voice called out to her, very softly. 'Steffi Holt?' it asked through the gloom.

At first she didn't know where to look for the owner of the voice. Then her eyes managed to pick out the figure descending from the second floor. It was tall, male, dark-clad and probably light-haired. It also sounded youngish and reasonably educated, not like the barbarous Lancs-speak that surrounded her all day.

It also startled her, though not enough to prevent her automatically answering: 'Yes? Who is it?'

The figure came closer. 'Might I have a moment of your time?' it enquired politely, now almost close enough to touch her.

'Do I know you?' she countered, defensively and rather resentful of the intrusion even a moment was going to cause. It was nearly six now, and she'd have to leave just after eight to be sure of catching a bus in time. She needed all of the intervening two hours to put herself back together after her heavy session at the Picadilly Plaza.

The figure's response was swift and unexpected. A hand shot out and caught her squarely on the breastbone, knocking her several feet backwards into her hall. Before she could cry out the door was closed, the figure now on this side of it, and she felt the pressure of a sharp and deadly point against her windpipe.

Keep calm, she struggled to tell herself. Don't do anything to alarm him. Play along, even if it means rape. Don't do a single thing to make him more excited than he is. That way you stand a chance of coming through this.

'We ... we'll be more comfortable in the bedroom ...' she offered. Her voice sounded small and weak and submissive. Good, she thought, that might help to placate this monster.

'It will do as well as anywhere,' Ennio told her. 'But move carefully and be very, very quiet. Just one twitch out of place, dear Steffi, and I'll cut your head off. Do you understand me?'

His voice had become a tense, dangerous hissing. She nodded carefully and, one hand to her aching chest, slid her legs beneath her, getting on to her knees and, eventually, her feet. The point of the butterfly knife followed her movements, never more than three inches from her throat.

She reached for the light switch but the knife-point flicked across, leaving a thin red stinging, bleeding line on the back of her hand. 'Not yet,' Ennio commanded. 'Let's wait a little longer, shall we?'

Steffi lowered her hand and clasped the other one across it to still the sudden pain. The cut had been less than a millimetre deep and very skilfully inflicted, but her fingers were shaking as they touched and depressed the door-handle. This sick bastard wasn't joking. He knew how to use that knife of his and he wasn't afraid to damage her.

The door swung inwards, its furniture dim in the pale light through closed curtains. Ennio's free hand pressed the small of her back further into the room, releasing the pressure only to step back and switch on the light. His blue eyes glanced at the bed, a generous single with silk sheets beneath a wildly-patterned duvet. He closed the door behind them.

'Tear some strips from the sheets,' he ordered, his voice now as calm and normal as if he'd been ordering a drink in a bar.

Her heart pounding, her hand stinging, her breath threatening to choke her with her stomach moving up like that, Steffi obeyed. She tried hard not to look at her tormentor once she glimpsed he wasn't masked. Not having seen his face could be the only thing that would keep her alive. She ripped the hemmed edges from one of the silk sheets, the stitch-holes making them tear away comparatively easily.

'That's fine,' Ennio told her.

'Shall . . . I make myself a blindfold?' Steffi asked, trying to keep herself from shaking too much.

'Why, whatever for?' Ennio enquired.

'If I can't see you I can't tell the police who you are,' she gabbled, her frayed nerves in danger of unravelling completely.

'But, my dear,' came the reply, her chin firmly grasped between thumb and fingers, her head twisted so that their noses were mere inches apart, her wide eyes staring into her tormentor's cold, blue ones, 'I want you to see me. Now lie down.'

She moaned softly, her limbs quivering, as she did as he told her. She'd seen him now and there was no going back on that. He'd have to kill her, even if that hadn't been his intention all along.

He slammed his fist into her mouth, breaking at least two teeth. Her head exploded with the pain but the frothing blood as incisors, doubled back and stabbed into her tongue, kept her from crying out. She frothed and coughed violently whilst he bound her hands to the bed-head, then struggled to look up and down as he repeated the operation with her feet, spread-eagling her.

Steffi began to cry.

Ennio knelt above her, slapping her hard and hissing for silence. Fresh agony blossomed inside her ruined mouth and stung up to her nose and eyes. Her head fell back and she fought for breath for an eternity.

During which he slowly unpicked the seams of her clothes until he was able to pull them away and leave her naked.

Perhaps one day he'd do this to Andrea Duncan. But not yet. There were other things to be done to Andrea before he could come to this. *Longer* things.

'A fine body, Steffi,' he congratulated her. 'A good body. Whoever you were with tonight was very lucky.

'Was he one of the Sons of Samael by any chance?'

Her mind reeled, even through the pain it had to cope with. Oh Christ! she thought. He knows! He knows about the secret.

The knife began to cut again, very carefully. As she felt the new pain Steffi began to howl, but the howl was cut short by another blow to her throbbing mouth. Slowly and cautiously the point of Ennio's blade traced around the aureole of her right breast. When he had finished and trickles of blood were flowing in several spidery directions he flashed her a smile, wetted his fingers and began to tweak the nipple erect.

'How do you know about the Sons of Samael, Steffi?' The question was polite, as if he were asking her to dance.

She was too aware of her own terror to make any reply. He grasped the nipple firmly and set the blade of the knife against it.

'Right nipple first,' he informed her. 'Then the left. And if that doesn't work I can start on your lips and clitoris. My,' he added, glancing at the bleeding breast, 'I seem to be making a mess. Excuse me a minute while I find some tissues. Or kitchen-roll. You'll have some in the kitchen? It's not as gentle as tissues, you see.'

He left her, weeping and shaking and moaning, not daring to call out because of what she knew he'd do if she did, and went off to find the kitchen. He returned

116

several dreadful moments later with the kitchen-roll and began wiping none-too-gently at her wound. When he finished she thought he'd sliced her right open. Instead, the realisation eventually formed, he'd run the hard corner of an ice-cube from the refrigerator down her rib-cage and abdomen. He held it up for her to see and smiled before pushing it, burning-cold, into her vagina. Her urethral sphincter relaxed and the contents of her bladder spurted out over the bed.

'You're . . . going . . . to kill me . . .' Steffi bubbled.

'Dear Steffi,' Ennio replied, 'I am.' He quickly slapped his hand over her mouth to stop her screaming. 'You are indeed a perceptive lady. Now, I can kill you one of several ways. The best way, for both of us, is quickly. There's less mess and less risk that way. And less pain for you to endure. But in order for me to kill you quickly I need good, accurate, *believable* answers to my questions. Now, knowing that you're going to die, you may decide to fuck me up by trying to lie to me. I assure you that to do that would be very unwise. You see, I have a knack of knowing when somebody is lying to me, and the pain gets worse and goes on longer whenever that happens. You're an intelligent woman. You've already made up your mind that the only way you'll get away from me is to embrace old Grandfather Death. So why not tell me the truth and make things easier all round? I'm a reasonable man. Really I am. And yes, I *do* enjoy cutting people up. But it's so much easier and more pleasant once they're dead. So just tell me how you know about the Sons of Samael and I'll kill you quickly. Do we have a bargain?'

He lifted his hand from her mouth a fraction, ready to replace it again if she tried to call out. She tried but the hand clamped down again.

'If I have to,' he said reproachfully, 'I'll cut your tongue out and make you nod through the letters of the alphabet to give me my answer. All I want is a name, Steffi. Just a name. Then all the pain can stop for you for ever.'

Ennio raised his hand again. This time Steffi stayed quiet except for a whimpering mingled in with her forced attempts to breathe. Tears were flowing freely down her cheeks and her eyes were glazed with pain and terror.

He was right, this man sitting on top of her with his pain-dealing knife. No one was going to help her. No-one was going to come to save her life. She was going to die, there, tied to her own bed. Whoever her tormentor was he knew she'd been told about the Sons of Samael. He also knew she'd told someone else, although only one someone else. If only she hadn't got drunk at that party and shot her mouth off to that Howard creep. He had to be the one who'd given her away.

Well, if this one knows, then chances are Howard's dead as well.

Ennio set the knife to her nipple again. 'The name, Steffi?' he asked without the slightest trace of impatience.

It was all over. No way out. Nothing left but to be dead and out of her agony as quickly as possible. She turned her head to the side and spat to clear her mouth as much as she could. Then she told him.

He stared at her long and hard. Then nodded. 'I believe you,' he told her, sending waves of relief flooding through her tormented being. Only when he fitted the gag to her mouth did she realise that he was the one who'd been lying.

He wasn't going to finish her quickly at all. He was going to take all the time in the world. Starting with what he'd told her he was going to cut off.

Then her eyelids. Then the lips either side of the gag. Then her ears.

And next, very very slowly, lowering the point of the knife a fraction of an inch at a time, tickling the surface with the point before he stabbed, her lidless eyes.

Wiping away the blood with kitchen-roll as he went on.

Steffi could only *feel* when he sliced away her breasts to either side, laid bare her rib-cage and began to carve out her heart. The memory of that final, awful ache delayed the embrace of death for several sickening moments.

By the time Ennio had cleaned himself up and left the flat the sun had risen, and Steffi was overdue for work. Not that anybody would have recognised her there without her face.

19

LEONARD GAUNT WAS disgusted to discover that his cheap return ticket prevented him from taking an early train back to London. Instead he sat in the station buffet drinking inadequate coffee and nursing the small roll of payment-to-come he'd extracted from his camera, watching the minutes creep by with agonising stealth.

As soon as he got back he'd have the film developed and pay a call on Mrs Buchanan. She wouldn't enjoy looking at the pictures, but she'd be impressed with the speed and efficiency with which he'd gathered the evidence of her husband's adultery. Maybe there'd be enough left out of her gratitude for him and Margot to have a cheap holiday somewhere. Weston-super-Mare maybe. He liked Weston. It was so . . . seasidey. Dirty postcards and giftey shoppes and hot dogs. All served with sand.

It was past noon by the time he was back in London, and the walk from Euston, down Tottenham Court Road, took him another twenty minutes. He checked in with Margot before taking a walk round to the photo-service, only to find out the one hour facility was down and he'd have to wait until tomorrow to see his mastershots.

Gaunt had abandoned his *Evening Standard* in the hotel after the third reading. The only story which had really stuck in his mind was the one about the man found dead and mutilated above a shop in Coptic Street. The details weren't exact, naturally, with the police holding something back to weed out any crank confessions, but the report was complete enough to make Gaunt wish that he could get himself involved with a case like that, instead of the common run of divorces and shoplifting. Perhaps if he'd known that he already was he might have changed his mind.

20

ENNIO ZABETTI TOOK the more direct M6–M1 route back to London, stopping at Nantwich services for an early lunch or late breakfast. He was feeling particularly vital and alive, every fibre of his being tingling with suppressed delight. Two sacrifices in two days. He hadn't felt this good, or had this much fun, in years.

He was only slightly cross with himself for having killed Steffi Holt. He'd known from the outset that she had to die, that it was impractical to leave her alive, but he'd wanted to all the same. One day there'd be one that he could keep alive indefinitely, mutilating it strip by painful strip. His god liked the sort of vibrations continued and unremitting agony produced, and it satisfied a craving inside Ennio as well.

At least he'd been slower with her than he'd had to be with that shopkeeper. And cutting her heart out with her still alive, her whole being one gruesome throbbing wound, had been good practice. He was beginning to learn exactly what he was capable of, and he liked it.

Maybe Andrea Duncan would be the one. Maybe he could keep her alive for days or weeks, if the circumstances were right. There was something thrilling about the concept of a continuous paean of pain descending to the deity, be it god or dog or goat or even some kind of superman. But he couldn't rush into that. He needed Andrea for other things first. It might even be a year before he could begin the slow, careful process of slicing her into separate living morsels.

Beside him, on the passenger seat as he drove, Steffi's heart lay wrapped in a plastic bin-liner he'd discovered in the kitchen. He wasn't sure exactly why he'd taken it, but it was going to be interesting finding out. Ennio knew that the concentration of muscle fibre wasn't going to make it easy eating, but if he minced it first it shouldn't be too tough. Worse things than hearts went into the average sausage, all said and done.

By the time he was passing Luton he'd almost forgotten about Steffi. The exhilaration persisted, but without conscious recollection for its reason. Instead he was beginning to think about that little creature they'd initiated the other night. Pravus the depraved.

The Magister never did anything without a reason, and that included his naming of the latest initiate. On top of that there was the fact that dirty little Pravus was a complete outsider, initiated on the Magister's orders alone. Usually the recruits were culled from people who could be made use of, induced by the discovery and careful manipulation of their vices, or simple blackmail if necessary, from the ranks of the professions or the police. Very few were shop-girls or truck-drivers pulled in off the street, unless they happened to possess some special and potentially useful skill. The present Porta Inferi coven numbered a headmistress, two solicitors, an accountant,

123

a dispensing chemist, three police officers, two above the rank of inspector, a madam and the superintendent of a children's home. All except one of the policemen had already proven their worth at least once, and the one policeman who had yet to be called upon was the lesser ranking of the three. Only Ennio and a girl known in coven circles as Medusa didn't fit the professional category, but had been inducted at puberty as the children of existing members.

For little Pravus to enter this select group, and the Porta Inferi coven was the senior coven of the Sons of Samael, was an honour indeed, unless there was some deeper reason behind her induction.

Still, Pravus was going to have to wait. Johnny Howard had led Ennio to Steffi Holt. Both knew about the Sons of Samael without being members of the brotherhood. That meant that someone, and someone on the inside, in a position to know, was talking. Find that person and expose them and the Magister was going to be very, very grateful.

There was, however, a snag. In the grade hierarchy Ennio, or Brother Ball-Phegor as he was known, was only a Chief Priest. As only the grade of High Priest, the next before Magister Inferi or coven leader, was permitted to know the identity of the Magister, he was going to have to find out who the Magister was before he could spring his revelation. Obviously neither that dumb-fuck Howard or Steffi Holt had been the big one. Wrong size, wrong sex, wrong status. He'd also have known if they'd been coven members, as they tended to discard their masks for some of the more physical rituals, except for the Magister.

Well, he reasoned, the next step was to check out the name Steffi Holt had given him. With this one he'd have to tread more carefully. This one had status and possibly some degree of physical strength on his side. There was likely to be more shit hitting the fan than the other two combined had generated if he turned up with his face missing. Still, a little careful planning would take care of that.

'If the shit's going to hit the fan, make sure it's already left your arse,' he chuckled to himself, driving through Swiss Cottage on his way back towards the West End.

21

THEY HADN'T ARRANGED to meet for lunch because Josh needed to maximise the time available with his regional team, and it was mid-afternoon before he learned that Steffi hadn't reported in for the day. The meetings carried him along until shortly before seven, when he finally let the others start home to wives and families.

He wasn't unduly concerned that Steffi had taken the day off, but he was beginning to wonder if she was all right, maybe down with something she'd eaten at the hotel the night before. If that was the case then a second night was going to be out of the question, and that wasn't going to fit in with Josh's plans at all.

There was no need to phone for a cab. He picked one up just outside the offices easily enough, giving the hotel as his ultimate destination but asking it to call around to Steffi's flat on the way. If she was okay and willing he could tip the driver to come back and collect her later. The meter clicked on to waiting time as he climbed the steps to the front door and rang Steffi's bell.

No answer.

He looked at the windows and couldn't see a light on the first floor, despite the fact that the bedroom curtains were drawn. Josh was about to give up when the door opened for a resident going out. He smiled and pushed his way in before the door could close again.

In the street outside the cab-driver picked up his paperback and started to snatch a few paragraphs. The light going on behind the bedroom curtains caught his eye. He looked behind him to make sure his fare had left his briefcase on the back seat. Some moments later the front door opened and Josh half-stumbled down the steps, shouting something incomprehensible. The driver looked up from his book, then swallowed hard.

His fare's features were chalk white, except for his staring eyes. He also appeared to be wearing blood-red gloves.

22

THE DAY SINCE her initiation ticked slowly by. In the comparatively timeless world of the black room Pravus never knew the exact hour, nor how the world outside was governed by the clock, crushing bodies into tube trains and buses, then spilling them out again to inhabit shops and offices and factories. She'd heard a little about it, of course. Man and Woman had both told her something of the outside world, the world ruled by the Enemy which she would one day be called upon to destroy, but she had yet to see it for herself.

Perhaps that will happen after I have a name, she'd thought. Perhaps then I will be able to go out and fight the Enemy.

One day passed. Then another.

She knew their passing by the meals she was given, and by the periods of sleep they made her take. She took them unwillingly, determined that she would be both awake and alert when the Magister came to see her. But two days had passed now and still the Magister hadn't come.

Perhaps he'd forgotten her.

Pravus unrolled the circle of lino with the design painted on it, covering the centre of the black carpet. Then she took out the other equipment and set it up. She wasn't supposed to do this except when Man or Woman told her, so she had to make sure she did it at a time when they were unlikely to interrupt, at a time when she'd have the black room entirely to herself. Then she could make the signs and say the words without fear of interruption.

Like now.

They wouldn't notice the smell of the incense afterwards. It was a part of the routine to burn a little every day, so the room permanently smelled of the mixture of myrrh, asphalt and cannabis. Getting rid of the ointment might be a problem, but the next thing they'd come to call her to would be a bath, and if she wrapped herself in a bath-sheet, that and the incense would mask the odour until she'd washed it off.

And, if they did find out, so what? She had a name now. She was an initiate. Surely that put her above them? And if the Magister truly was coming he wouldn't want to find her marked, would he. He'd be cross with them if they marked her now. It would spoil his special purpose, the one he was coming to tell her all about.

She didn't know that she could die tomorrow and no one would even notice. Her birth had never been recorded. On those rare occasions she had left the house it had been night, so the neighbours hadn't seen enough of her to realise that she lived there, even if they'd noticed her at all. She'd never been to school, outside the black room. In fact she had only seen the sun twice, and it had frightened her both times. No, there were none of the usual giveaways to inform anyone that there was a teenage girl in the house. No young men calling and taking her out. No howling heavy metal or acid house screaming out through the windows. No sunbathing in the garden or giggling girlfriends playing there. For fifteen years there had been no one there at all. Not a person. Not a name.

But that was different now.

It had to be different. Certainly she didn't feel the same any more. That was how she could dare to set up the circle and say the words, at a season when the man and the woman hadn't told her to.

Slowly she had become aware that something else was taking over from Man and Woman as the ordering factor in her life. It embodied a feeling of growing independence, of willingness to challenge and make decisions of her own. This was one of them, one of the first and one of the most important.

As the Magister wasn't coming of his own accord she was going to call him to her.

It was, of course, unheard of, even undreamed of. Without a name she would never have dared to contemplate something like this. She wouldn't have had the strength to stand in the circle before the long mirror, her young body lit only by the wavering light from the red, white and black candles burning in their holders, yet not seeing herself because her eyes were turned inwards upon her purposing. Unheard of, yes. But she felt the power within herself. She felt it rippling through her being with a force and vitality that made her previous workings pale and insipid shadows of this awesome present.

At first it was simply a tenseness throughout her limbs, a tenseness which reached even into the tips of her fingers and her toes until her whole body became rigid and swaying on a precarious balance. Then, slowly, the rigidity gave way to a tingling sensation as the words became stronger, more normal, less like the gutteral whispering which they always began as. And as the tingling began to generate a warmth her sense of presence, of having a body at all, began to fade. The warmth replaced everything else as she stood there, wearing nothing, holding nothing.

The hard part, when she'd first started to do this, had been forgetting the soles of her feet, the only part of her body which was in contact with anything except the air about her. The trick was to forget them without remembering that you had to do it, to make it an instinctive reaction to the onset of the warmth. It had taken her several years to master, and Pravus could still remember how delighted Man and Woman had been when she finally achieved it once. Yet their delight had coloured her next attempt and set her back, so they took no notice until the time came when she proved her success by completing the tasks they set her, the tasks which demonstrated her mastery of the technique beyond dispute.

Now her mastery was so complete as to be automatic, and with her naming and initiation the force it generated felt all the more formidable and stark in its total, unremitting reality. Those whom she had served two nights before couldn't do this. Perhaps even the Magister Inferi himself couldn't do this.

She'd soon know, anyway.

Her feet forgotten, she set about transforming the heat from thermal energy into total energy, a power which could be directed according to the dictates of her will. A power which had *become* her will. With an ease that was more down to her naming than her practice she lowered the temperature to room heat whilst retaining the full presence of the energy. Then and only then did she focus its direction.

And release it.

Pravus felt her legs weaken. Her body was suddenly back, heavier than it ever normally felt, forcing her to her knees with its weight, all ninety-eight pounds of it. Her hands weighed her arms down and they fell to her sides where she knelt. Her head, unable to support itself, nodded forward until her chin was just above her breasts. Her waist doubled over and she dropped onto her side like an oversize foetus.

She was still lying there, in the circle, when the woman came in to her. With a cry that was half concern and half fury Woman dropped down beside her and raised her head up by its hair, glaring into the relaxed features. Slowly Pravus opened her eyes. When Woman looked into them she released her hold and started back with a suppressed gasp.

'I have summoned the Magister,' Pravus informed her. 'He will be here tomorrow.'

23

IT WAS JOSH Buchanan's turn for nightmares.

They began well enough, with him playing his love-games in the lounge of Steffi's flat. She played them back and they drank wine and ate and kissed.

'Why don't we take tomorrow off and go up to the Lakes?' she asked him teasingly. 'We've never really been anywhere but bed, Josh.'

He nodded to himself. The reproach was real enough despite the gentle manner of its delivery. As Steffi wound her arms around him he felt work beginning to fade away. Her idea was a good one. He deserved some time with her. After all, he gave Andrea enough, so why shouldn't there be the opportunity to make Steffi happier?

'Why not?' he smiled back. 'A few phone calls first thing and it can be all arranged. Okay?'

'Ohh . . . kayy,' she breathed back. 'Now that's worth something extra special.'

She got up from the floor where they'd been sitting and began to walk towards the door. 'Hey, where're you going?'

Josh called after her.

'To the bedroom,' she pouted back. 'And don't you come in until I call you, right?'

He shrugged and pouted back. Steffi left him alone there and he climbed to his feet, suddenly feeling very heavy and exactly how old he was. The flat wasn't quite as it usually was. It had a soft-focus about the corners which would have worried him off to the optician's if he hadn't known he was dreaming. He pointed his finger at the CD player and Enya's voice floated back at him, haunting and eloquent though not quite seductive.

The heavy silver frame set up on the side-table held his photograph. Josh picked it up and stared at it, deciding he didn't quite like his expression. That wasn't the right look to be frozen for eternity. He'd find a better one.

Maybe Steffi could take one at the Lakes tomorrow. If it was a cold day he could stand there in his overcoat, looking windswept and Byronic.

'Ready yet?' he called into the bedroom.

'Not yet, big boy. Have a little patience,' Steffi called back.

She was playing with him, teasing him. Okay, he'd short-circuit that easily enough. He decided to climb out of the rest of his clothes while he was waiting. That went smoothly enough until he came to his trousers and found the zip fly firmly stuck shut.

With an oath he undid everything he could and forced them down over his hips. Yes, the time was coming when he'd have to lose a little weight. All those corporate lunches were having a bad effect on his corporation.

His underpants followed and he stood there, looking down at his socks. For the first and only time in his life he was wearing sock-suspenders to hold them up. They made him feel like the depraved villain in a bad Victorian melodrama, so he decided to leave them where they were. If Steffi could look good in suspenders so could he.

'I'll give you a count of ten,' he called towards the lounge door. 'Then I'm coming in. One . . .'

'God, you're a ram, Buchanan.'

'Two . . . three . . . four . . . five . . .'

'I hope you can handle this, big boy. It really is going to be something special for you . . .'

'Six . . . seven . . . eight, nine, ten!'

He sprang out of the lounge, his solidity waggling and slapping against him as he moved, and leaped through the bedroom door. Steffi was standing on the bed, her back to him, pouting over her shoulder.

'Stay there,' she ordered. Then: 'Are you ready for this?'

'I'm ready for *anything*,' he leered back.

She turned slowly, wobbling a little to keep her balance on the oversprung mattress. One hand was shielding her pubic bush whilst the other covered her breasts. Just like Botticelli's Aphrodite, Josh thought. Christ, she's a fine looking woman!

The hands moved slowly, teasingly away from the areas they covered. Then Steffi spread out her arms like a female Jesus, one leg bending slightly at the knee.

'I can hear my heart beating,' she whispered.

Josh listened hard. He heard his own, then Steffi's. Slowly the beating of her heart grew louder. And louder.

'I can *feel* my heart beating, Josh.'

He couldn't keep his eyes off her. Without trying to work out where the light was coming from it was bathing her entire body, leaving it shadow-free and slightly luminescent. For a moment he wondered if she had three breasts, then he realised that the third was her heart, beating just beneath the flesh, pushing it outwards as it pumped, a little further forward each time.

135

Her smile threatened to devour him. She reached out, invitingly. 'Let me give you my heart, Josh,' Steffi implored.

The skin began to crack as she stood there. The crack widened and deepened until a trickle of blood streaked down towards her navel. He felt his eyes widen, first in surprise, then with concern.

'Steffi,' he mumbled. 'Steffi. Stop it. Stop it!'

'What's the matter, Josh?' she enquired sarcastically. 'Don't you want my heart?'

The skin split again and again, the wounds forming a bloody star. Josh wanted to shut his eyes or look away, but he was unable to do either. He simply stood there, his erection waning, the colour draining from his features, as the skin peeled back between Steffi's breasts, revealing her naked, beating heart.

'Here it comes, Josh,' she cooed. 'All yours . . .'

With a smacking, sucking sound that continued to echo in his ears, with a reek of hot blood that flooded his nostrils, with an eruptive spattering that drenched the room like a garden-spray, the heart flew from her breast and shot towards him, smashing into his gaping mouth with tooth-jarring force. Its juices filled his throat and he began to choke. His fingers clawed at the protruding portion, trying to tear the organ loose, to ease the pressure on his stretched lips and cheeks before they gave way and destroyed his face. He writhed and twisted, ripping, clawing, prying, tasting his own adrenalin and the iron-flavoured saltiness of the blood.

He was still fighting to dislodge it when he realised he was in bed, and that there was nothing in his mouth. Gentle fingers were stroking the sweat from his forehead.

'Hush, baby,' Steffi soothed. 'Just a nightmare. You're all right now.'

136

Josh sighed with relief and turned towards her, feeling the stickiness of the bed as he moved. As he yelled and leaped away the covers came with him, stuck to his body with the same red liquid that had stained them.

Steffi lay there, laughing softly, her chest empty and ruined, half-severed breasts flopping uselessly to either side.

'No!' he gasped. 'You're not real. You're a dream! That's all, a dream!'

She sat up and blew him a kiss. Her lips came with it. Her eyes exploded. The skin peeled away from her face strip by strip, leaving crimson furrows that dripped and grew until they replaced her features altogether.

His sweat washed the bedclothes from him. He felt them sliding down his belly and legs. 'Go 'way!' he howled. 'You're not real! Not real!'

She clawed out for him blindly. He backed away as she stumbled off the bed and kept backing until he felt the wall pressing his shoulder-blades inwards. The hands grasped his head on either side and pressed his face towards the ruin of her own.

'One last kiss, big boy,' Steffi whimpered.

Josh felt his legs and bladder give way together. He was still urinating over his tight-pressed thighs when he realised that the room was empty. Suddenly conscious of the warm dampness he stopped himself and stood up, disgusted by the liquid trickling down his legs.

A trail of bedclothes led from the bed to the corner where he stood, shaking and ashamed. There were no red stains. Outside the closed curtains the day was starting to become light. He looked at his watch. The time was quarter to seven.

With a groan he staggered towards the bathroom and clicked the light on. Its yellow reality was comforting, enabling him to seek out the mirror and check for tell-tale signs of that last gory kiss from Steffi's flayed and reddened mouth. He saw instead the rings beneath his eyes and the stubble on his cheeks.

He opened the mirror-fronted cabinet and looked inside it at his toilet things. No razor. Probably forgot to unpack it. Leaving the cupboard open he turned to go back into the bedroom and check his luggage.

'Shave?' Steffi asked him from the doorway.

It had to be Steffi. He couldn't think of anyone else who'd be standing there with no face and no heart, dripping red and brandishing a cut-throat. At least, he thought it was a cut-throat. As it wavered menacingly closer he could see that it wasn't, that it was some kind of folding knife with a split handle. That it was incredibly sharp and very, very eager . . .

There were other dreams before Josh finally came round with his alarm call ringing in his ears. He reached for the receiver expecting it to spurt blood out at him, or to burst Steffi's tongue out of the mouthpiece. It did neither.

With an effort he swung his legs out of bed, trying to replace the image of Steffi's corpse with that of those suspicious policemen the night before. The cabbie and, in a little while from now, the hotel staff and his own people would have alibied him, though. Nobody was going to suspect him, which was as it should be.

Slowly the nightmares began to fade away and he remembered traces of his other dreams. One in particular nagged at him because of its formlessness. Yet even without being fully recalled, even without having any clear image that he could remember at that time, it worried him by its implications.

He found his razor in the bathroom, where he'd put it two nights before. After shaving and showering he looked around the room, feeling brighter and more human once again. One corner of his top sheet was damp, but it wasn't damp anywhere where he could be thought by the staff to have soiled it in the way he knew he had. He was always careful about dreams involving urinating, just in case he actually was.

Jesus Christ but that had been some night! And the day that followed wasn't going to be much easier. The police would want to talk to him again, as they'd be talking to his staff. Still, at least that would put him firmly in the clear, once and for all. And being honest up here might just keep things away from Andrea. She'd want to know what he was doing calling on an attractive underling in the first place.

He dressed and steeled himself for the day. He was about to go down to breakfast when he thought he'd just make a phone call first.

24

GAUNT PICKED UP the photos from the processors and looked through them. Definitely some of his best work, he decided.

Margot agreed.

Well, they had to be good if Margot agreed they were. That meant he could bump up the expenses and make something over and above what he'd already planned on. He'd known right from the beginning that this job for the Buchanan woman was going to be lucrative.

He decided to drive out and see Mrs Buchanan, so he walked round to the parking space he hired for an exorbitant price from a nearby solicitor's and forced his rusting Allegro into life. He'd never liked the car, either as one for him or as a make, but it had come cheap after a repossession job. The Austin Allegro wasn't part of the PI image. The only virtue it had, with its cornflake-coloured paintwork, was its virtual anonymity if ever he had to follow anyone. There were so many cornflake-coloured Allegros around, all of them old and battered like his.

The only problem was they all seemed, to Gaunt, to be driven by complete morons.

Still, any car that had started life with a square steering wheel, as the early Allegros had, was doomed before it began. The only wonder left was that it had stayed a production model as long as it had. Must be a lot of square-brained motorists around, Gaunt decided.

The large brown envelope containing the prints sat beside him on the passenger seat as he chugged through the traffic towards the M25. He didn't like the motorway and wasn't alone in his dislike. At least one comedian had risked the Prime Minister's wrath by describing it as a 'designer car-park' and, although he usually found Jasper Carrot tedious, he was forced to agree. As a good Tory he shouldn't, he knew. Maggie had firmly told the faithful not to 'carp about a great British (Great British?) achievement', and Gaunt felt disloyal for not liking the road.

He turned off the M25 at Slough, following signs for Gerrards Cross and, eventually, Abbots Ringley. Margot had telephoned ahead to make sure it was convenient for him to call on Andrea Buchanan, and he was by now fully confident that the contents of the envelope would justify both his visit and his account, when he put it in after a decorous delay of two or three days.

The countryside, with its occasional dotting of houses and farms, sped by as Gaunt motored on. He could have been almost anywhere in the country now, except perhaps for the highlands of Scotland or approaching the Vale of Evesham from the east. Or Wisbech. He hated the fens, those countless miles of flatlands where the trees looked like alien invaders, when they happened at all, and the whole countryside felt like the wrong end of a vacuum cleaner. When he finally reached Abbots Ringley he looked

141

in at the Bell and Horns – with its garish modern sign which was forty per cent name of brewery and the rest a picture of a bellwether-ram, except for the thirty per cent which displayed the name of the pub – more for directions than for lunch, although he managed to get both.

Gaunt climbed back into his car feeling better fortified for the work ahead and reached into the glove compartment for the packet of extra-strong mints. One or two would at least take the worst of the beer off his breath before he reached the Abbey and that all-important interview with Mrs Buchanan.

He followed the road out of the village and passed by the long row of aspens which now, with the coming of spring, were beginning to screen the ancient building more effectively. Some bloody pile, he thought to himself by the time he was turning into the drive, between the gates Andrea had insisted Josh have fitted. Maybe I should find a way to up the price even more.

Oh, what the hell, he consoled himself. People with this much money can be picky. Chances are I'll do better by staying reasonable. Less hassle that way.

The gates stood open but the electric eye picked him up. By the time he'd parked and walked over to the two-arched porch beneath the oriel window Mrs Haigh, who came up from the village every day to 'do' for the Buchanans, was standing in the open doorway looking menacing, her eyes taking in every detail of Leonard Gaunt's ill-fitting best suit.

'I'm Mr Gaunt,' he announced. 'Mrs Buchanan is expecting me.'

In the same way that Gaunt had spent most of the day so far preparing to be received by Mrs Buchanan, so Andrea had spent a great deal of it wondering just how she was

142

going to react to Gaunt. She'd managed a rare good night's sleep, only to be awakened by Josh ringing her sometime around eight. He'd told her a long and rambling tale of finding one of his employees murdered the day before, protesting a little too much about how he'd done it and ostensibly calling to prepare her in case she had a visit from the local constabulary. Not that she had.

Since then she'd managed to get up and have a bath, spending the morning hunting through the outhouses for nothing in particular, simply deciding it was time she knew what was lying about out there. One of the things which impressed her most as potentially useful was an old metal travelling trunk, nearly five feet long and with its metal lid dented in by something heavy having sat on top of it at some point of its abandoned history. It seemed to spark off obscure memories in its quiet, ginger-brown-painted, unassuming way.

Josh's call hadn't worried her unduly. In fact she'd felt much calmer than he sounded as he'd explained that it was likely to keep him away for a day longer than usual. Details to clear up with the police. Nasty business, etc.

The wander through the outbuildings had set her mind working in a way it hadn't been called upon to do for some time. One wall of an old barn had been studded with a variety of bygone agricultural implements, and Andrea had spent nearly an hour looking at the cobwebbed, rusted items, trying to assign a use to each of them from her early memories.

Early memories.

Since the night before the night before two faces had kept floating unbidden before her inner eye. One was that of Tim Garfield, good old Tim, still ready and willing to be at least friendly and probably something more than friendly, given an ounce of encouragement. There was still a lot of

143

good that Tim could do her, especially if she wanted to pay Josh back for what she knew Gaunt was going to tell her about. And she wanted to pay Josh back. At the very least she wanted to pay Josh back for not being there to comfort her after Ennio had bitten her lips off in that dream.

Ennio.

She hadn't given him a name yet because she didn't know what his name really was. She thought of him as the *other* one, the *other* face which haunted her, threatening and teasing with its promises of pleasure to be experienced and pain to be endured, and the possible merging of the two. Did she hate him or love him? Fear him or want him? The decision was beyond her conscious mind, and it could be left to circumstances to decide it for her. Sooner or later she'd see him again. That was as certain as New Year following Christmas, in any universe you cared to name.

Lunch had been a desultory affair eaten off a tray prepared by Mrs Haigh in front of a video of *Poltergeist II*. Andrea was finding it increasingly difficult to come to terms with the way that the horrors she watched, and was slowly becoming immune to, had no effect of lessening the horrors of her dreams. Maybe it was because she knew that they were simply the artificial products of other people's imaginations, an agglomeration of perverse writing, special effects, directorial vision and money, whereas her dreams came unprompted from within herself. No matter what special effects could do in terms of talking severed heads and exploding bodies, no matter how much gore could be sprayed over a mattress, mistress or witness, no matter how creepy the old house or the half-glimpsed figure in the moonlight, they were deliberately created for an audience, unlike the private imaginings she produced for herself without even trying.

144

What could *she* do with an old tin trunk and a pair of sheep shears? And a human victim? Maybe she was going to find out.

Mrs Haigh announced Gaunt. She received the detective in the great hall. She always received visitors to Ringley Abbey in the great hall. Unless they were born to it, which the people she knew never were, the high, ancient surroundings awed them, keeping them from being entirely at their ease, giving Andrea the edge she'd always craved for in those early days as a girl puppet in the hands of accountants and lawyers and account executives.

Like Tim.

She was beginning to realise that the only way she could stop thinking of Tim Garfield was to transmute his face into the other's face, to make him into that handsome, disgusting person she'd only ever seen twice, both times in the same graveyard in Norfolk. She took some relief at Gaunt's rotund, hairless appearance, shaking his plump hand with positive pleasure, knowing that this fat, bald man would never turn into either of her haunters.

'Nice little place you've got here,' Gaunt remarked.

Andrea missed his irony as she waved him to a seat. His breath stank of beer and peppermints, with the latter having a slight edge over the former. She offered him a whisky and he accepted readily.

You can never be too prepared for an interview like this, he told himself.

Sheep shears. The old one-piece kind with triangular blades and the spring in the loop-shaped handle.

Rusty and blunt.

'Acting upon the information you gave me I followed your husband to Manchester, Mrs Buchanan,' Gaunt informed her. 'He's staying at the Picadilly Plaza Hotel.

Now, I know it's not the cheapest place in the city, but I had to stay there myself in order to keep tabs on him, you understand?'

'Quite so, Mr Gaunt.' The great hall was making him apologetic. It did that to people.

Would they cut, though? She'd have to take them off the wall of the barn and try them out sometime, just to be sure.

'I regret that I do not have the most felicitous news possible for you, Mrs Buchanan, though from your engagement of my services I doubt that it will be entirely unexpected.'

Get on with it, her mind hissed. She'd forgotten just how verbose this unappealing hireling could be.

'I have here,' Gaunt continued, prominently displaying the envelope, 'a series of photographs which, I presume to believe, offers incontrovertible proof of your husband's adultery. If you have no objection I propose to show them to you in the order in which *I* took them.'

Why wasn't she surprised? Why hadn't Gaunt left her feeling shattered, or at least a little moved, by his pedantic annunciation? What sort of Archangel Gabriel was this, anyway?

And the angel came in unto her, and said, Hail, thou that art highly favoured, the Lord is with thee; blessed art thou among women.

Maybe they'll need sharpening a bit. I want him to suffer, but not at the price of my own *inconvenience*.

'I see, Mr Gaunt. Yes, I think I'd better see them.'

He reached inside the envelope and removed a wad of black and white prints. Turning them towards himself first he selected one and laid it down on the surface of the table separating their respective seats. It showed Josh Buchanan and Steffi Holt kissing in the Starlight Bar.

146

Andrea looked at it in silence for several moments, then picked it up with trembling fingers. Her heart was suddenly beating wildly and her mind was focusing in on the sheep shears once again.

'And there're more?' she asked at length.

'I regret to inform you that there are. Is it your wish that I show them to you.'

'Most certainly, Mr Gaunt.'

'Then here they are.'

He laid them down on the table, the most innocuous – two rearing sets of buttocks taken from the bedroom doorway – on top. The others, following his progress around the bed until fragments of both the faces in the first photograph were both present and recognisable, lay underneath in sequence. Andrea looked hard at each in turn.

'I see.'

Her voice was flat, unemotional despite the continuing tremor of her fingers. She laid the pictures back down and stood up. Gaunt followed suit.

'Mr Gaunt, I require the negatives of these photographs,' Andrea stated flatly. 'Once I have them, and your assurance that you have not retained any prints, you may name your own fee up to £5000. I am prepared to add the same amount again for your assurance that my name does not appear in your business records. Have I made myself clear?'

Gaunt felt his own heart leap. The sum Andrea proposed had exceeded even his most padded account. 'Indeed you have, Mrs Buchanan,' he told her. 'I shall deliver everything into your hands at this time tomorrow.'

'Very good. My cheque will be here waiting for you. And should it make things any easier,' she added, 'I think I can manage about £3000 of the amount in cash.'

147

'That will be most satisfactory,' Gaunt responded, trying to suppress a sudden compulsion to grin with delight.

'That's fine, then. Until tomorrow.'

Andrea stood up and extended her hand for the detective's firm grasp, then showed him to the door.

Once he had gone she told Mrs Haigh not to bother about leaving her anything tonight and resumed her examination of the outhouses, though in a more preoccupied manner than she had before lunch. Time and again she came back to the wall with its ancient implements, the others fading from her sight altogether as the shears began to dominate, set up like the crucifix on the high altar of a demonic cathedral.

A movement through one of the grimed windows showed Mrs Haigh, done for the day, taking the back path through the fields to her own home in Abbots Ringley. Andrea breathed a quiet sigh of relief and looked back at the shears. She was feeling progressively more uncomfortable at sharing the house with anyone, even on a temporary basis. And if his infidelities gave her more time for her own perverse indulgences, then were they really such a bad thing?

Of course they were, the shears informed her. They were a betrayal of her love, of all their time together. Behaviour like that cried out to be punished. Cruelly.

Snick-snack.

Andrea shook her head. They couldn't really have moved on their own like that. The tracery of cobwebs surrounding them would have stretched and ruptured. Flakes of rust would have fallen from the sprung-loop handle. And they would have dislodged themselves from that old clout-headed nail which was keeping them in place.

148

She looked at the tin trunk again, and at everything piled up on top of it. She hefted a few of the mouldering cardboard boxes out of the way, the bottom of one of them collapsing and showering her feet and legs with old springs and locks and hinges that bit and scratched through her tights. This would be better done tomorrow with a pair of old jeans on, if she still had any.

For the first time, as she stood in the doorway and looked back at the trunk, Andrea began to wonder if it actually contained anything. Her initial assumption had been that it was empty, but the amount of clutter piled around it was beginning to persuade her otherwise. Besides, the small padlock fitted through the hasp didn't have the same dull, crusted, forgotten finish as the other brassy objects out here. It looked newer, as if it was actually there to do its work today, and not in the times before their purchase of Ringley Abbey.

A pair of bolt-croppers stood propped up just inside the door. They looked heavy and unwieldy and it took Andrea several attempts to set them in position above the lock. When she tried to squeeze the handles they moved only slightly, refusing to give in the way they always did in films. She squeezed again and felt them close a little further. Finally she gave up on her ruined tights altogether and, half-squatting, fitted the ends of the handles past her knees and pressed with hands and legs together. With a muted click the hasp of the lock gave way and it dropped into the litter on the wooden floor.

Good. At least she could now get into the trunk when she wanted to.

Andrea replaced the bolt-croppers, both her palms and her knees feeling abused by her exertions. Outside, the sky was starting to alter into a premature twilight as rainclouds, black and heavy and threatening, gathered across the face of the sun.

Snick-snack. Punish him.

Her gaze shot back to the shears, which were still in their original position, a fat-bodied spider making its way cautiously through the mess of cobwebs towards a struggling fly. Then a thought occurred to her and she walked slowly back into the house, careless of the first spots of rain beginning to fall heavily about her.

In her bedroom she found the bag she'd carried on her visit to Gaunt's office and turned its contents out onto her bed. The small card had fallen face down and Andrea looked at it without touching it for several minutes as her brain attempted to dictate a course of action. Her hands were shaking in the same way they'd shaken over Gaunt's photographs as she reached out and picked it up, flipping it over like a coin between her fingers.

PHANTASTICADS. And a phone number.

Andrea put the card down beside the bedside phone and lifted the receiver. Her other hand had dialled the number and she was listening to the ringing tone before she realised what she'd done. Then the voice came on line, sounding young and pretty but probably fat and fortyish. At least, Andrea found herself hoping it was fat and fortyish, if not even older.

'Phantasticads,' it informed her. 'Thank you for calling. How can I help you?'

Andrea paused as long as she dared. She could still put the phone down, couldn't she? And Gaunt could still go back to that hotel in Manchester and not take his wretched photographs, couldn't he? And nobody'd cut the lock off the tin trunk, and the sheep-shears hadn't spoken to her, and she still lived in St John's Wood.

'Mr Garfield, please.'

The sound of her voice surprised her, but the sound of the name she'd just spoken almost pleased her.

'I'm afraid Mr Garfield isn't expected back this afternoon. May I take a message for him?'

Not there? Didn't he know what it was costing her to make this call? How dare he not be there when she needed him. Absolutely typical. Just like Josh.

'Men, dear, are all the same,' was one of her mother's favourite expressions. Andrea found it on her own lips and struggled to check it. Instead she just said: 'Tell him Andrea Buchanan called,' and put the phone down.

She took off her dress and examined it, a little surprised by the number of strands of cobweb and brushes of dust it had collected. Then she peeled off her ruined tights and ran a bath while she got out of the rest of her clothes and pinned her hair up. Half a bottle of Andrea Duncan Luxury Foam Bath later she was ready for a good soak.

Not too good, though. Not hard or long enough to leave her fingers looking like desiccated liquorice sticks.

Why hadn't she left her phone number?

Maybe because she didn't really want to see Tim again. Maybe he was just a way of expressing her protest at Josh's behaviour. After all, Josh had his good points, lots of them. And even if they didn't love each other any more she didn't want the hassle that getting rid of him was going to cause.

Tim could be married now. She'd not asked him when they'd met in the museum, and there was nothing to stop someone like himself, looking good and doing well, from making a good match. She could be asking him to behave in the same way Josh was behaving.

She remembered his call that morning. He'd told her he'd had some nightmares after his experience the day before, and Andrea had struggled hard to keep the pleasure out of her voice and try to be soothing. Maybe the

151

murdered girl was his mistress. That would serve both of them right. It could even be punishment enough.

Snick-snack.

I shouldn't still be hearing that, she thought. Maybe Freddy's razor-clawed hand is going to reach up out of the water between my legs and cut me to death.

No.

The videos were losing their power. She'd try to disprove that tonight, sitting alone in the vault by the light of American International red twisty candles, drinking midnight wine and watching something very nasty. A splatter movie like *The Last House On The Left* should prove it, one way or the other.

But if they really were losing their value as a counterbalance to her nightmares, what was left? A return to the world of the businesswoman, the world she'd already conquered and abandoned? Settle down to being the well-to-do housewife, all tweeds and Barbour and charity works? That was unthinkable. Not even the successful businesswoman, let alone the little girl from rural East Anglia, could play lady of the manor. There was too much old money around Abbots Ringley, as the few dinner parties they'd given at the Abbey had shown her. Too many people who knew their wine and their shooting and which end of the table who sat at. Andrea would be sure to give herself away and lose whatever respect the recluse – mysterious and probably regarded through her efforts as better-looking than she actually knew herself to be – had built up for her individuality.

The same question came back. What *was* left? Suicide? A lover? Both sounded too much like stock ingredients of her videos. Maybe she should try some SM porno.

She reached down through the bubbles and touched herself, then shuddered. Pauline had shown her how to do that years ago, but the only time she'd actually wanted to was that night in the churchyard at East Bilney. Ever since, the action had held too many confused and frightening memories. It was all right for someone else to do it to her, but not for her to do it to herself.

No, porno, SM or otherwise, was out.

This wasn't something that could be worked out in a hurry, she decided. Besides, she hadn't put it to the midnight test in her own secret world yet.

Andrea was speculating as to whether or not to eat as she dried herself, examining her body carefully in the mirror as she did so. Her breasts were still firm and her body was keeping its lines well. Maybe that was the price she'd have to pay for happiness. Maybe she should give in to the natural feelings she'd pretended she didn't have for so long. Maybe she should have a baby. Something that squalled in the night and leaked at both ends, mostly when she wanted to go to sleep.

But did she actually want to go to sleep? Getting up to change the creature, or to burp it or feed it or just plain comfort it, could be a way of disrupting her nightmares. And if it got too much for her she could hire a nanny, someone plain and motherly that Josh wouldn't want to bed.

It made as much sense as anything she'd come up with so far, and with what she knew about beauty preparations she needn't even lose too much of her figure. Or be cobwebbed with stretch-marks.

Andrea slipped into a bra and panties and lingered through her wardrobe. It was going to have to be her Mortitia dress tonight, she finally decided, the black one with the full-length sweeping skirt and plunging neckline and belled sleeves. It went so well with the red twisty candles in the Georgian silver candelabra.

When she'd dressed she let down her hair again, whitened her cheeks and reddened her lips to a devastatingly vampiric carmine. A small drop of that unmarketable liquid she prepared for herself from deadly nightshade widened each eye hauntingly, completing the effect she wanted. Finally prepared, ready to face the mutterings of the old house and the shrieks from the video, she lit the candles and swept down the crepuscular main staircase like a refugee from *The Addams Family*.

This was to be her night of trial, she decided. Tomorrow she would know for certain what her world was going to be.

25

ENNIO WAS RELAXING with a large brandy in his flat above a Greek Street delicatessen when the ring came on the street door. He set the glass down and crossed the room, lifting the door phone and simply stating: 'Yes?'

'It's Carole Vanbrugh,' said the voice at the other end.

Carole? By the Great Dog's prick this was a surprise. He'd wanted to get to Carole, red-haired big-nippled Carole, outside the ritual chamber ever since he'd first set eyes on the delicious Sister Hagiel, as she was known amongst the Sons of Samael.

'C'mon up,' he said with feigned nonchalance, tripping the switch.

He checked the room for anything he might not want a bed-partner to see and found nothing overtly offensive. The Evening Standard lay open on the table where he'd left it, the better part of a page devoted to two murders, one in Manchester and one in Coptic Street, which the police had decided were linked. Photos of both victims, before receiving his ministrations, stared back off the page at him, acquiescent rather than accusing.

Yippee! If Carole's come to see me then the sacrifices must be working. I was going to cool it for a while, but maybe I should chase the next one up faster than I'd intended.

Not only that, the voice at the back of his head whispered. Sister Hagiel is a High Priestess. She has access to the Magister Inferi. She can be your link to his favour, handled carefully.

Oh, but he was going to handle her carefully. And lovingly. That hot, slightly-plump body of hers deserved all the attention he could give it. And then some.

He opened the hall door to her and found her dressed in innocuous sweater, slacks and jacket, her red hair tied back at the nape of her neck. With a smile and a mock bow he motioned for her to enter, but she stayed firmly where she was, at the top of the stairs.

Ennio's eyes narrowed. This wasn't what he'd expected. She ought to be more pliable, more . . . involved than this. Especially as she was the one who'd done the seeking-out.

'Get your coat,' she commanded, her voice hard and unyielding. She reminded him of a sex tyrant in a bad porno movie.

'We'd be more comfortable here,' he invited.

'Don't fuck me around, Zabetti,' Carole said wearily. 'The Magister wants to see you.'

This wasn't something he'd expected. But then, he hadn't expected Carole either. Things were starting to move quickly. Perhaps too quickly.

Ennio shrugged and did as he was ordered. Carole led the way down the stairs, her arse jigging with unfulfilled promise, and stood aside at the bottom for Ennio to open the street door. She followed him out, grasping his elbow and steering him towards a double-parked car with its engine running and a stranger sitting behind the wheel. The man

156

leaned back as they approached and opened the nearside
rear passenger door.

'Inside,' Carole said flatly.

He got in and slid across the seat, trying the other door
surreptitiously and finding it fitted with a child-proof lock.
Carole sat down beside him, her perfume stimulating him
despite his growing sense of unease. The driver, whose face
Ennio had yet to see, flipped something over the front seat
which Carole caught. It was a large black bag of heavy fabric
with a drawstring around the neck.

'Put this on,' she told him.

He was beginning to get rather annoyed by this monosyllabic set of commands, more so than with the idea of the
blindfold. Still, if putting up with a little hassle would get him
on the right side of the Magister it was going to be worth it.

'As you desire,' he muttered, complying. Then, through
the fabric: 'Is there anything I can persuade you to do to
entertain me through the journey?' he asked her.

Her reply was a sudden and violent tightening of the
drawstring which threatened to strangle him. As he began
to choke and thrash about the pressure lessened and he
heard Carole's reply.

'Don't ask me silly questions, Zabetti,' she answered,
yawning. 'I have better creatures to squash than you. If
the Magister hadn't ordered it I wouldn't be here at all.
Now shut up.'

The car threaded its path through the West End and
up into Camden Town before branching across in the
direction of Hendon. At that precise moment Ennio was
probably the most wanted man in Britain, and he would
not have been pleased to know how close he came to the
Metropolitan Police College on that blindfold journey.
Unable to see his watch he had no real idea of how
long the journey was taking. All he knew was that it was

157

beginning to feel interminable. His first indication that they were approaching their destination was when he felt the car swerve around several corners in rapid succession, telling him that the straight, long roads were behind them and they were into a warren of side-streets.

When the vehicle finally stopped it was parked under a broken street-lamp. Residents of that particular road felt it was strange how the vandals always put that particular light out, though they never thought it was in any way connected with the residents of the house it would have mostly illuminated. The driver got out first, then walked around the front of the car onto the pavement to open the rear door for Carole and Ennio, who had to be helped out and guided up the path to the front of the house. The door opened without any ringing or knocking and the change of air as he mounted the steps and crossed the threshold told Ennio he was now inside.

He reached up to remove the bag. Carole's elbow connected painfully with his rib-cage. 'Not yet,' she hissed. 'We'll tell you when to take it off.'

They led him through another doorway and helped him to sit down in an armchair. He heard their footfalls, soft on a thick-pile carpet, as they withdrew, then there was the sound of an inner door closing.

Badly disorientated, beginning to feel afraid for his own safety for one of the few times in his life, Ennio strained to catch something, anything, through the heavy fabric. It was a sense, rather than any physical evidence, that told him he was not alone.

'Why *did* you choose to call yourself Ball-Phegor, Ennio?' came a familiar voice from the other side of the room. 'I've seen it written down, so I know it's more than a simple mispronunciation of Baal. And you're too intelligent to have simply spelled it wrong.'

It was Astaroth, sure enough. The Magister Inferi himself.

Ennio touched his face, or rather the cloth still covering it. 'Can . . . I take this thing off, Magister?' he enquired.

'Hmm? Oh, the hoodwink. Yes, take it off if it's bothering you.' The acquiescence was unconcerned, as if Astaroth hadn't noticed Ennio was still wearing it. But it was important. It did three things for Ennio Zabetti.

It enabled him to remove the blindfold and look about him, putting himself more at ease.

It started his brain working again.

And it told him, by the use of the term *hoodwink*, which he had never heard any of the brethren use before, that the Magister was probably a Freemason as well.

He surveyed his surroundings briefly. The room was large and comfortable, with an open fire burning in the hearth between two solid banks of bookshelves. The ceiling was corniced and high and had three doors. One was by the chair he was sitting in, and was probably the one he'd been brought in through. The second was further along the same wall and the third was in the end wall adjacent, also surrounded by bookshelves. If there was a TV or any other electrical equipment it was out of sight, most likely in the large bay window he assumed faced the road behind him.

The Magister Inferi sat on the other side of a double-pedestal desk at the inner end of the room. A table-lamp shone neutrally down onto a leather blotter tooled with gold on the otherwise clear surface. No other lights were burning but the fire sent flickering gleams dancing around the room.

'Ball-Phegor?' Astaroth reminded him, standing up.

The goat-mask looked incongruous above the dark business suit and pale shirt, but it had been too much to expect to meet the Magister without it. Only with his initiation to the next grade up would that particular cherished secret be revealed to him.

If he lived that long.

He wanted to turn around, to see if there was anyone standing behind him, ready to carry out a swift execution. It was always possible that he'd offended in some way he didn't know about. Brothers sometimes disappeared, never to be seen in the ritual chamber or heard from outside it again. And the whim of the Magister Inferi, Lord of the Porta Inferi and possibly several other covens of the Sons of Samael, would be quite sufficient to explain those disappearances.

'I've . . . always enjoyed the flesh . . .'

'Then why not simply Belphegor or Baal-Phegor? By far the more usual spellings for the demon of licence.'

'It's a double pun. On testicle and dance. Sort of dance of the testicles, which is what licentiousness is all about.'

Had he said it too quickly? It was the real explanation, thought up by a fifteen-year-old boy initiate. Now, almost two decades on, it sounded hollow and unconvincing.

Was that it? His name didn't fit? That simple and that fatal? His stomach began to churn with apprehension in the depths of the chair. Here he was, having killed several times in his years with the brethren, before the man who had killed far more often and with far less reason, if there ever could be a reason for killing.

Why hadn't he been born a Catholic?

'Good.' He felt the features behind the goat-mask smile and relax. The Magister sat down again. Silence resumed, except for the crackling of the fire in its hell-mouth grate.

'Is . . . that all?' Ennio asked nervously.

'Hmm?' the same absent response as he'd had before, as if the Magister was a preoccupied but indulgent uncle with a favourite nephew tugging at his sleeve. 'No, not quite. Have a drink.'

160

He followed the sweep of the masked figure's arm and was surprised not to have noticed the decanter of whisky, together with a water-jug and a cut-crystal tumbler sitting on an occasional table beside him, facets winking with reflected flames.

'Thank . . . you.' He gave the pouring of whisky and water his full attention to make sure his hands didn't shake too much. He'd almost finished when the Magister, now standing less than three feet away and towering over him, his approach completely unobserved, said: 'Ennio, I want you to close the circle.'

His hand wavered and a few drops of water spilled from the jug onto the surface of the table. Deciding to ignore them rather than weaken his position still further by trying to mop them up he picked up the tumbler and took a hefty swallow at its contents.

'I . . . I didn't know it had been broken, Magister.'

'It has never been completed. But you think I mean the ritual circle, don't you. My dear boy, I don't mean that at all. I mean the *blood* circle.'

'The blood circle?'

Astaroth's goat-head nodded indulgently. 'This shall be your test for advancement, Ennio,' the Magister continued. 'Many years ago, when you were little more than a boy, you began the rite of the blood circle, although you didn't know it at the time and have not known it since. The circle has remained open all that time, and now it is appropriate that it should be closed.

'Tell me, what do you think of your status within the Sons of Samael?'

The question caught him by surprise, but the whisky and the Magister's tone together were beginning to convince him that he had nothing serious to fear. Already this session was starting to feel more like a job interview than anything else.

'I've tried to do all that could be asked of me.'

'And more?'

He didn't see where the *Evening Standard* came from, but it landed on his lap folded open to the page with his victims' photos on it. His heart leaped violently and his rectum tightened. The drink nearly slopped over the lip of the glass.

'You know . . .?'

'There's little I don't know, Ennio. For the time being I want you to do nothing about the person Steffi Holt named. He won't trouble you or affect the Sons of Samael in any way I can't control. Concentrate on your main task, which is to discover the nature of the blood circle and complete it.

'Now, you came here in company with Carole Vanbrugh, yes? Of course you did. It excited you. You've always wanted Carole, haven't you, Ennio? But she's above your station in the brethren, and so untouchable. Isn't she?'

The question demanded a spoken answer. 'Yes,' Ennio agreed, sulkily.

'Wrong. She is your reward when the blood circle is complete. Not until then, mind. In the meantime I have a certain little sweetmeat with which to thank you for coming here tonight. Come now.'

Astaroth moved towards the inner end of the room, beckoning for Ennio to follow him. He swallowed the rest of his whisky and stood up, obeying with greater confidence than he would ever have dreamed he'd be able to muster when he first arrived. For a moment he half-dreamed of tearing the goat-mask from the Magister's face, exposing his features and saving himself the trouble of further advancement by the blood circle, whatever that was, but even as he formed the thought the figure ahead of him uttered a brief but disturbing chuckle that seemed to imply the thought was both read and understood.

162

They left the room through the innermost of the doors in the side wall and entered a wide hall which narrowed towards the front door. A staircase led up to a first-floor landing in one broad, unbroken flight warded with an ornate wooden bannister. Tiffany-shaded lights hung from the slanting ceiling above them at regular intervals, providing a dim, particoloured illumination. Once on the landing the Magister turned and continued towards a door at the farther end. This he opened, disclosing a completely white room within. Floor, walls, ceiling, furnishings, everything was white. His fingers punched a number into a control panel beside the door and the light slowly deepened to the red of fresh-spilled blood.

Ennio followed his master into the room, the middle of which was occupied by a huge circular bed. A huge mirror set floor to ceiling in a white frame swung inwards and a figure stepped through it out of the darkness beyond. The figure was smallish and pale, and completely naked. The Magister turned to Ennio.

'You remember little Pravus from the initiation, Ball-Phegor?' he enquired.

Ennio remembered her all right. Her combination of agony and desperation and pleasure had been difficult to forget. Not that he'd even wanted to.

The mirror-door swung closed behind her, sealing her in the room.

'As I suspect you have guessed,' the Magister continued, 'Pravus is very special to me, to all of us. And especially to you, Ennio. Anyone who is capable of summoning me into her presence, as Pravus has done, commands a real and very substantial power. Now, she is yours to do whatever you wish to do to her, but with the proviso that not one drop of her blood is to be shed. And you, my dear,' he added, turning to Pravus, 'are to perform whatever this brother wishes, but in the way we discussed before his arrival. Is that clear?'

Ennio was too busy removing his clothes to worry about what Astaroth was saying to Pravus. By the time the Magister had withdrawn and closed the door behind himself Ennio was as naked as his companion, and very proud.

They moved towards the bed from either side. Pravus reached it first and spread herself across the covers. Ennio sprang on top of her without hesitation or further ceremony. He was pumping with the same unbroken rhythm towards his first climax when he realised that she was now on top of him.

He reached up to jiggle her young breasts, her hands beating a tattoo on his chest in time with his plunging strokes. Her movements seemed stiff, somehow awkward in their rigidity, then grew more relaxed as her touch became warm and ethereal. As Ennio reached his climax and let fly he suddenly became aware that she was shimmering slightly, her outline wavering like an uncertain hologram.

Only then did he hear the words.

The tightness of her muscles around him seemed to stick, to burn. He struggled to get free, even as his member kept on pumping. The sensation was strange, dangerous, and the sudden fear of being left a eunuch began to take an irrational hold over his mind.

He twisted and turned. She had next to no weight to keep him down and he should have been able to throw her off easily. He tried to focus his mind on the words she was chanting, but they meant nothing to him. Even the scraps of Latin and Basque and whatever he'd heard during her initiation made more sense than the words Pravus was chanting.

He arched his back, digging his heels into the yielding

mattress, trying to dislodge her before she ripped his penis off altogether. His world became a battlefield of increasing agony, a jagged series of migraine flashes searing up his spine from groin to brain. If this kept up, if he didn't manage to pull out of her soon, the blood circle was going to be torn out of his groin.

Her face bent towards his own, wild and ecstatic. Her eyes widened until their pupils became tunnels down which he could pass, both at once without dividing, like something out of quantum physics. Whatever her talent might be, and he was no longer in any doubt that it was special, very special indeed, he'd be lucky to come out of this without an important piece of himself lost forever.

Oh hell! his mind screamed. Jesus fucking Christ! This little cunt is sticking to me like Superglue!

And then, even as he felt the muscle fibres begin to pop and tear, even as he knew his worst ever fears were about to be realised, the lovely, glowing, menacing apparition above him suddenly relaxed. With a heave he hadn't believed himself still capable of he threw her clear and fell back across the circle of crumpled bedclothes, panting wildly.

The words had stopped. Slowly, carefully, he raised himself up on his elbows and looked down towards the expected ruin of his manhood. It lay there, detumescent, a little red and limp but otherwise unscathed.

Between breaths he heard the click as the hidden video cameras were switched off from behind the two-way mirror. He should have expected that, he told himself. He should also have expected to see the Magister's goat-mask peering down at him from the door-side of the circular bed.

The Magister walked around to where Pravus lay and extended his hand to her. She took it in her own and sat up. As the mirror swung open again Ennio turned his head and watched her slowly leave the room.

The Magister remained with him as he threw an arm across his eyes and tried to pull himself together enough to get dressed.

'An interesting experience for you, Ennio, in more ways than one,' came the voice from behind the mask.

He pulled himself together and hobbled over to find his underpants. The Magister punched a code into the control panel and the light returned to brilliant white.

'That was your first experience of incest, wasn't it?' Astaroth asked, as courteous as if he were discussing trivia at a cocktail party.

Ennio stepped into his pants and looked over at his master. 'Incest?' he queried. 'That was *incest*?'

'The girl is your daughter, Ennio. She was conceived atop a tombstone in a Norfolk graveyard some fifteen years ago. You remember the occasion?'

He tried to fight an answer past the shattering revelation he'd received. 'I . . . remember. Her mother . . .'

'Let's not think about the dead, Ennio. But use your memories to guide you in the task you've been set tonight. Pravus will be able to assist you with her special talents.

'Now, you may leave this house whenever you wish and return to it as you may decide proper. Your car has been brought here and is parked a few doors up. Doubtless you will notice the address as you leave.

'I'm pleased with you, Ennio. Just remember what you've been told tonight and you have a good future, a great future, amongst the Sons of Samael. Once the circle has been completed.'

166

26

LEONARD GAUNT HAD hardly touched Margot's shepherd's pie. Or the Heinz Treacle Pudding she followed it with. Instead he sat in the small front room of his terraced house in Morley Gardens, Catford, his eyes glazed and the *Evening Standard* open before him.

It was all too much of a coincidence, he decided at length. He worked less than a mile from Coptic Street, where the bookseller had been killed. And he'd photographed the other victim, the Holt woman, just hours before her own horrible death in a flat in Manchester.

Somewhere there had to be a connection. It didn't take Sam Spade to work that much out.

Certainly the connection with Steffi Holt and himself was clear enough. According to the newspaper she'd been found by her employer, a Mr Buchanan, after failing to go to work. That was the same Buchanan whose wife had hired him. But what about the other guy? How did the link between the Manchester and London killings come about?

He'd explained it all to Margot, who was sitting beside him watching Coronation Street on TV. 'Sounds like you oughta tell the police, Lenny,' was all the advice she'd offered him. It was sound enough, but this was the closest Gaunt had come to his big case and he was reluctant to relinquish what he knew.

Maybe the police already knew that Buchanan and Steffi Holt were sleeping together. Probably he'd be wasting his time, and theirs, if he made any approach to them. What they didn't know was the same thing that he didn't know: how exactly the two deaths were related.

If he could find that out he'd be half way to solving the case. That would be the time to tell the police, and the papers as well. He'd have built up enough kudos to turn Factfinders into one of the leading London detective agencies.

P.I. PROVIDES PRIME CLUE, sang the headlines in his mind. GAUNT HELPS CATCH DOUBLE KILLER.

This was the big one, all right. If only he could crack it.

Tomorrow there was nothing pressing in the office that Margot couldn't handle. He'd ask a few questions around Coptic Street and see if that got him anywhere. He'd also have a good session with Mrs Buchanan in the afternoon. There might just be something she knew which could tip him off.

His one reservation was that he'd be dealing with a knife-killer. Leonard Gaunt had never liked knives, and he took the dislike as far as shaving electric. Knives were nasty things. They sliced and stabbed. They could make even more of a mess of you than a small calibre bullet could, in the hands of someone who knew what he was doing. And this maniac obviously did.

Uh-huh. He'd try Coptic Street and Mrs B. If something came out of either he'd work out whether to follow it up himself or give it to the coppers. *If* anything came out of it. Which, knowing his luck, was as likely as replacing his Allegro with a brand new Mercedes.

27

IT WAS ABOUT half-nine when Andrea realised the electric eye in the drive had been tripped.

Christ, that thing was going to have to go. The doorbell alone was bad enough, without that device giving its extra warning. An intercom to the gates and an electric catch could do both jobs with half the hassle.

She'd been watching the main evening news on BBC1, slowly working her way through a bottle of wine and feeling more mellow than she'd done for some time because of it. This one news broadcast a day was as much as she wanted to see of the world outside. It kept her abreast of happenings in the one-party state Britain was becoming. Although she'd never particularly liked America or Americans she found herself grudgingly admiring their freedom of information and the jealous safeguarding of individual liberty they pursued with such vigour.

Andrea climbed to her feet from the depths of her comfortable seat in the great hall and wavered towards the front door, ready for the inevitable ring. Probably Josh coming back early to see if she played the same games as he did. Well, she didn't. So fucking there.

Whoops. Such coarseness. She'd never get to be lady of the manor if she said fuck.

Fuck it, she thought. I don't want to be lady of the manor anyway. I want to be . . .

How was she going to react to Josh? Was she going to confront him with Gaunt's photos? Would she simply be cool and withdraw, which he'd probably take as her acting naturally? How about a blazing row?

How about just plain wait and see? Maybe he'd slouch back in looking guilty and wanting to confess and grovel. Not that he ever had done before, but he'd never been found out before, had he?

Andrea checked herself. He didn't know he'd been found out this time, so why should he come back grovelling? It had never been Josh's way, and she was pretty certain he wouldn't be starting it now.

She waited at the foot of the stairs, surprised to find her world swaying slightly. She only remembered the one bottle of wine. Maybe she should check the bin in the kitchen in case there was another one, empty and forgotten, waiting to chastise her there. Come to think of it there probably was.

Fuck you, Josh. How about fucking me for a change?

The bell rang. Andrea was sitting on the bottom step, though she didn't remember the act of sitting down at all. Her legs weren't working very well tonight, and her head didn't feel overly competent either. Maybe another glass or two would straighten her out.

Snick-snack.

Look you, shut it, will you? That's the bell. I'm supposed to be answering the front door, *if* you don't mind.

It's time, Andrea.

She peered up at the ceiling. It hadn't spoken to her for ages. Hardly at all since that first day. Funny time for it to start again. Still, this was crunch night, after all. Yeah, something was going to happen tonight.

Something was happening tonight. The doorbell rang again.

Not Josh? He'd have given up and let himself in by now, wouldn't he? Then, if not Josh, who'd be calling at this time of night? Some escaped rapist or loony bent on mayhem? Someone who'd do what she wanted and then strip all the skin off her face and leave her to die screaming?

Now what made her think of that? That was only a part of her nightmares, nothing more. Unless you lived in Coptic Street, and Abbots Ringley was a long way from being Coptic Street.

She lurched to her feet and struggled with the door, finally swinging it wider than she'd meant to. The porch-light was on, glaring against the inner stonework of the two arches supporting the high oriel window above. And nothing else.

In the porch, that was. Outside, a dark blotch in the night, a figure turned its pink face back towards her.

'I . . . didn't think you were going to answer,' said Tim Garfield.

She peered at him through the wine-haze. 'Tim? Is that you?' Her hands reached for and found the door-frame. She clung to it for support. 'What the fuck are you doing here?'

She *must* stop saying *fuck*.

'I'm sorry. It was a mistake. I'll go.'

'Stay right where you are,' she commanded, releasing her grip so that one hand could point. 'No, don't do that. Come closer. Come in.'

He stepped under the arches, his eyes hurt and confused. His hands were at his sides, the fingers stiff with his

172

effort to appear relaxed, to belie his expression with his body-language. He looked at her with that hurt puppy expression he'd always been so good at and her outstretched, imperious finger wavered and dropped to her side. Then the arm swept upwards and in, pointing through the hall to her inner magnificence surrounded by the minstrel gallery.

'C'mon in, Timmy.'

She was obviously drunk, both from her behaviour and from the way she turned and lurched away from the open doorway to make room for him to follow her. Her eyes were too wide and she looked more like a lost little girl than Mortitia Addams, despite the dress and the smudged carmine around her mouth. He felt his heart going out to her, while his mind wondered why she should be in a state like this. Oh, he'd seen her drunk before, but always happy drunk. Never in this state of exuberance bordering on total and abject despair.

He still knew her. He believed that he could still read her moods. But this was a mood he'd never seen before, and he followed her into Ringley Abbey with hesitant and uncertain steps.

Tim knew she'd done well from the sale of her business, but he'd never suspected that the little girl from East Anglia would have ensconced herself in so fabulous a pile as this. She'd never been very good at spending her money, naturally careful rather than mean, and Ringley Abbey came as something of a shock to him. Josh's work, obviously, he decided. And so, most likely, was her current state of drunkenness, one way or the other.

She waggled back into the great hall, sawing her buttocks and turning occasionally to pout at him, and flopped onto a sofa, legs crossed and breasts thrust forward, looking worryingly uncomfortable. 'Have a drink,' she waved at the bottle of Bulgarian Cabernet Sauvignon, standing alone without a glass.

Tim shook his head. 'Sorry, Andy, I'd better be going,' he told her. He was feeling too much pity, and too much desire at finding her like this, friendly, vulnerable and doubly appealing because of the combination, to trust himself to stay.

'G'wan,' she leered, struggling to her feet. She meandered over to the Chinese cabinet, touching every piece of intervening furniture on her way, and found him a glass. She filled it too full and handed it to him with a miraculous display of self-control, not spilling a drop. For several moments he stood and looked at it, then took it from her fingers a fraction of a second before it would have slipped through her failing grasp.

'Sit,' she commanded.

He gazed at her, helpless, lost and so very, very fragile. 'Woof,' he said gently, obeying.

She sat beside him, too close for his comfort. Maybe she wasn't that magnificent a beauty but she'd pulled something out of that old book of her grandmother's that gave her a distinct and, as far as Tim Garfield was concerned, infallible allure. Her hand stroked his arm and her face turned up towards his. He smelled the wine on her breath and that so gentle other perfume she'd never put on the market, saving its secret for herself alone.

'Hi, Tim,' she whispered.

'Hi, Andy,' he responded, more gently, more affectionately than he'd intended to.

Her arms were around his neck before he could fight them off. He didn't want to take advantage of her obvious weakness. It would be so easy to regret when they parted, as part they must. She was married. She belonged to somebody else now. Someone called Joshua Buchanan.

174

His Andy wasn't his Andy any more, hadn't been for too many painful years.

What the hell was he doing here anyway?

He reached out and grasped her face to keep it away from his own. He had to tell her how he'd deliberately sought her out, trying to arrange an appointment with her husband and discovering he was out of town. Pumping Josh's secretary for details she shouldn't have given him, then spending several hours torturing himself before finally deciding to use them to cool himself off once and for all.

She should have turned him away on the step. She should have told him not to be such a weak, selfish fool and sent him packing. That was what he'd come for. One last kick in the balls. One last spurning which would have finished it for ever. Not for this. Not for her lips seeking his own. And finding them.

He broke away. 'Christ, Andy, this is silly. I shouldn't be here,' he gasped before she silenced him again.

It wasn't right. It just wasn't. And it was all his fault. But oh, how he wanted her. And how he was going to give in to his desire.

He didn't remember that broad, ancient staircase the following morning. He didn't remember anything but the feel of her strength around him, soothing his doubts and lulling him from post-ecstatic recriminations into sleep, the smell of her in his nostrils like balm on his blistered soul. She woke him in the same way that she'd sent him to sleep, and he adored her for it. Every little look, every touch, was treasured and secretly enshrined in his memory. It could still be the last, he told himself. This could still be the end, the real end, instead of a new beginning.

But it wasn't. They both knew that, although neither of them went as far as saying so. When they eventually parted they parted with a kiss and a promise that each would

175

contact the other very soon, with a renewed addiction to each other's company. And for Tim Garfield there was an added bonus. Some few precious words that he'd never thought he'd hear.

She'd told him over breakfast, her in her night-dress, he in a borrowed robe of Josh's. 'It was a mistake, Timmy. *My* mistake. I should never have let you go in the first place. I don't know what's brought you back into my life and I don't care. On this particular twenty-seventh of April I love you more than I've ever loved anyone in my life, including Josh. In fact I don't think I ever really loved Josh at all. Just you, Timmy. Just you.'

For Andrea the night of crisis was passed and she finally knew where her life was going to take her. She'd slept without nightmares in the arms of the man she loved, and the world was a better place without her even having to leave Ringley Abbey.

Sun shining. Birds singing. Wind whispering in the tree-tops. The script was perfect and the leading man was the one she'd always wanted. The one she could settle down and have children with. In Brixton if she had to. All the melodrama of her life lacked was a villain, and there wasn't a villain anywhere to be found. Even Ennio Zabetti was forgotten.

Though Ennio Zabetti had not forgotten her.

28

ENNIO DROVE BACK across London and squeezed his car into the expensive little space behind his flat. All the way he'd been trying to puzzle out exactly what the evening meant to him, without any particular or lasting success.

If the Magister told him that Pravus was his daughter, then she was. He'd had plenty of opportunity to remember that night recently, with his discovery of Andrea Duncan again. There'd never been any doubt that the girl he'd fucked on the table tomb had conceived and borne a child, though he'd never actually seen or heard of the infant from that day to this. It had been spirited away by the order and, he'd imagined, gone the way of most unregistered births in a ritual sacrifice or a snuff movie. To discover it alive and on top of him all these years later was an incredible shock.

And what the hell had little Pravus been doing to him? How had she learned to inflict such pain? Was it pain?

The question took Ennio by surprise. Certainly it had hurt enough at the time, and he'd walked out to his car with a definite ache between his legs, an ache sufficient to keep him from wondering how they'd got hold of his car in the first place. Yet in retrospect, analysing his recollections of the experience, there had been pleasure as well. And something else that he'd never felt or even imagined before.

Whatever they'd done to Pravus in the intervening years was doubtless connected to the teachings of the brotherhood, the inner teachings which he wouldn't be privy to until he was promoted to the same grade as Carole Vanbrugh and her peers. She'd undergone some very special form of training that went beyond the ritual mummery and fornication that the rest of them practised.

No, he was going to have to wait before he could find out what made Pravus special, he decided. But if, as the Magister said, he'd have unrestricted access to her from now on, he might manage the odd short-cut now and again and gather the odd fragment of extra information.

That access was worrying in itself. Why had it suddenly been granted after all this time? Answer, so that he could complete the circle.

What circle? The blood circle.

And what exactly was the blood circle?

That was for him to find out, the Magister had said. Maybe Pravus knew. He'd drive over and ask her in a little while, when he'd got his head together and had some sleep.

He got himself ready for bed and clicked the light off. As he stared at the ceiling his mind tried to work through any clues he might have forgotten. That night when Pravus had been conceived must have something to do with it. The chant had been standard enough and he still remembered most of it. There wasn't going to be anything to help him there. Pravus' mother? He shook his head on the pillow. Hardly. Pravus herself? No, she'd only been there as seed and egg, not as a conscious entity.

Andrea Duncan?

Now *that* might mean something. He was thinking round it as his eyes closed. Behind his eyelids he visualised the scene again. Andrea had been there quite long enough to know what was going on, even if she didn't understand why. Pravus' mother could only have been a few months older than Andrea was at the time. They'd both have been about the same age as Pravus was now . . .

He began to tumble into sleep. Pravus and her mother and Andrea, all the same age, danced in a circle about him as he lay atop the table tomb. Other members of the Sons of Samael, robed and skull-masked, kept their torchlight vigil, chanting monotonously, beyond the circle of freshly-spilled blood which surrounded them.

A blood circle?

Too blatant. It burst into flame as he questioned it, burning in a way that blood never did, vividly without boiling away into a sticky blackness.

Mother and daughter? A blood link, certainly. He got up off the tomb, not particularly surprised to find himself naked, and tried to push past the three dancers to look something up. Their faces all merged into one and they pushed him back.

He studied their features, finding traces of each in the three identical faces. Andrea's nose. Pravus' eyes. Her mother's mouth. All three the same.

They came to him on the tomb, one by one. The only one he hadn't had before was Andrea, and he wanted her badly. She was last and as she approached, led willingly by the other two, their nails turned into claws and Ennio felt for his knife, only to find it missing.

'Let us say the words,' they chorused.

They said the words, Ennio realising he didn't know what they were and remaining mutely in his place while

179

they chanted. At each phrase a strip of skin peeled from one of their faces, transforming them slowly into bloodstained zebras. He found himself unable to move, unable to escape or turn away. He could only watch as the chanting continued and the three faces flayed themselves, drawing ever closer, looming ever larger in his sight.

'Quautem, virius, ad in hastibus homec . . .'

He'd never heard anything like it before. It wasn't Latin. Not proper Latin. He knew enough to realise that much.

'Vestis, qualibus, et ab horridus graumec . . .'

He shuddered before the hidden mystery which must lie in this gibberish. Could it be pure sound, pure barbarism, with the sounds themselves having a meaning that was denied to the words?

'Maugam, tassigus, os har demandius mordec . . .'

The sounds began to deteriorate as their lips fell away, becoming thick, bubbling mumbles from behind their exposed teeth. Beyond them, in the torchlit circle, the skull-masks became real skulls, clacking their teeth in the same unhallowed rhythm.

Clack-clack. Clack-clack-clack. Clack clack clack-clack-clack-clack clack-clack . . .

The three peeled faces hovered nearer, bending to kiss or bite or simply press their naked teeth against his features. Their eyes exploded and the vitreous humour spattered into his gaping mouth.

He woke up choking, sweating, staring at the daylight.

'Faugas, massius, in vos cavaribus laudec . . .'

Only as he made the effort and swung his feet out of bed did he realise that the chant was lingering, echoing, still calling from his nightmare in the dawn.

29

IT DIDN'T TAKE Gaunt long to discover the exact nature of Johnny Howard's mutilations. The shop was open, his assistant continuing to keep it running until its exact disposal was known, and only too eager to drum up trade by telling all and sundry the grisly details of the dead owner's missing face.

Gaunt shuddered. His fear of knives had so far only consisted of a respect for their ability to slash and stab. The thought that they could peel somebody's face off as easily as they could take the skin off an apple went beyond the simply unpleasant and into the downright *nasty*. As he left the shop, walking as normally as he could with one hand firmly pressed to his stomach to stop it heaving, the assistant's satisfied grin following him to the door, he wondered once again about leaving this to the police. If they'd linked this death with that poor bitch in Manchester then it implied the same method was being used in both cases. Two missing faces. Probably both removed by the same foul pervert.

A pervert with a knife. A pervert Leonard Gaunt was in no hurry to meet up with.

He stepped out of the shop into the world of car-parks and traffic-lights and pizzarias. Little antique shops with dim windows sold coins and Egyptian *ushabtis*. Bookshops displayed first editions of Bulwer Lytton and *Alice*. People pushed at the junctions and the cabs vied to see who could come closest. Gaunt felt himself pushed along with the rest, finding solace in the very nearness of the crowd about him in exactly the opposite way to Andrea.

Until he realised the killer might be any one of them.

He headed for a coffee shop. The day was fine after the rain the previous night and tables and chairs were set out to trip unwary pedestrians on the pavement of New Oxford Street. A cappuccino, all froth and sweetness, helped to calm him a little and let him put his thoughts in order.

The police probably knew everything he did anyway, he reasoned. Buchanan had doubtless had to tell them about his relationship with Steffi Holt to explain being in her flat. Could Buchanan have killed her?

Doubtful. The police weren't fools. If they had any doubts they'd be holding Buchanan and the paper would have said so. What about Mrs Buchanan? She might have followed her husband to Manchester, then tailed his lover home and sliced her face off.

Gaunt shook his head. No way. Point one, Buchanan and Holt had been together in public in the Starlight Bar, and only in the Starlight Bar. If Mrs B had turned up as well Gaunt would have seen her. Point two, if she already knew Holt's identity, why hire him to find it out? And point three, what possible motive could she have for the shopkeeper's death? Apart from anything else she had her husband at home that night to give her an alibi. He'd come in late, but he'd been there from ten-ish on, and the paper gave

Howard's time of death at round about then. She'd never have got from Coptic Street to Abbots Ringley in time to meet him on the doorstep.

Not that Ringley Abbey had anything as common as a doorstep.

So, she was out as a suspect, and her husband as well. That left an outsider.

With a sigh Gaunt drained his coffee and wondered about a doughnut. He was no farther on than when he'd climbed out of bed that morning. If Andrea Buchanan couldn't tell him anything that afternoon he'd have to drop the whole thing, and his dreams of glory with it.

Yet there was something still nagging away at the back of his mind, some vague connection waiting to firm up. He'd always prided himself on doing his homework and a friend in a press-cuttings agency had managed to find him chapter and verse on Andrea Buchanan, nee Duncan. At least, there'd been an article in *Cosmopolitan* a few years back, when she was the rising star of the beauty world, which had provided a great deal of biographical information. The art-coated pages were folded up in his pocket, and he ignored the doughnut, ordered another coffee and settled down to read them.

Born, and early years: Woodbridge in Essex. Moved to her grandfather's farm at East Bilney near King's Lynn at twelve, when her father died. Started work in local salons on leaving school. And the rest.

Intuitively Gaunt felt the rest didn't matter. What he was looking for was right there, in the first two decades of Andrea Buchanan's life.

He found a phone and rang Margot at the office. She told him about the mail, mostly bills as usual, though there was a small cheque among the rest of the junk. Then he asked her to check something out for him.

'Shelves by the door, there's a copy of McCain and Vickers' *Unsolved British Murders*. Have a squint in the index and tell me if there's anything for East Bilney in Norfolk, will you?'

'You still worrying that murder business, Lenny?' Margot asked, reprovingly.

'Look, this thing's eating money. Just do it will you, Margot?'

'Okay. Hang on.'

He heard the phone go down on something crinkly. A carrier bag, no doubt. She'd been going on about that sweater in Westaways although they both knew she couldn't afford it. Yet. Damn her, she'd gone out and bought it anyway, counting her chickens . . .

Gaunt was still cursing mentally when he heard the bag crinkle once more as Margot put the book down and lifted the receiver again. 'One about fifteen years ago,' she told him. 'Teenaged girl found in a hedgerow. Given birth recently. Badly mutilated.'

He felt his heart shudder slightly, then carry on working overtime to cope with his bulk. 'How mutilated?' he asked.

'Let's see. Just a minute, Len.' A pause. A riffling of paper. Silly cow had shut the book before he'd finished. 'Here we are. Head and neck . . .'

Her voice tailed off and he knew they were both thinking the same thing. 'Okay, thanks,' he said quickly. 'See you tonight, after I've been out to the Buchanans'.' He put the phone down quickly before she could start in on him.

About fifteen years ago. Andrea Buchanan would have still been at East Bilney then. And if the crime had been unsolved when McCain and Vickers' book was published it would still be unsolved today, three years later.

The police hadn't given away any details then, and they weren't giving away any details now. The link was there, though. Gaunt knew beyond any shadow of doubt that the girl at East Bilney had died without a face.

Shit! he reproached himself. I should have asked Margot for her name. Then I could have tried it on Mrs B and seen if she knew her from her reaction. Still, we'll work it out anyway.

I've got what I was looking for, he smirked. I've got a clear link to the Buchanans *and* I can tie these present killings to an unsolved murder in the past. It's all starting to come together.

And while Mrs B probably hasn't got anything to do with them herself, I'd bet my soul against the Devil that she bloody well knows who has.

30

THEY TOOK HER to Westminster Abbey and told her it was the House of the Enemy. She thought how powerful he must be to live in such a splendid place, so high and spacious in comparison to the house in Mill Hill with its black room. Yet despite his display of ostentation the house was unwelcoming, without a ritual chamber or even somewhere comfortable to lie down.

After that they showed her the Palace of Westminster and went up into the Strangers' Gallery. This was where much of their work was being done, they said. Pravus looked down and listened for a while. She found the building tall and exciting, but those silly men down there bored her. There were much more exciting ways of doing their work, and she already knew many of them.

At lunch-time they went to a restaurant and met the man she'd performed the ritual with the night before. He seemed nervous and ill at ease, uncertain as to how to behave with her. At one point he became arrogant and noisy and told her sternly that she wasn't to think of him as any kind of a *father*. She didn't. Not knowingly, anyway. She didn't even know what the word meant.

It hadn't been a part of her training that she should. She simply was. That's all. She was Pravus and she existed. Did there have to be anything else?

This new person called Ennio looked at Man. 'What exactly *can* she do?' he asked him.

Man shrugged and looked across the table to where Woman was sitting. Woman replied: 'We don't know, exactly, Mr Zabetti.' They were using his real name in public. He in turn obviated the need for theirs – which he still didn't know – by looking at them as he spoke. 'Only the Magister knows that for certain. It was he who first conceived the project which has resulted in Pravus. He has made all the decisions concerning her upbringing. Where she's lived, what she's learned. How she's developed. He could probably tell you, but it's possible she's developed in ways that even he didn't anticipate.'

The answer only served to puzzle Ennio even more. The Magister had made it clear the previous night that he'd told Ennio everything he was going to, and that the rest was up to him. He'd tried questioning Pravus before they went to table, but all she could say was that they were going to be working together, very soon.

'The season is growing stronger, you see,' she told him, smiling the enchanting, innocent smile of a girl young for her fifteen years. Only her eyes were older.

No, not older. They weren't *old* eyes. They were powerful eyes. Eyes that looked out of a mind that was unlike any mind Ennio had encountered before. Or would again, he thought to himself, shuddering a little.

Here they were, half-way through spring, and she was talking about the season? He asked her what she meant.

'Our girl has been brought up in a constant environment,

Mr Zabetti,' Man answered for her. 'She has been taught to recognise seasons other than those of nature. While she's been told about them she has no real experience of them. So, when she speaks of seasons they are not the natural ones. They are ritual seasons, the times when the rites may best be performed for their greatest efficacy. Is that a little clearer?'

'Sort of. So you're telling me we've got to do this working soon, Pravus?'

She nodded.

'How soon?'

'The night of the day after tomorrow, *Father*.'

That was when he'd shouted at her. Not too loudly or too long because he didn't want to draw attention to himself in public. But hard enough to get his point across.

And then he sat and thought about it, sipping his gin and tonic. If she'd been told he was her father then it must have been by the Magister. Maybe that was why she'd behaved as she had the night before, when he didn't know. Maybe it was to cut incest out of their relationship for ever for some reason. Certainly he felt disinclined to repeat the experience, or the nightmare it had induced. Usually Ennio slept well and soundly, free of conscience as he was of morality, without that sort of fantasy intruding.

The food was good but Ennio didn't eat very much. His mind was too preoccupied by what Pravus had told him about the *season*. There had to be a way of slotting that in with what the Magister had said. Nothing in the work of the Sons of Samael was left to chance, and his introduction to Pravus meant that she had a role to play in the closing of the blood circle. Now he knew *when* it had to happen, and he wasn't altogether surprised. May Eve was the traditional time for dark and Sanatic workings, the famous *Walpurgis nacht* of Dennis Wheatley and the witches. It was also one of the brotherhood's times for announcing advancement and he'd been surprised that no ritual had been announced at their last gathering. Now, though, he knew that there was going to be a ritual after all.

Okay, he reasoned. I know when. What I don't know is *how*. But I think I'm going to. There's an answer in all this somewhere and the Magister must be reasonably confident I'll find it or he wouldn't have risked not telling me.

Maybe it's got something to do with the name that Holt bitch gave me. No, not if the Magister said do nothing about that for the time being.

He looked across to where Pravus was slicing her way through a blue fillet steak, ignoring the vegetables and garnish that went with it. Just another pretty little cunt with fair hair and a young figure. Until you got to the eyes.

'Yeah,' he muttered into his wine. 'Why not? Okay, kid, call me father.'

She looked up from the oozing meat in front of her. The juices running out of it were gathering in a slight depression at the rim of the plate, forming a circle around the steak.

'Hallowed be thy name,' she told him.

He shot a blazing glance across to Man and Woman, sitting there as if suddenly frozen, Woman with her glass half raised. 'Where did she hear that?' Ennio demanded.

'She . . . didn't . . .' Man hesitated. 'There's no way she could have heard it. We've been scrupulous about that.'

Woman agreed, then turned to Pravus. 'Where did you get those words?' She asked gently, though the hand which had lowered her glass was trembling slightly.

'I made them up,' Pravus beamed. Then, looking at the three confused faces at table with her: 'They seem to be powerful, don't they?'

'They're forbidden,' Woman told her sternly. 'Don't say them again.'

Pravus shrugged. 'Okay.' She returned her attention to the meat.

She ate in silence for some time as the three adults slowly resumed their own food and conversation. Then she asked: 'Are they the words of the Enemy?'

Man nodded. 'They are, child. The Enemy gains strength from them. Remember that you denied the Enemy at your initiation.'

'Oh, I remember that clearly. That was good,' she added, pushing her plate slightly away from her. 'Can I have some more?'

Woman ordered her another blue fillet instead of a dessert, this time without garnish or vegetables. Then she lifted her handbag up in front of her and opened it. Reaching inside she took out a sheet of folded paper and held it out to Ennio.

'The Magister told me to give you this,' she informed him.

He reached over and grasped it, trying to keep his hand calm. Too much was going on in his life for him to feel completely comfortable about any of it. The paper was plain white, A4 size and folded to tuck together and form its own envelope. A small piece of sellotape held it closed.

Ennio turned it in his fingers for a few moments, then picked up his unused steak knife and cut the tape. Opening the sheet out, its folds dividing it into nine compartments, he read in the middle one:

> Andrea Buchanan
> (nee Duncan)
> Ringley Abbey
> Abbots Ringley
> South Buckinghamshire

That was all.

31

THE ONLY THING Andrea found herself regretting about the night before was the moment when Tim had produced a packet of Mates and asked her to fit one over his best feature. Without that she might have conceived his child, and that would have cemented them back together for ever.

He'd gone by the time Mrs Haigh came up from Abbots Ringley for the day, and Andrea was dressed and in her working clothes, jeans and sweater, announcing her intention to do some more sorting out in the outhouses. The daily thought how bright Mrs Buchanan was looking, though she knew better than to say anything about her unpredictable employer.

The sheep-shears were still in their cobwebbed place on the wall of the outhouse when Andrea stepped inside. She looked at them long and hard but they neither moved nor spoke beneath her gaze, as if they recognised the change which her renewed relationship with Tim Garfield had wrought in her. Now all that remained was to fill in the time until she and Tim could meet again, and her mind was busy attempting to devise excuses which could keep her away from the Abbey for the occasional, and hopefully regular, night of renewed love.

She moved the boxes and packages off the lid of the tin trunk, often struggling some distance with a heavy burden without finding a space she could put it down in. The work was hard, but she felt strong and determined, a different woman to the one who immersed herself in horrors in her own private crypt. It was only when the lid was clear and the only thing preventing her from seeing what was inside was herself that she thought of the futility of the exercise. With this done, she wondered, what the hell was she going to turn out next?

Andrea postponed the moment by going back to the kitchen and making herself and Mrs Haigh a cup of coffee. She sat there, only slightly in the way, sipping hers and flipping through a copy of *Good Housekeeping*. Once she became aware that somehow she'd managed to collect some cobwebs in her hair and she plucked some of the sticky fibres away, making a mental note to clean herself up before Josh got back that evening.

Before Josh got back.

That was what she had to do next. In the afterglow of Tim's unexpected visit she'd almost completely forgotten about working out how to handle her errant husband. Her position of strength as the faithful wife had been eroded through the night, but Josh didn't have to know that. Tim was hardly about to tell him and she certainly wasn't going to herself. Well, she'd open the old trunk and sort out its contents, which were probably going to be intensely disappointing, and then settle to the business of how to tackle Joshua Adulterer Buchanan.

Snick-snack.

192

She ignored the sound in her head. Her thoughts had wandered back towards Tim's baby. Their child. *Her* child. A part of Tim that would be hers for ever. They'd started together, then drawn apart. Now they were fated to come back together, like points tracing the circumference on either side of a circle, which had begun in the same place and would eventually close together to complete it.

The trunk lid lifted slowly, protestingly as the metal hinges grated against themselves. It creaked like a door with Vincent Price coming through it. Inside, beneath the dust and dead spiders, a piece of sacking covered the contents. Andrea lifted one corner carefully and peered down at the shiny, crinkled surface of a plastic rubbish bag.

She pulled the sacking out and threw it away, watching it land on top of a jumble of netting and flower pots in a corner, dust-motes rising and scattering lazily in its path. The black rubbish sack gave no clue as to its contents, but whatever was in it had been packed, and the sack sealed with adhesive tape, before it was laid on its side inside the trunk. She wasted a minute or so looking round for a knife and, not finding one, finally ripped the bag open with her fingernails. A faint smell of something perfumed and sickly wafted up at her.

Fabric. Some kind of garment. Fat coloured candles and carved wooden holders for them. A censer and a tin containing a blackish, gritty powder that smelled the same as the other contents of the bag. A length of stick with cloth wrapped around one end and stapled in place. A packet of self-igniting charcoal. And a large cardboard box, a cube about the size of an album sleeve, tied with string and sealed with gobs of purple sealing-wax.

She'd see them better if she took them out, but this wasn't the place to do it. They'd pick up the general filth of the outhouse. Besides, Mrs Haigh might decide to come round to tell her something and she wanted to look her discovery over in private.

Andrea had seen quite enough videos to know black magic paraphernalia when she saw it, and something told her she was seeing it now. It all looked so familiar, like some left-over props from *The Devil Rides Out*. And dated. All so dated. Did they really bother with this shit any more? Wasn't it more likely to be the brutal, vicious, deformalised Satanism of films like *Angel Heart* and *The Believers* that reigned today? This was strictly old hat, or old hood she corrected herself, smiling.

She closed the lid again to keep the contents clean and tried to lift the trunk by the handle at one end. While it would probably be too heavy for her to carry she could at least manage to drag it. Her biggest problem in taking it to the vault was going to be getting it down into the cellar, but if she took it slowly she could bump it down the stone stairs a step at a time.

The hell with it! That was the hard way. The easy way was good enough, especially as Mrs Haigh never went down to the cellar for anything, having her cleaning materials in a cupboard in the utility room. She looked around for something to keep the lid shut with, eventually finding an old nail and jamming it through the loop which had taken the hasp of the lock. Mrs Haigh could give her a hand into the house and down the steps. Then Andrea could drag the trunk into the vault herself. There she could examine the contents till the cows came home, or Josh did, without any fear of interruption.

The only real fly in this jar of ointment, she remembered, was that man Gaunt. She'd have to get the trunk down and then take care of him before she could rummage through what it contained.

Andrea found Mrs Haigh and called her out of the house to help with her burden. Together the two women, backs bent, the daily mentally threatening to quit if there was going to be much more of this, managed the trunk into the cellar. Mrs Haigh went back to her cleaning and Andrea opened the concealed door leading to the vault. A few sweaty minutes later it was hidden away in her private sanctuary, ready for inspection later.

With Mrs Haigh upstairs she washed off the surface grime in the downstairs cloakroom then went to the wall-safe which had been installed in Josh's study. From a thick wad of banknotes she counted off £3000 in fifties, then sealed the bundle, about the size of a thin paperback, into a brown manilla envelope. It wouldn't do for Gaunt to see her getting the money out, so it was best to get that done before he came.

Andrea took an early lunch and settled down in front of *Exorcist II: The Heretic* to wait for Gaunt's arrival. She'd never completely understood the film, being puzzled by director Boorman's use of locusts as a diabolical symbol instead of going for the more dramatic physical special effects of the original. Rather a waste of Richard Burton, she felt. She could forgive that dead but desirable actor anything, except for his being Welsh. She'd caught her dislike of Welsh people off her grandfather, who'd told her once: 'If yhu find a good Welshman, Andy, yhu'd best shoot 'im before 'e turns bhad.'

She could hear him saying it now, though his voice sounded more like Mrs Haigh's.

As Gaunt entered, carrying a battered leather briefcase that no yuppie would have been seen *zombie* with, she clicked off the video with the remote control, not bothering to rise as he extended his hand, fat and clammy, for her to shake. She did as was required of her, then motioned him to a seat across the low table from where she was sitting herself.

'Have you brought everything, Mr Gaunt?' she enquired.

'Indeed I have, Mrs Buchanan, and I venture to persuade myself that my endeavours have been in total accord with your wishes.'

Christ, he was at it again. Andrea tried not to yawn and temporarily succeeded. 'Good,' she told him. 'The negatives?'

He opened his briefcase and stood up to hand her a large envelope. As he sat down again she opened it and scattered its contents on the seat beside her. They consisted of a photoprocessor's wallet, several sheets of handwritten paper and the printed form with the Factfinders heading she'd filled in. Glancing briefly at the pages, which constituted the notes Gaunt had taken during their interview and some jottings made on the way back from Manchester, she opened the wallet and held the negatives it contained up to the light from one of the big windows.

Just like the photos. All of them.

'Thank you, Mr Gaunt,' she said, taking the envelope she'd sealed earlier from beneath a cushion beside her and sliding it across the table to him. 'There's £3000 in fifties in there, and I'll write you a cheque for the balance now.' Her cheque-book and a lacquer-finish Parker pen followed the envelope out from beneath the cushion.

Gaunt didn't like to look in the envelope. It felt bad form. Instead he contented himself with feeling its thickness and weight. All that lovely cash he wasn't going to have to declare to the rat-fingered taxman.

Andrea scribbled out the cheque and passed it to him. He checked the details, just in case she'd made a mistake, then put both cheque and envelope inside his briefcase.

'I'm most grateful, Mrs Buchanan,' he told her.

The trunk called out to her. 'Then I'll bid you good day.'

He stayed where he was. 'There was just one other thing,' he ventured.

196

'Not more cash, Mr Gaunt. You've been well overpaid as things are . . .'

'No no,' he interrupted. 'You've been most generous.'

'Then what is it?' She didn't manage to stifle the yawn this time.

'Have you heard about the murders?'

'Murders?' There'd been something on the news last night, but there was always something on the news. This man expected her to remember everything?

'The girl in Manchester, the one your husband was with . . .'

'Oh . . .'

'And the man in Coptic Street, Bloomsbury. They both died the same way, Mrs Buchanan. Faces flayed off.'

He watched her carefully for her reaction to his words. There wasn't one that he could see.

'Really?' The voice was flat, uninterested.

'Just like that girl at East Bilney, all those years ago.'

'Well, the police seem to have a coincidence on their hands.'

'I haven't told them, yet,' Gaunt pressed her. 'You were living in East Bilney when that girl died. Probably you knew her. You'd both have been about the same age.'

'I didn't go into the village much. I lived on my grandfather's farm. I feel you're implying something, Mr Gaunt. What is it?'

'I merely felt you should be apprised of a possible future direction of the police investigation, Mrs Buchanan,' he replied. This wasn't getting him anywhere.

'Then you have my gratitude again. I don't think the police will be very successful talking to me, though.'

Now, was that simply ambiguous phrasing, or was this woman on the defensive? One last thrust might sort things out a bit.

197

'You haven't said you didn't know her, Mrs Buchanan. You might not have gone to the village much, but you'd have both gone to the same school. And things like that stick in a young mind. Can you tell me her name?'

Andrea opened her mouth, then closed it again. Had she recognised the girl on the table tomb or was it just some confused imagining out of her past? Searching her memory wasn't going to help. Her thoughts were confused, and to try to draw any conclusions from them would have been speculative at best. Across the table Gaunt's eyes, piggy as they were, had taken on a new light, a new fire. She'd seen that fire burning on old newsreels, out of the eyes of the man called Adolf Hitler. To have it sitting across from her now was, at the very least, rather disconcerting.

Tell him something, her mind shrieked. Tell him something so that he'll go away. You'll be safe again once he's gone away.

'There . . . was a girl called Pauline Stafford,' she offered, placatingly. 'She got pregnant and her parents took her out of school. I never saw her again after that. None of us did.'

That would do. It would have to.

Where are you, Timmy? Why aren't you here to protect me from this maniac? You should be here, you know. None of this would be happening if you were here. I didn't even dream last night.

Snick-snack.

Gaunt's manner seemed to change. He relaxed and the fire went out of his eyes. 'I'm sorry to have troubled you, Mrs Buchanan,' he told her, picking up his briefcase and rising.

She rose too, eager to actually watch him leave. Once he'd done so she watched the rest of the film and waited for Mrs Haigh to finish. After all, there might be a question the daily needed answering which might take her down to the cellar to look for Andrea. And if she wasn't there the secret of the vault would be blown.

The film was half-run again when she finally heard Mrs Haigh leaving. Andrea leaped down the cellar steps, pausing only to set the electric eye in the drive so that she'd have some warning of Josh's return. She still hadn't worked out how to handle him, but by this time she'd decided that the only way to play it was by ear, and damn the consequences.

Now that Tim Garfield was back in her life again.

With the trunk open she carefully lifted its contents out of the remains of the rubbish bag and laid them down on the carpet, one by one. The garment she held up and opened out, discovering it to be a hooded robe, made all in one piece and large enough for a substantially-built man to wear.

The man she'd seen in the graveyard, perhaps?

The thought chilled her, despite the warmth from the heating installed in the vault. She carried the robe over to her chair in the centre of the double row of squat pillars and draped it across it.

She examined each item in turn, saving the sealed cardboard box for last. The charcoal was ordinary enough, as was the censer, though it had been made out of a heavier brass than most. The candles, red, white and black, had yet to be burned, though the candlesticks, eight of them made from turned wood, oak maybe, covered with a durable black finish, showed signs of wear. The powder in the tin was obviously an incense, intended to be burned in the censer on top of the self-igniting charcoal in its modern foil packaging.

Modern? Andrea suddenly realised that everything she'd seen so far was at most a few years old, and no more. This Dennis Wheatley rubbish was persistent, if nothing else.

Two items remained, awaiting her attention. One was the cardboard box. The other, more of a puzzle, was the length of stick with the cloth stapled to its end. As she held it out to look at it a sudden vision flashed into her mind.

A robed figure, skull-masked, holding a burning torch aloft.

So that was what it was. Now she knew it for a torch, the cloth waiting to be soaked with petrol or some other inflammable substance, she could guess only too well what was waiting to be discovered inside the cardboard box. It had to be the skull-mask that went with the torch and the robe.

No messing about this time. She'd brought a sharp knife down from the kitchen with her, ready to cut the string and open that cube of cardboard. She approached it and cut through the strands on one side. Then the other.

A simple loop of string now held the box closed. Nodding to herself with grim anticipation, not bothering yet to ask herself what this stuff was doing there, why it had come out of her past to haunt her present, Andrea set the knife to the string and prepared to cut through the final obstacle, the chanting ringing in her ears.

The chanting. Ringing. In her ears.

It wasn't chanting, though, when she stopped to listen to it. It was something quite different. More modern. More electronic than a chant could ever be. It was the sound of the alarm filtering down through the stonework from upstairs. The sound that told her someone or something had tripped the electric eye in the drive.

The sound that told her Josh was home.

32

THE STILL REASONABLY young, and quite attractive, head of Vanbrugh Personnel Consultancy Services picked up her private line within moments of it starting to ring. She always kept that line *extremely* private, and only a handful of business contacts and one or two others, apart from British Telecom, even knew of its existance, let alone the number that would get them through.

As usual the only thing she said was 'Yes?', giving away neither her name or the number. The voice at the other end offered no identification either, launching straight into her instructions.

'The party is yours tomorrow night,' it told her. 'Please bear in mind that it will not be the only party in progress.'

She had no doubts at all about who she was speaking to. The call, and to a great extent its contents, had been expected. 'You won't be visiting?' she enquired.

'I'll be looking in elsewhere. Somebody has to carry the torch.' This last comment was made with some humour in the caller's voice.

'Then you know it's all been worked out?'

'Not for certain, my lovely. Our friend is really quite bright. Sometimes your dislike makes you overlook that. The pieces will all be in place by the time I arrive.' A pause. 'Is there anything else you need to know?'

'Will I be able to contact you if anything comes up before then?' Carole asked. She was trying to sound competent and in full control, though the question itself belied the image she was struggling to project.

'Not unless it's absolutely vital. I'm taking a few days off to smooth things through. Things will have to be kept under tight control, and the happenings of the last few days may have eroded my standing. I'd rather be safe than sorry, to coin a cliché.'

'I understand. I'll try not to disturb you. And I'll be delighted to host the nearer party for you. It's a rare opportunity.'

'Then I'll bid you a good afternoon.'

Carole heard the phone go down at the other end and replaced the handset of her own. Then she took a cigarette from a lacquered silver case and lit it with a match, splitting the wood-end with a manicured fingernail before blowing it out with a cloud of exhaled smoke and tossing it into her onyx ash-tray.

The Magister Inferi was doing her a great honour by leaving the group ritual to her. He'd delegated his position to her on two previous occasions, both of which had gone reasonably smoothly, although Brother Ball-Phegor (stupid name to pick) had come close to disrupting one of them. That young man was dangerous. He wanted her and he was prepared to challenge her authority within the Sons of Samael if he had to. One day a small accident might be necessary to calm him down. Castration whilst carelessly handling a power-tool, perhaps. That could easily happen to someone living alone, and it would certainly limit his future ambitions.

Carole flipped open her Filofax and wandered through its index pages until she found the number she was looking for. Then she dialled, using her private line again. A voice answered.

'Party Sunday night,' said Carole, then put the phone down again. The others would be contacted in turn by the person she'd spoken to.

The one factor in the equation she wasn't entirely certain of was the new initiate, Pravus. She'd waited behind at the house in Mill Hill to listen to the tape of the Magister's conversation with Ennio Zabetti and, later, to view the tape of his performance with the girl. Naturally Carole knew that the Magister's offer of herself as Ennio's prize for completing his assignment was a total fabrication. She'd certainly make sure that it was anyway, if she had to. Outside the ritual chamber she had no intention of letting that Cockney Wop anywhere near her.

No, that didn't worry her. Nothing about Ennio Zabetti worried Carole Vanbrugh more than slightly. Pravus, however, was something else. Anyone who could control the actions of a serious lecher like Ennio, even appearing to cause him some discomfort, had mastered skills Carole didn't possess herself. And when the person performing this hitherto impossible feat was a cloistered girl of fifteen, both a precedent and a *non sequitur* had been established. It shouldn't have been possible, and without the evidence of the videotape she wouldn't have believed that it had happened.

Even more than Ennio, little Pravus was going to take some watching in the future.

For now, though, there was the support ritual to administer. This was to be the last phase of the Magister's longest-standing scheme. The closing of the blood circle. After fifteen years father and daughter and witness were to come together in a new combination, a combination that would possibly unlock the latent powers of one of them. A combination that would provide the Sons of Samael with the Satanic equivalent of a nuclear weapon.

She would have liked to have been there, if only as an observer, but her place and duties were with the rest of the Porta Inferi coven, providing the support that would be required to contain whatever was released that May Eve. Carole had to confess to herself that she didn't have the faintest idea of what that was likely to be. All she knew was that after fifteen years of planning it was likely to be something quite remarkable, be it from Pravus or Ball-Phegor or from this Andrea Duncan woman. Or from all three of them.

Well, speculating wasn't going to make the outcome any clearer. The best thing Carole could do was to settle down to taking care of the support details. The rest, including the result, would be made plain by the Magister in due course.

33

WHEN LEONARD GAUNT left Ringley Abbey he'd already made up his mind where he was going. Instead of heading back towards the office or Catford he branched off the M25 onto the M1, then cut off at Northampton on the A45 for Cambridge. Once there he took the A10 north through Ely to King's Lynn.

By the time he'd arrived and booked himself a room in the Duke's Head on the Market Square it was too late on the Friday night to see anyone or do anything. The fact that the following day was Saturday was going to make his task immeasurably harder, but he felt deep down that to wait until the weekend was out of the way would queer his investigation. He needed the time now, not on Monday.

He took possession of his room, his lack of luggage being noticed and deplored by the hotel staff, and borrowed a Yellow Pages from the lobby. It wasn't quite six o'clock yet and there might just be someone left on the premises if he could find the number quickly enough. And sod the snooty locals. They'd bow and scrape soon enough once he'd cracked his case and the press had made him famous.

Yellow Pages tortured him with its pedantic classifications. *Schools* ought to be a clear enough heading, all on its own, first thing alphabetically. He came to *School furniture & eqpt suppliers*, then progressed down the page past *School outfitters*, *Schools – agricultural*, *Schools – commercial* and six other categories before finally finding what he impatiently sought under *Schools & colleges*.

E for East Bilney . . . nothing. Shit! Try B for Bilney . . . double shit! So, what's left?

Oh, East is East, and West is West, and never the twain shall meet, 'Til Earth and Sky stand presently at God's great Judgement Seat . . . Who the hell was this Kipling character anyway?

W gave him the now West Bilney Middle School. He had to go through the hotel switchboard to get the number. It rang. And rang . . .

And answered. Jesus, there was luck dripping off the ceiling!

'West Bilney Middle,' said the voice, a woman's.

'Who is that, please?' Gaunt began. Attack was always the best form of defence, even without reading Caesar, and Gaunt hadn't read Caesar anyway.

'Mrs Shuttleworth, Deputy Head.'

'Hello, Mrs Shuttleford . . .'

'Worth!'

'. . . Sorry, Worth. My name's Gaunt. I'm a private enquiry agent helping the police with a murder investigation.' A small lie, though only very tiny really. He did intend to help the police, eventually. 'Were you there fifteen years ago?'

'Er . . . yes, I was . . .'

'Then do you remember a girl called Pauline Stafford?'

206

'Pauline . . . Oh, yes. That's a hard name to forget Mr
. . .'

'Gaunt. She was the girl they found missing her face, right?'

'That's right. It was a dreadful thing. They said she'd had a baby. Certainly she had to leave the school because she was pregnant. We never heard anything about the child, though. It would have been in our . . . no, it would have gone on to an upper school in Lynn by now. Heaven only knows what happened to it. I don't think the police ever did.'

'Do you remember a girl called Andrea Duncan?'

'Oh yes. Very hard worker. Never particularly good at her schoolwork, but I believe she's done quite well for herself since then. She'd have been about the same age as Pauline, though I don't think she was as *advanced*.'

The stress on the last word left Gaunt in no doubt as to Mrs Shuttleworth's exact meaning. Pauline Stafford, dirty little cow. Andrea Duncan, pure little innocent.

Little goody-goody's made good, Gaunt caught himself thinking.

'I don't see why you're asking me, though, Mr Gaunt,' the deputy head continued. 'Pauline had left school when she was . . . at the time of her death. So had Andrea, for that matter. Could I ask why you're interested in Andrea at all?'

Gaunt ignored the question. 'Pauline's parents? Are they still around?'

'Goodness, no. She was orphaned before she came to school. She lived with her grandmother. Strange old lady. Everyone thought she was a witch. People weren't at all surprised when Pauline came to a bad end.'

His hand was beginning to sweat against the receiver. Come to think of it he'd done quite a bit of sweating over this affair. *Witch* was one of his favourite words for disliking, and in the context of missing faces it weighed heavily in his thinking. He wanted to put the phone down and consolidate the dead end he'd come to, getting out of the game once and for all. But he had to ask one last question before he could do that, for his own personal satisfaction if for no other reason.

'How come Pauline didn't go to school at East Bilney? She lived there, didn't she?'

'I can tell you're a stranger to this area, Mr Gaunt,' Mrs Shuttleworth replied. 'East Bilney is one of Norfolk's lost villages. All that's left of it . . . was left of it fifteen years ago . . . are three or four old houses, a ruined church and two or three farms. Andrea Duncan grew up on one of the farms, you know.'

'And Pauline Stafford and her gran lived in one of the houses?'

'That's right.'

'Many thanks, Mrs S. Look, can you give me your home number in case I think of anything else?'

'I doubt if I will, Mr Gaunt. If I do, though, I'd like to know how I can get hold of you.'

'I'm staying overnight at the Duke's Head.'

They swapped phone numbers and Gaunt rang off. Next on his list was a courtesy call to Margot to tell her why he wasn't home, and also to reassure her that Andrea Buchanan had come across with the boodle. Once that was out of the way he settled down to review what he'd learned before he went down to the green dining room for dinner.

Andrea Duncan knew Pauline Stafford. Pauline Stafford died without a face. Josh Buchanan knew Steffi Holt. Steffi Holt died without a face. Who knew that man Howard in Coptic Street? Answer, the person who'd taken the faces off the other two.

Andrea Buchanan? Motive for Steffi, yes. Opportunity, no. Motive for Pauline? Hard to say. Pauline's gran was supposed to be a witch. Andrea liked weird videos. Nobody transmitted the wacko stuff she'd been watching that early in the day, which meant it had to be on tape.

Click.

Howard ran an occult shop. He's dead. Pauline's gran was a witch. She's dead. Steffi Holt was sleeping with Josh Buchanan who's married to Andrea who watches weird videos. She's dead.

But I'm still lost, he conceded to himself. I still don't know anyone common to the three of them. Andrea Buchanan fits in somewhere. She must do. I can't link her to Howard, though. And that fifteen-year gap between Pauline Stafford and the other two worries the hell out of me. It's as if those years were spent waiting for something to happen. Trouble is I don't know what it is.

He sighed and abandoned his speculations for the time being. He'd have his night at the Duke's Head and a bloody good meal out of Mrs Buchanan's cash. Then he'd head back to town and, if nothing had occured by then, give up on his investigation.

Not that he wanted to. He simply didn't have anywhere else to take it.

His hand was hovering over the receiver before he realised what the call was he intended to make. Fighting the switchboard for an outside line he rang the number Mrs Shuttleworth had given him and waited for a reply.

'Dick Shuttleworth,' said a man's voice.

'Mr Shuttleworth? My name's Gaunt. Look, I've spoken to your wife already. She knows where to reach me. Can you have her call me when she gets in? I need to know if Pauline Stafford's gran is still alive.'

34

'HI, JOSH.'

She'd wanted to run and hide, to tuck herself away in the vault and not come out until she knew what she was going to do. She'd wanted to ignore him altogether, to stay down in her inner sanctum and finish opening the old cardboard box. She knew, though, that he could follow her in there, was the only one who could follow her in there, and he would if he didn't find her anywhere else in Ringley Abbey. And then he'd find the old tin trunk.

Whether the trunk had been put in the outhouse for her to find or not didn't really matter. All Andrea was concerned with were its contents. Already they were beginning to bring odd snatches of memory out of her past, odd fragments of that night in the graveyard at East Bilney when she had said goodbye to a normal life for ever . . .

She checked herself. Not for ever. Not when she'd been with Tim. Not now that Tim had come into her life again. She was going to lay the ghosts of her past and build a new and different future, a future with the man she should have said yes to those few sad years before.

Is that really what you want, Andrea? the Abbey asked her as she closed the entrance to the vault behind her and went up to the entrance hall to greet her returning husband. Isn't there something else? Something darker?

She didn't bother to reply to the house's mutterings any more. They'd come to mean less and less to her the longer she lived there. At first she'd listened dutifully, but as she became more and more fond of the old heap she'd learned to ignore its promptings, only occasionally using them as a sounding-board for her own emotions and desires.

And now, with Josh coming up the drive, was not the time for that.

He fitted his key into the door and opened it. Andrea had just finished turning the alarm off and came to meet him, looping her arms around his neck, looking up into those weary features, kissing him firmly and saying: 'Hi, Josh.'

'Hello, Andy,' he replied, dropping his overnight bag where he stood and wrapping his arms around her in turn, hugging her close. Just like the dutiful returning master of the house.

She ran her fingers over his brow. 'Poor old thing,' she cooed. 'It's been a hard trip this time, hasn't it?'

She listened to herself, a little surprised by the depth of her duplicity. Say nothing, she told herself. Act normally, perhaps a little warmer than normally. That way if he thinks you suspect he'll also think he's forgiven. Won't he? That's it. Keep him sweet until you've had more of a chance to consolidate things with Tim.

'Could have been easier,' he smiled wanly, mentally heaving a sigh of relief at his reception. He reached down and patted her buttocks. 'How about a drink?'

211

She helped him out of his coat then went through to the main hall and poured whisky and water from the Chinese cabinet. Josh heaved his bag off the floor and onto the old oak staircase, then followed her through, retaining his briefcase. He dumped the briefcase, unopened, in the study, then took the drink his wife was holding out to him and sank onto one of the sofas.

Archly, she began to question him about the murder, mentally still a little resentful of Gaunt's interrogation of her that afternoon. She pried out unwilling details of who the murdered girl was, what her position with JB Enterprises had been, how Josh had got into her flat without a key (He didn't have a key, did he?) and what he'd seen there. She made him more drinks as and when he needed them, which seemed to be pretty regularly, and gloated at the way he skimmed over the exact details of Steffi's mutilations, paling visibly.

She held her trump card till last. As Josh threatened to turn as white as a good girl's bikini-mark she patted his arm and stood up. 'You must be hungry,' she insisted. 'I'll fix us a couple of steaks out of the freezer.'

Before he could protest she'd vanished into the kitchen to fulfil her threat. Bloody meat was probably the last thing Josh felt like just then, but that was absolutely what he was going to get.

Keep him sick and he'll stay out of my bed tonight, she told herself. I don't want him in my bed. Not after sleeping with that woman. I've enough nightmares of my own without sharing his.

Snick-snack.

Just the sound of knife and fork meeting in rare meat.

He drank plenty of wine with the meal, not seeming to notice that she'd served him some of her own cheap plonk instead of one of his château-bottled Medocs. Afterwards he rose unsteadily, waving coffee aside for a while, and headed into the study. 'One or two things that won't wait,' he smiled at her, the smile painted on with steak-blood and Bulgarian wine, the features behind it mottling into an unhealthy red and white willow-pattern.

Snick-snack.

Andrea snorted mentally at the sound. They wouldn't really sound like that anyway, she told herself sternly.

She turned on the television but all she could find was Wogan. The bland Irish charm threatened to dilate her nostrils with its blend of concern and playing to the gallery. A science programme on another channel was looking at a new development in mechanical shears for industry. They purred their way through leather, sheet metal, thick card and even, with the right attachment and setting, sheet glass. Just a purr and a whisper.

No snick-snack.

This was intolerable. She ought to be able to banish that sound whenever she wanted to. It wasn't even the noise those old shears would make. Was it?

Andrea left the TV running and Josh in his study and went into the kitchen. There she turned on the exterior lights so that she could see her way round to the outhouse and took a torch from one of the drawers. She'd never set foot in the place after dark and had no reason to suppose that the lights inside were working, not from the general condition of the interior anyway. Then she opened the back door and started off to solve her mystery once and for all.

Taking the torch had been a good idea. The ancient light-switch inside the outhouse door did nothing when she clicked it, and the light from outside wasn't enough to guide her way through the jumbled boxes and stacks between herself and that back wall. She pressed the torch on and its yellow beam caught small scuttling things that

213

vanished to either side almost at once, except for one huge spider which froze and invited her to squash it. She'd always liked spiders and was careful to step over it.

Once at the wall she turned the beam on the shears, then onto a bench beside her to find something that would drag the worst of the cobwebs away. A long, wooden-handled screwdriver, its blade brown with the patina of old rust, was the only likely looking object, and she took it up in her free hand, drawing brackets on the wall to either side of the shears, looping congealed lumps of grey-brown fibres around the tip.

She put the screwdriver back down on the littered surface of the bench without trying to wipe the cobwebs off and reached up for the old shears. They seemed to drop into her hand willingly almost the moment before she touched them, their surfaces gritty with dirt and rust. Setting the torch down she held them in its beam and slid her grip along to a point just behind the blades. Then she pressed.

They were stiff. A great deal of the spring seemed to have gone out of them. They groaned in her one-handed grip, refusing to perform. Andrea tried with both hands and the shears groaned and ground together, the noise nothing more impressive than a sort of rough scraping, an ancient and consumptive coughing.

Not a snick-snack to be heard.

Maybe if the metal was cleaned up and oiled . . . it would go *shaa-click*.

Andrea hooked the shears back onto the wall and returned to the doorway. Once there she shone the torch back at them and listened hard. They said nothing. They just hung there, abused and naked without their comfortable shrouding of cobwebs, accusing her mutely of disturbing their peace. Eventually she closed the door behind herself and returned to the kitchen.

Josh was out of his study, still a fraction green around the gills, she fancied, and making coffee. 'Here,' she told him, 'I'll do that. You go and sit down.'

He kissed her and obeyed. She made up a tray with milk and sugar and two cups and set the glass jug from the coffee-maker on it as well. Then she carried it through to the main hall and set it down on the low table. An inane comedy was rattling out of the box and Josh, looking drained, had slumped before it. Either he'd taken the Holt bitch's death particularly badly or he had other things on his mind that were equally sickening.

Snick-snack.

Thank Christ she'd put the tray down. Josh was too wrapped up in himself to notice the tremor in her fingers as she poured the coffee. That bloody sound had no right to be here. Not any more. She'd exorcised it, once and for all, in the outhouse a few minutes before. It couldn't be back. It shouldn't be, anyway.

But it was.

So it's not the shears? Then what? She glanced at Josh.

He'd folded his arms across his broad chest and was smiling occasionally at the antics on the TV screen, slowly coming out of himself again. He'd obviously heard nothing that wasn't a joke or canned laughter. It wasn't fair.

Not the shears? Then what was it? Andrea had first heard it in the outhouse and it had followed her ever since. Into the house. Into the vault beneath where she was now sitting.

Into the vault . . .

They sat together through the interminable evening, Josh saying little, Andrea saying even less. While her eyes were on the television her ears were elsewhere, straining down through the floor and the stone vaulting beneath it for any sound that might be rising to them. Finding none.

There'd been nothing in the tin trunk that could have made such a sound, had there? She'd been through everything it contained except for that old cardboard box with the string and sealing-wax around it. And she knew what was in that already. It had to be the skull-mask that went with the robe. And there was no way a lump of latex, probably perished by now anyway, was going to go snick-snack, was there?

You have to know, don't you, Pandora? You'll have to open it up and see.

Josh finally hauled himself to his feet. 'You ready yet, Andy?' he asked her.

She shook her head. 'I'm going to stay down for a while. You get a good night's sleep in your own bed. You'll feel much better in the morning.'

He nodded at her wisdom, not commenting or showing any sign of having perceived the irony that also whispered through her words. He stooped and kissed her gently, then headed off towards the stairs.

Andrea gave him the full length of an old black and white on Channel 4, ignoring the now cold coffee and working her way through another bottle of wine. Maybe if she drank enough Tim would come back for her and Josh and snick-snack and robes and skull-masks would all become irrelevant. For ever. Yet she knew that Tim wasn't going to come tonight. She'd told him that Josh would be home, told him not to, that she'd contact him over the next day or so.

Boris Karloff (once an Englishman called Pratt) shuddered his last on *The Isle Of The Dead* and the hero, who'd spent most of the film trying to stop Karloff killing the heroine, found something nice to say before the final credits flashed up. Andrea sighed and wondered about running one of her collection. There was still the tape of *The Last House*

On The Left waiting in the VCR in the vault, and she could always stretch to another bottle to go with it. Yes, she *was* drinking too much, and she didn't know whether to blame Josh Buchanan or Tim Garfield. Or that other one she'd seen in the graveyard at East Bilney. That one wasn't done with her yet.

Neither was that sound. Snick-snack.

So, it comes and goes as it wants to, does it? I'll fix it. I'll settle its little haunting, now and for ever.

She lurched up off the sofa and clicked off the TV. Even if she ended up watching splatter she'd do it in her own little world, two floors away from sleeping Josh. So there.

Her steps were far from steady as Andrea headed down into the cellar and fumbled at the entrance to the vault. Leaving the shelf-door open she stepped through into the L-shaped corridor and opened the inner door. Standing at the entrance, surveying the vaulting and its supporting pillars, the worn carvings at the capitals now all surveyed and forgotten, having challenged her in vain to determine which saint was doing what to whom, if at all, she suddenly felt like one of those things that had scuttled away from the beam of her torch, small and dirty and about as significant as a grain of sand in the Sahara.

There ought to be rats down here with her. There ought to be scurrying, scuttering things that could keep her company in the artificial light of her own private mausoleum of the soul. And there ought to be something that goes snick-snack as well.

The trunk sat there, open, almost at the centre of the vault. On the seat of her chair sat the cardboard box. Around it, on the floor, were the other items the trunk had contained, except for the robe which was still draped over its back.

She put her bottle down in the doorway but kept the glass with her as she wove across to the trunk, her eyes looking past it to the knife beside the box and the tendrils of cut string curling out from beneath it. One last strand to cut and she could lift the lid off. Maybe she'd try the skull-mask on, if it wasn't too hideously dirty by now.

Are you in there, my little noise? she asked the box.

I'm in here, Andrea, it told her. I'm in here waiting for you to find me. Snick-*smack*. That's the password, isn't it?

Not quite. It's snick-*snack*. Or are you just trying to fool me?

Not really, Andrea. It's been so long. I forget sometimes.

So long? I don't understand you. What are you trying to tell me?

You'll know soon enough. I'm waiting for you. Now.

She looked around for somewhere to put her glass down. Most of the furnishings were against the outer walls, and she finally settled for the top of the TV beside her chair. Now all she had to do was pick up the knife and cut that last loop of string. Then she'd know.

It wasn't that easy, though.

Andrea picked up the knife easily enough and set its edge to the string. A slight pressure and the sharp blade would cut through the dirty-white strands and the top would come off. For ever. Yes, for ever. No putting it back on and pretending you hadn't seen what was inside. No telling yourself you didn't know what had been calling out to you ever since you found the old trunk in the outhouse. Nothing like that, Pandora. Either you master your desire to know and leave here now, sealing the vault behind you and never setting foot in it again, or you cut the string. Cut the string and there's no going back. You're a part of whatever is waiting for you inside here.

Yes, for ever.

She pressed. The string parted and fell away. She lifted off the lid.

She didn't look inside yet. That would have been cheating. Instead she found her glass and drained it, then looked around wild-eyed until she located the bottle by the door. Shambling across to it she refilled her glass and carried it back to the TV.

Take the box off the chair and put it aside. Watch the film.

Andrea sat there staring at the blank screen, the open box held in her lap. Her eyes struggled to see something, anything, except the one thing they were being drawn down towards. A hump of discoloured tissue-paper surrounded by cardboard walls. A rubber skull bricked up in a pasteboard niche. But not for ever.

She reached inside and pulled out the yielding bundle, feeling it give beneath her fingers. As she stripped the tissue away she felt the box begin to move, to topple from her lap towards the carpeted floor.

A rubber skull-mask grinned at her vacantly, saying nothing.

You haven't found me yet, Andrea. Have you?

You lied to me, she fumed. You lied to me. You're not snick-snack. And you weren't in the box.

But I was, Andrea. And I'm still here. Look again.

She turned the skull every which-way, feeling inside with wary fingers which encountered nothing. She tossed the skull-mask up and down but nothing rattled or fell out.

Snick-snack.

The sound came from her feet. Andrea looked down.

At a small bundle of tissue that had spilled from the box as it fell. A small bundle she might have thought was just packing and ignored. About six inches long and an inch

219

and a half wide. A tissue-paper penis that concealed the mysteries of life. Or death.

She picked it up and unwrapped it, feeling the weight of the object at its centre. As the last layer came away she held it in the palm of her hand and smiled. The handle spoke to her.

E.J.P., it said. Edward James Pickingill. Her grandfather.

Andrea held it so that she could hook a finger over the projecting spur of metal and open it.

Snick.

With an ease that made her feel positively practised she flipped the cut-throat razor closed again.

Snack, it announced. Triumphantly.

35

AFTER THEIR MEAL they returned to the house in Mill
Hill and spent the rest of the afternoon sitting in the
downstairs room. Most of the time was spent in silence,
as Ennio struggled to fit the pieces of the Magister Inferi's
puzzle into place. Occasionally he would fire a question at
Man or Woman, but never at Pravus. He was already more
than a little afraid of his strange daughter.

Neither Man nor Woman was a great deal of help to
him. Both had been recruited after Pravus' conception
and neither had ever been a member of the Porta Inferi
coven. They could offer no details to supplement Ennio's
distant memories of that ritual so many years before. He'd
only been a young initiate himself in those days, awed by
the ceremony he now despised and by the obvious power
being secretly exercised by those about and above him.

Woman took it for granted that he would be staying for
most of the evening, if not all night, and disappeared to
prepare a light meal about seven. She left Man, Pravus
and Ennio to their deliberations, still mostly silent. Man

fixed gins for Ennio and himself and a glass of red wine for
Pravus, then distributed the drinks, slipped a tape into the
stereo stack and returned to his seat.

The music proved to be ecclesiastical. Ennio recognised
snatches here and there, the odd few words of *Ave Maria*
and *Salve Mater* being sung in Gregorian chant by a convent
choir. It was an odd choice but his thoughts were elsewhere
and he didn't bother to challenge it. The only recognition
he offered was the mental reflection that there were no
virgins, immaculate or otherwise, amongst the Sons of
Samael. Initiation saw to that.

And yet perhaps it was relevant after all. While Man and
Woman obviously didn't know any of the details he was
struggling to resurrect they would be under orders from
the Magister to offer hints, perhaps even plain statements,
that meant nothing to them but could assist his own
deliberations. The point of the ritual that May Eve at
East Bilney had been to conceive a child. A special child.
In that, at least, if Pravus was anything at all to go by, it
had been spectacularly successful.

Of course it had. He'd been selected by the Magister,
who held his office even in those days, because of his
fertility. The task of his initiation four years before, when
he was only fifteen himself, had been the fathering of a child
for later sacrifice. Since then it had been his pleasurable
duty to repeat the exercise at least three times. Fucking a
village girl on a tombstone wasn't going to be any different.
Nor, he suspected, would be the fate of the child.

He fingered his shirt collar. It was warm in here. There
was an even warmth which seemed to belie the presence
of the open fire. Usually they cooked the side nearest and
left the rest of you half-frozen, but this one seemed to
be spreading a gentle, pervasive warmth throughout the
atmosphere of the room, a warmth that lulled you towards

222

sleep, even with the sharp fizz of a gin and tonic to bring you out of it at will.

Ennio looked at his glass and found it empty. He looked across at Man, who came and took his glass and refilled it, setting it down on the table beside him rather than offering it to his hand. That was the sensible thing to do. His fingers were't that ready to take hold of anything at that moment.

The tape hummed in the background. *Ave Maria, gratia plena, Dominus tecum, benedicta tu in mulieribus . . .*

Pravus finished her wine and set the glass down without looking at it. Her eyes had grown larger, more luminous, without so much as a suggestion of reflected firelight. Almost bright enough to burn him. Almost large enough to engulf him.

Visitasti terram, et inebriasti eam, multiplicasti locupletare eam . . .

Yes, that was Latin. A single gentle, female voice singing forbidden phrases from the House of the Enemy. But was the name it was singing always Maria? Ennio began to wonder, sitting there, relaxing beneath the warmth of his daughter's gaze.

He tried to listen harder.

On the periphery of his vision Woman returned with a tray, then took it away again, untasted. Pravus drank more wine, her enormous eyes never wavering away from him for a moment.

Ave Andrea, gratia plena, Dominus Inferi tecum . . .

They prepared him in the ritual chamber, then took him muffled to the car which was waiting, the big, fancy car he'd never seen before. Nor had he seen the man who drove him out of London on that long, twisting journey north to Norfolk. He sat in the back, like the

Queen, with the privacy panel up between the driver and himself.

The car stopped only once, outside a quaint little cottage. The driver left him in the back and went inside, emerging robed and skull-masked with a girl draped only in a blanket. Then they continued along a night-dark lane until the trees broke and ruined stonework jutted up amongst the gravestones. Skull-mask parked the car and led them up to a table-tomb which had been cleaned of dirt and lichen. The girl, really very pretty, took the blanket from her glistening limbs and spread it over the stone, then lay down and parted her legs enticingly. As he relinquished his own garment Skull-mask lit a petrol-soaked torch he'd taken from the boot of the car and began to chant.

Ave Andrea, gratia plena, Dominus Inferi tecum . . .

The girl had been well-prepared and he slid into her easily. At first there was no sensation, but after a few strokes her muscles contracted around him and began to grip. The night wasn't particularly warm but Ennio didn't notice that. Neither did the girl, her limbs shining and a little slippery, smelling of something dark and secret and organic. She began to moan beneath him, then the moans started to form words. Words that matched the ones he'd been taught to say himself, that he tried to force through gritted teeth in place of moans of pleasure.

Skull-mask continued with his own chant. Gradually the three took on a rhythm and began to merge.

Ave, Andrea, gra ti aplenado minus . . .

Gaute, mandius, har de horrenadus minec . . .

Faugas, massius, in vos cavaribus laudec . . .

The words no longer had any meaning of their own. They were purely sounds. Vibrations. Barbarous names of evocation screamed out to the mute and unprotesting heavens where the Enemy was supposed to dwell. Ennio gave up on trying to speak them and concentrated instead on reciting the doggerel mentally.

Doggerel . . .

He turned away from the bucking, arching girl who had spasmed into her climax beneath him, suddenly aware that someone else was there, standing quietly, watching, a plastic carrier-bag floating from surprised fingers down towards her feet. For a moment the chant from Skull-mask wavered, then took on a stronger, more triumphant note.

Ave, Andrea . . .

She watched for a few moments, mouth agape, hands wandering, her face etching itself into Ennio's memory. As he climaxed into the girl moaning beneath him the newcomer seemed to awaken from a dream. Awaken and run away.

After that there was only the present to come back to.

Pravus was nodding like a little old man, sipping a diminishing quantity of wine from her glass. For a moment she reminded Ennio of that wizened dwarf Jedi, master in *The Empire Strikes Back*. Her eyes had returned to normal size and the appearance of age melted away, leaving only her youth in its place.

'I . . . was remembering the night you were conceived . . .' Ennio began. She seemed to be so obviously waiting for him to say something.

'I know,' Pravus replied gently. 'I was there. Remember?'

He noticed his gin and tonic and took a good swig at it, then started at her. Andrea? No, no resemblance to Andrea. But he saw traces of what he remembered of the girl who had been Pravus' mother, in the days when she still had a face.

225

'Yes,' he conceded without really understanding her remark. 'You were there. And you will be again.' He was speaking with a greater certainty than any he'd felt since this whole thing began. Man noticed and peered at him keenly.

'You know what the blood circle is?' he asked.

Ennio nodded. 'I know what it is. I don't know how to compose it, though. The blood circle is the family. In our case the *Unholy Family* that will rival the root and essence of the Enemy's faith. Father, mother and child.'

Man looked puzzled. 'So what's the problem, Mr Zabetti?'

'The problem is working out who's who. If I concede myself as father, then Pravus ought to follow as child. Her mother's dead, though. At best she can only have a foster-mother.'

'The Son of the Enemy only had a foster-father,' Pravus told him.

Man eyed her sharply. Her reference to St Joseph had been clear enough. That made twice in one day she'd shown a forbidden knowledge of the faith of the Enemy, a knowledge they'd struggled for fifteen years to keep her from. She hadn't even set foot in a church until that morning.

Ennio didn't notice. He was too busy considering the meaning of her words to worry about their import. Strictly speaking Woman was Pravus' foster-mother, to all intents and purposes. But something had led Andrea Duncan to be there at the moment of his daughter's conception, and now the Magister himself had brought Andrea's name and address to his attention on that folded piece of paper.

Hail Andrea, full of grace. The Infernal Lord is with thee. Blessed art thou among women.

'Tell me where you learned of that?' Man asked Pravus gently.

She smiled at him, her eyes hungry, her young body relaxed in an adult, rather than a childish sprawl. She sipped her wine, then said: 'Our Lord is the Father of Lies. Will you believe me if I tell you?'

The words were gentle, softly-spoken. Ennio, involved with his own deliberations, hadn't even heard them. But Man had. He'd heard and remembered, and later he would tell Woman. And he'd be certain to tell the Magister when the opportunity arose. This wasn't the Pravus he knew speaking to him. This wasn't the abused and degraded child they'd held a prisoner for fifteen years. This was someone, something else. Some *thing* else.

And Man had suddenly realised that he was becoming afraid of it.

36

By the time Dora Shuttleworth rang the Duke's Head with the information Gaunt wanted, the evening was too far gone for him to be capable of doing anything with it. He'd already had dinner and was settled into the bar to see how much of £3000 cash he could drink his way through in one night. Christ, but it was some contrast with his halves of bitter in the Starlight Bar of the Picadilly Plaza in Manchester.

Reception paged him, of course, but his consolation prize at reaching a dead end on his big case, which it had to be because that bloody teacher hadn't phoned him, had grown a little large for his senses. It was only later, when he staggered up to his room, that he noticed the message in an envelope taped to the handle. As soon as he was inside he ripped it open and struggled to read the contents.

'Mrs Shuttleworth rang and left this name and address. Mrs D. Fortress, 37 Lynn Street, West Bilney. No telephone.'

He flopped onto the bed and held it above him, the light shining through the paper, distorting the wavering script. Morning was soon enough, he decided. His only problem was going to be remembering. Mus' finder wayy thru thattt.

Gaunt rang the switchboard and arranged an alarm call, slurring his words heavily. Then he dropped the receiver back onto its rest and propped up the note beside the phone. As the room began to spin a tunnel opened up behind him and he fell into the blackness which would take him to tomorrow.

Which began with an ear-splitting jangle beside his head.

He'd slept fully dressed and hadn't brought a change of clothes with him, so he scrubbed himself heftily with hotel soap and shaved with the courtesy Bic razor on the washstand. Breakfast seemed an unappealing experience to have to face, but he was paying for it and he'd bloody well eat it. After forcing his way through bacon and eggs he returned to his room and re-read the message from the night before. Then he called the switchboard and asked for Mrs Shuttleworth's number. He was beginning to feel a little more human again when she answered.

'Sorry to be a pest,' he began, aware of the coolness in her tone when he'd identified himself. 'I just wondered if there was anything else you could tell me about Mrs Fortress. You know, something *useful*.'

She didn't know, and she didn't understand his stress on the last word either, but she tried her best all the same. Dolly Fortress, well-known local character, now in her mid-eighties and tougher than ever. Moved out of her rented cottage in the remains of East Bilney to a council house in the surviving village shortly after Pauline's death. Seemed to be a bit more prosperous for a while. Even bought herself a colour TV and a synthetic fur coat. Started drinking more, but that was understandable, wasn't it?'

Gaunt nodded into the phone. Understandable. But for what reason? He could think of at least two. 'And the witchy bit?'

'You know what these villages are like, Mr Gaunt.' He didn't, but he agreed anyway. 'People get these funny ideas. Old Dolly was never very pretty, and any scruffy old lady who's a bit odd and . . . well . . . ugly, is automatically a witch. The fact that nobody ever saw her in church helped as well.'

'Yeah. 'Course it would. Okay, Mrs Shuttleworth. Thanks again.'

He paid his bill and felt the sigh of relief from behind the reception desk as he took his lack of luggage out towards the car-park. His rusty steed awaited him and even expressed its pleasure by starting reasonably easily at the third attempt. Better than average for its age and the state of its battery, Gaunt decided. This was going to be one of his better days.

He threaded out of King's Lynn past the incoming streams of Saturday shoppers and found West Bilney reasonably easily. Lynn Road, he'd reasoned to himself, ought to be the main road running through the village, the A47 to Norwich. It wasn't, though. He found it nearly a quarter of an hour and two asks later, tucked away in a depressing thirties council development on the edge of the back of beyond. All the houses looked much the same, except for two with different front doors which had obviously been bought by their tenants and sported brighter paintwork.

Gaunt found 37 and cruised past without stopping, driving back to a small parade of shops he'd passed to pick up some inducement at the off-license. Once armed with

230

a bottle of cheap scotch (MacDoughty sounded like an inversion of the porn-buyer's standard dress) he returned to the Fortress residence, parked old faithful and strode up the weed-strewn path.

His first knock brought no response, but he persisted, sneaking side-glances at the grimed lace curtains to see if they were twitching. Sure enough a slight movement caught his eye and he shifted the bag with the bottle in it to the hand nearest his hidden watcher, then knocked a third time.

The catches clicked. The door creaked inwards the full length of its safety-chain, a vision of ugliness peering through the narrow opening. Mrs S had been right. Old Dolly Fortress certainly wasn't any kind of beauty.

'Mrs Fortress?' he asked mildly.

The vision sniffed evilly. 'What yhu want?' it demanded.

He took out a business card and held it through the opening, making sure the old crow could see the bottle as well. 'Mind if I ask you a few questions?' His nose was starting to wrinkle at the indistinct but pervasive odour floating out past her into God's clean air. 'Thought we might have a spot of elevenses while we're about it?'

Gaunt held the cap of the bottle to the gap. Dolly's rheumy eyes wavered from his card to the MacDoughty logo. 'Priyvate, yhu say? Not poliyce?'

'Private. Not police,' he repeated after her.

The door closed long enough for the chain to be slid off, then opened again. The narrow hall was strewn with free newspapers and junk mail, all of it unopened. A venomous-looking yellow cat sat on the threadbare staircarpet, two treads up, sneering at Gaunt. One of its ears was shredded and a snaggle-tooth stuck wickedly out through its muzzle. Definitely about as appealing as its owner.

Dolly was wearing a floral apron over something brown and shapeless. Her dirty-white hair was wild and thin, showing the liver-spotted scalp beneath it. Her eyes were dark and squinty and one of them was slightly off-target. The nose didn't have the expected hairy wart but the receding chin sported a cluster of four or five. Her lips were thin and pinched and the alternate yellow stumps behind them most certainly weren't a National Health replacement set. A fine network of lines, like a slipped hairnet, criss-crossed her features and the skin on the backs of her arthritis-clawed hands.

And she stank. Gaunt could almost see the odour emanating off her like a psychic aura.

She kept his card and led him into her cluttered sitting-room, knocking a pile of old books out of a grimy armchair for him to sit down. His card was tucked behind an ancient clock on the mantelpiece, its hands woven together in an asexual embrace at twenty-seven minutes past five, and she lumbered off towards the kitchen to find a couple of cleanish glasses. He'd got the cap off, relying on the MacDoughty to sterilise whatever he was going to have to drink it out of, when she returned, holding the chipped and cracked tumblers, different sizes, for him to pour.

He filled them up and she handed him the smaller of the two. He took a good pull at the cheap scotch, which by now he regarded as antiseptic, like a hero dressing a wound in a fifties Western, and watched her seat herself in the room's only clear chair, pulling a threadbare rug over her knobbled legs.

'Tell me about Pauline, Dolly,' Gaunt began.

She glared at him malevolently for a moment, then raised a finger and wiped the beginnings of a tear away from one eye. 'She's dead,' Dolly declared, her voice ringing with finality as if to say *so there*.

'But she didn't die in childbirth,' Gaunt continued. He'd decided that this monosyllabic old woman wasn't going to volunteer anything, so he might as well speculate aloud and watch for her reactions. 'She died screaming with her face being peeled away. After she had the child. Wasn't that about the time you started spending money, Dolly? The payment you got for the child and for Pauline's carrying it?'

He looked around for the colour TV but it wasn't there. Probably packed up and thrown away years ago. He checked Dolly's features. Her eyes were moist and her lips were quivering slightly.

'That's the way it was, Dolly, wasn't it? You sold Pauline to that maniac who killed her and you sold her child as well. That's the way it happened. You'd be denying it by now if I wasn't right.'

She glared at him through the moisture. 'Poliyce never proved it. Yhu can't prove it neither, Mr Priyvate man. I hain't sayin' nuthing. Paul . . . Pauline's dead. Hain't nuthing goin' tu bring her baack.'

He reached over and topped her glass up. 'How could you do it, Dolly? How could you sell your granddaughter and her child for money?'

She swigged her scotch, her free hand picking at the ancient rug. Her throat worked more than it needed to. Her lips trembled again.

'Just for money, Dolly. Even an old witch like you must know about Judas. Thirty pieces of silver and a colour TV.'

Dolly glared up at him, then looked down at her glass, which she raised and drained. Gaunt filled it again, then replenished his own.

'Just for money, Dolly. And how she suffered so that you could pocket a few coins. Aren't you ashamed? Doesn't her screaming haunt your nights?'

233

She looked up, all fire and venom. 'Yhu shut your face!' she snapped. 'Yhu doan't know. It weren't like that!'

'Then what was it like? Tell me what really happened, Dolly. I'm not the police.' He was careful not to say he wasn't going to tell them, though.

'They were good people. *My* people . . .'

'Family?'

She couldn't mean that. She was Pauline's only family and Pauline was hers.

'Like me. *Like* me. They knew the words. They spoke 'em.'

'You mean witches? They were witches, Dolly? Witches who buy babies and peel young girls' faces off?'

Careful, Lenny, he told himself. Don't press too hard or you'll blow it. She's starting to talk, so let her do it in her own time. Just keep the whisky flowing and listen.

'Not . . . witches. *Like* witches. And all they wanted was the baby. It 'ad to be made special, on May Eve. An' it were goin' to be special for 'em. They said so. My Pauline weren't goin' tu be 'urt . . .'

Her old frame shook. She'd degenerate into the tears of self-pity if he didn't do something to check her. He poured more MacDoughty into her glass.

'But she was hurt, Dolly. We know that now, don't we?'

Dolly shook her balding head in wordless denial of the facts. It was as much an affirmation as if she'd agreed. Gaunt swallowed some more of the whisky, suddenly aware of every nerve-ending in his body. He'd wanted his big case and he'd got it. Maniacs, black magic and baby-selling.

'They said she weren't goin' tu be 'urt. An' I believed them. I *believed* them. I still want tu . . .'

'Who were they, Dolly?'

234

She shook her head again. 'I doan't know, mister. They came up from Lunnun an' toald me what they wanted. They spoke the words so's I'd know 'em. Then that May Eve I 'ad my Pauline ready an' one came for 'er. They went to the old graveyard an' she came back with chiyld. We'd go there sometimes arterward an' she'd show me where.'

'Will you show me where?' He was counting on the hotel breakfast to absorb the whisky. If Dolly had been in East Bilney in those days the graveyard wasn't going to be in walking distance. 'I'll take you, in my car.'

She sighed and finished her glass. 'Why'd yhu want to know all this?' she demanded.

'Because it's happening again, Dolly Fortress. Other people are having their faces cut off, slowly and painfully like your poor Pauline's was. If I can find out who they are they can be stopped. Other lives can be saved. If not . . .' he shrugged, 'your Pauline will have died for nothing. Now, shall we go?'

What the fuck was he going to do about this old crone? He'd have to tell the police what he knew, eventually. But did he have to drag this pathetic old woman into it?

Oh yes, the answer came back. You'll tell them the works. That way you'll get the credit you're looking for.

Take her to the graveyard. Keep on working on her memory. Maybe she'll come up with a name sooner or later. A name, or anything. Anything to stop this being just another dead end, like it was threatening to become right now.

He waited while she found her coat, then helped her into it, trying not to feel how greasy it was. On the path he waited again as she fumbled for her keys and locked the door, leaving the yellow monster on the stairs to keep vigil in her absence. Then he helped her into the car, leaning through her foul breath to fasten the seat-belt for her. She

235

stank of nothing he could identify, and he finally decided it must be the smell of her approaching death.

He followed her instructions, vague and often late as they were, and finally found the old churchyard at East Bilney. They left the car at the side of the road and made their way through the tangled grass and weeds between the tombstones until they reached the table-tomb where Ennio Zabetti had ritually impregnated the departed Pauline Stafford.

Gaunt read the inscription to Joshua Samson. The quaint name didn't mean anything to him. Nothing at all. Just some old rustic now a few fragments of earth discoloured bone. At best.

'And this was where it happened? You're sure?'

'Dolly nodded. 'At's ruyt. She weren't 'arf surpruysed when 'er friend showed up in the middle, an' all.'

Gaunt felt his ears prick up like a gundog's. 'Her friend?' he asked. 'Showed up? While it was going on?' He wasn't entirely sure what *it* was, but he had a fair idea. His mind kept showing him pictures of a succulent young thing with no face getting well and truly broken in.

'That she did,' Dolly affirmed. 'Pauline were ruyt surpruysed, she were.'

'Did she say which friend it was? Did she tell you her name?'

A witness. Assuming she was still alive he had a witness. He could give the police more than just an old woman's ramblings. If only he had a name.

'Ar. Fair shocked 'er, it did. She never expected to see 'at young virgin standin' there a playin' with 'erself. Waatchin' 'em at it.'

'Which young virgin?' He wished he'd thought to bring the remains of the bottle and the glasses with them. That might have speeded things up.

236

''At Andy Duncan, 'at's who.'

Andy? A boy? A man now . . .

Oh no. No, not a boy or a man. A girl and a woman. A girl and a woman who'd hired him just a few days before.

'You mean *Andrea* Duncan, Dolly?'

''At's who I mean, all ruyt. Made good, she 'as.'

Too bloody true, Gaunt reflected. He took Dolly back to the car and returned her to the house in Lynn Road. The old lady hadn't given him everything he wanted. Nothing outside a name would have been enough. But at least he had a further link to Andrea Buchanan, a link that could give him a little more leverage next time they spoke. Maybe she hadn't exactly lied to him about Pauline Stafford, but she hadn't been over-generous with the truth, either.

And there had to be a reason for that.

37

BREAKFAST AT RINGLEY Abbey was a desultory affair. Andrea had slept only a little, having spent most of the night in the vault. The fact of discovering the skull-mask and the razor together worried her. Whilst there could be no doubt that the razor had belonged to her grandfather it was impossible for him to have been the man in the robe and mask that night in the churchyard. He came of stocky Norfolk folk who had never produced any offspring capable of filling that substantial garment. Nor had he ever shown any inclination towards the kind of interests which would have accompanied the grim ceremonial Andrea had witnessed those many years ago.

Josh, for his part, seemed aware of his wife's preoccupation and left her alone with her thoughts, intruding as little as possible. In actuality he was glad of her preoccupation. Some of her questions the night before had come uncomfortably close to the truth of his relationship with the late Steffi Holt and this would not be the ideal time to have to explain away his adultery. There were too many other things to occupy himself with right now.

Mrs Haigh came in on Saturday mornings, though she didn't stay all day as she did during the week. Breakfast was out of the way by the time she arrived, Andrea having announced her intention of going up to town for the day. Josh retired to his study and left her alone to get ready for her expedition.

By the time Andrea was ready to go Mrs Haigh had arrived. Josh gave her strict instructions not to disturb him and explained that his wife was going out. As if to emphasize this Andrea came in and pecked him on the cheek before leaving. Her manner was absent, even distant, and Josh felt himself fighting down a sudden pang that she might not be inclined to return to Ringley. As the sound of her Escort Ghia drawing away came to his ears it was rivalled by Mrs Haigh beginning to hoover the room directly above him. Andrea's bedroom.

He finished checking over the contents of his briefcase from the night before and decided to make a few notes for his secretary to incorporate onto the files on Monday. Opening the desk drawer which held his rough paper he discovered a brown envelope lying on top of the stack. It didn't seem at all familiar and he lifted its flap and inverted it, scattering its contents onto the top of his desk.

Several sheets of handwritten paper. A photocopied form with familiar writing on it. Some photographs.

Of himself and Steffi Holt. Of the sort the papers called compromising. Taken in Manchester two nights ago.

To conclude that Andrea knew was superfluous. No way would Mrs Haigh have inserted the contents of the envelope into his desk, and that only left his wife. He felt a rising surge of panic, then managed to check it and began to look through the material in front of him for some clue as to its originator. The Factfinders logo and address were on the form, as were phone numbers for both in and out of office hours.

He picked up the phone and dialled the office number first. An answerphone told him it wasn't manned at present but if he'd like to leave a message Mr Gaunt would get back to him. Sam Spade might be the hero but Jim Rockford sat on the answerphone.

Josh dialled the second number. It rang for a while before a woman's voice answered with a simple: 'Hello?'

He took his cue from the previous call. 'Mrs Gaunt?'

'Yes? Who is this?'

'British Telecom directory check,' he lied. 'We have your number listed as 01–324 2988. Will you confirm your address please?'

Margot hesitated. She'd never come across this before. 'Did you say British Telecom?' she queried.

'That's right, subscriber. We just want to confirm that your address is printed correctly in the directory. Could you read it back to me?'

Her concern vanished. The man wasn't asking for anything that hadn't already been published. She complied.

'Morley Gardens, Catford,' Josh repeated, writing it down. 'Number eighteen. Thank you for your co-oper-ation.' He put the phone down again and sat back, grinning quietly. He'd already seen the wallet of negatives in with the photographs and drawn his conclusion from that.

Upstairs Mrs Haigh was still using or abusing the vacuum cleaner. Josh dialled another number and listened to it ring. After counting twelve rings he decided that no one was going to reply and dialled again.

A man's voice answered. Josh spoke slowly and carefully, choosing his words. Then he replaced the receiver.

38

TIM GARFIELD'S FLAT above an antique shop in
Kensington Church Street was as austere and business-
like as the offices of Phantasticads. Prints of artwork
from his most successful campaigns, including the one for
Andrea Duncan Salons, decorated the pale-washed walls.
Austere *objets d'art* stood on glass shelves. A bookshelf
contained back Penrose annuals and an array of library-
cased videotapes and the main room was dominated by
a 27' TV and a Hitachi VCR. Unlike normal people,
however, who recorded the programmes, Tim Garfield's
collection consisted mainly of commercials.

He'd risen and washed early, wondering whether or not to
go into the office and work on the new campaign for the fast-
growing chain of music stores that looked set to rival Richard
Branson's Virgin. The thing that stopped him, keeping him
drinking coffee in his towelling robe instead of dressing and
going to work, was the same thing that had rendered him
next to useless in the office the day before.

Andrea Buchanan.

He shouldn't have gone to Ringley Abbey that night. Even though he'd given in to the compulsion he shouldn't have received the reception that he did. Andy should have been as distant and hostile as ever. Not drunk. Not yielding. Not appreciative. It hadn't been right. She should have still hated him, like she'd pretended to when they split up the first time.

He shook his head and poured some more black Kenyan into his cup, sipping it slowly and appreciating the flavour. No, it wasn't right being involved with Andy again. She could destroy him with a snap of her fingers. She almost had done once already. To risk that a second time was as close to madness as he ever intended to come. And in any sort of creative profession it came even closer to committing suicide. A woman like that could get inside your head and fuck your thoughts up.

For now and always.

His bell rang just as he was thinking about getting finally dressed for the third time. He flipped on the videoscan and identified his caller, his heart leaping wildly. That shouldn't be Andy on his doorstep, but it was.

He let her in and waited for the small eternity it took for her to climb the stairs, door open and eyes eager to worship. There were no two ways about it. She reduced him to Plasticine, except for that one part she could make as hard as iron. He didn't like it, didn't trust it, but he gave in to it just the same.

She appeared at the top of the stairs, mouth parted, eyes inviting. He showed her into the flat. 'Coffee's made,' he told her. 'Want a cup?'

Her answer to his question was as welcome as it was unexpected. She kissed him firmly, even determinedly, undoing the tie that held his robe. Then she stood back and began to undress herself.

242

They never made it to his bedroom. Instead they went for carpet and couch and chair. His timescale altered, as it always seemed to do when they were together, and the better part of two breathless hours passed out of their lives in just a few minutes.

She lay back and smiled at him. Nothing hidden. Nothing to be ashamed of. 'Just thought I'd say hello,' she told him.

'That's one hell of a way of doing it,' he conceded.

'Thought you'd like it. Are you going to buy me lunch?'

There was a little Italian place just up the street, its basement cheap and cheerful with gingham tablecloths and good Chianti. They dressed, Tim for the first time that day, and wandered up to claim a table. Andrea murdered a spaghetti vongole, the baby clams in the sauce hardly touching her throat on the way down. She compared it mentally to the way that steak with Josh had stuck the night before, then blanked errant husband out of her thoughts and concentrated on the sharp wine in its raffia-wrapped bottles. Tim and herself were floating together in a passionate, never-ending present when he spoke again, destroying the dream.

'So, what gives, Andy?' he asked over the espresso.

She looked at him. The man she really loved. Had always really loved. 'I need you, Tim,' she answered.

'Why now? Why all of a sudden after all this time?'

Should she tell him the truth at last? That she'd never wanted to say goodbye in the first place? Would it sound right?

Would it sound any better than Josh-is-going-to-leave-me and I could end up alone? Wasn't that the hard core of her feelings? Good old Tim picking up the pieces of someone else's fiasco?

'Because,' she answered vaguely, 'I shouldn't have said goodbye, Tim. That was the biggest mistake of my life.'

And, she conceded, that was probably the truth.

'But you did, Andy. You've no right to expect me to be here now.'

'I had no right to expect you to be at Ringley,' she told him. 'But you were, Tim. Do we have no right at all to each other?'

The question was a fair one, he decided. Even if he couldn't answer it. Instead he asked: 'And what about Josh Buchanan? He's still your husband, isn't he? He must have some say in what's going on between us. Have you told him?'

She sighed and drank more wine in preference to her coffee. 'He's got enough on his plate at present. His mistress was killed a few days ago. Someone sliced her up and cut her face off.'

'That woman in the *Evening Standard?* That was Josh's mistress? Jesus!'

'Joseph and Mary as well. He had it coming. He's been cheating on me for most of our marriage.'

'And I'm a way of paying him back a bit?'

Andrea shook her head. 'You're a way of making me happier than I've ever been,' she answered. 'In case I haven't said it yet, I love you, Tim. I always have. It's that blatant and that simple. Josh can go fuck himself for all I care. With you I have my best chance of being happy.'

He reached over and took her hand. 'Me too,' he told her. 'Why'd we break up, anyway?'

'Because I wasn't ready. But I am now, Tim. I just need this weekend to work things out with Josh, then I'm all yours.'

She knew that she was going to have to go back to Ringley Abbey, sooner or later. It clouded the prospect of the afternoon. She left Tim Garfield shortly after they

244

finished their lunch, promising to be in touch with him as soon as circumstances permitted.

He wanted to ask her what circumstances she was talking about, but that would have been pushing things harder than he wanted to be seen to be doing. Instead he agreed and left her work things out for herself, unaware that there were others who also had designs upon Andrea Buchanan's future. Others like Ennio Zabetti and Leonard Gaunt, both of whom intended to be in touch with her very soon.

For Andrea, leaving Tim back at his flat, the return to Ringley Abbey was a time to think, a time to work things out. For Leonard Gaunt the drive back to town from darkest Norfolk gave him the chance to mentally rehearse all those questions he'd meant to ask Dolly Fortress but forgotten. He knew deep inside himself that something was going to break soon, that his big case was going to crack wide open and leave a lot of pieces for someone to pick up. He intended that someone to be himself. That's why he didn't contact Margot again. That's why he turned off the M1 onto the M25 and headed towards Slough. And Gerrards Cross. And Ringley Abbey.

It was time to watch the comings and goings at the Buchanan residence. He stopped off in Slough and picked up a vacuum flask in Boots that a roadside cafe could fill up with coffee when he bought a stack of sandwiches. The day, maybe even the night, was going to be a long one, and the great detective intended to be fully prepared for his vigil.

It would be too easy for Andrea Buchanan to deny everything Dolly had told him, if he simply confronted her. That's why things had to be done in a more roundabout way. That's why he parked the car in a hedgerow and made his way up to the house on foot, bypassing the electric eye which still stood sentinel along the drive.

Shortly after he'd taken up his position Andrea returned home. If nothing happened tonight he'd tell the police what he'd learned and leave the rest to them. For now, though, there was still the chance of solving this muddle of black magic and missing faces on his own.

39

'MRS GAUNT?'

The door was open only the fraction that the safety chain permitted. Margot preferred it that way, fully aware as she was of some of the dubious characters her husband dealt with. This one, though, was different from the usual run of them. True, his hair was a fraction long, but he was clean shaven and good looking, with the bluest of eyes and a nice smile. And there seemed to be a hint of promise in his expression as he surveyed what he could see of her.

She felt herself tingle. Lenny hadn't looked at her that way for a long time. And while he was away . . .

Margot tried to dismiss her little fantasy. She forced herself back to the present, to the handsome man in the business suit on her doorstep. 'I'm Margot Gaunt,' she told him. 'What is it?'

'I need to see your husband, Mrs Gaunt. Is he home?'

'Sorry, he's not here.' She thought for a moment. 'How did you get this address, Mr ..?'

'Zabetti. Ennio Zabetti. Look, it really is important I get in touch with Len. I've some important information for him. Do you know where I can reach him?'

Such a nice man. So very earnest in his desire to help.

Margot shook her head, wishing her hair looked better, mentally kicking herself for not having taken more trouble with her make-up. 'Sorry,' she repeated. 'He should be home later. Maybe you could ring late this afternoon. Or tonight?'

A cloud passed over the caller's handsome features. 'That could be too late.' He chewed his bottom lip thoughtfully. Then: 'I wonder . . . Would it be possible to come in and leave a message for him for when he contacts you? It's quite detailed, so I'd need to write it down.'

'Wait right there,' Margot answered. For a moment he thought she was going to pass a pad and pen out through the gap in the door. Then it closed briefly and he heard the chain come off. The door swung wide open.

'Come in, please,' Margot instructed him.

He thanked her and compiled, treating her to a dazzling smile on the way past. She showed him into the sitting room, noticing for the first time the executive case he was carrying. 'Do you need a pen and paper?' she asked.

'No, thanks. But I do need a minute or two to pick what Len needs out of some papers.'

'Of course. Sit down there and I'll make some coffee. I was just about to, anyway.' And tidy myself up a bit. Get out of this old houserobe into something a little more . . . She mentally sawed the air with her hand looking for the word she wanted.

Kitchen first. Fill and switch on the kettle. Then up . . . the . . . stairs . . . which were starting to leave her a little breathless if she took them too quickly, and try and turn the beast into some sort of beauty. She sat down in front of her dressing table, wishing her buttocks weren't quite so big and heavy these days. That meat could have served her better up front.

Margot slipped off the robe and surveyed herself. There were worse bodies around, but they didn't attract people like Ennio Zabetti. Now, a good bra and something to hold her stomach in . . .

What on earth was she thinking of? All he wanted was to leave a message for her husband, for dear old fat old Lenny. He wasn't interested in brightening her day at all. Not even slightly.

That was why he was standing in the bedroom doorway, peering over the unmade bed at her reflection in the dressing-table mirror. Margot felt her mouth fall open, then checked it. Her hands instinctively came up to cover her breast, but she checked that movement as well. She turned on her stool slowly, mentally trying to firm up those sagging areas and put some fire into her eyes. She'd been a beauty once. She could be a beauty again. Especially with a man like this, a man who stood there with his jacket off, removing his shirt and tie.

She stood up and walked over to him, swaying her hips and holding her stomach in. His torso was fit and athletic. Powerful. The muscles in his arms flexed slightly as his hands undid the buckle on his trouser-belt. Margot knelt in front of him and finished the job herself, sliding down his underpants and directing his firmness towards her mouth. Ennio reached down for the tangle of her hair and forced himself deeper in, smiling as she gasped and made little choking sounds.

This was going to be a pleasure, in its way. A small diversion from the larger issues he'd spent most of the night wrestling with. Man had offered Pravus to keep him company in that circular bed, but Ennio had declined.

It wasn't so much that he had scruples about sleeping with the girl he knew to be his daughter. Rather he'd become just a little afraid of that young, apparently fragile creature. She seemed to exercise a strange power that was more than just a simple fascination, a power that had as much of pain about it as it did of pleasure. Unlike Margot Gaunt.

He stooped and scooped her up, placing both of them down on the bed. He buried his face in her breasts, working at the nipples with his lips and tongue whilst his fingers found and explored and penetrated lower down. She was gripping him firmly now, almost stifling him in her eagerness. He broke free long enough to slip inside her, feeling her moist and warm and flaccid around him. Then she tightened and eased into a rhythm to match his own.

Margot looked up at him from the pillows, her eyes wide open, her lips pouting, occasionally whipping her head from side to side and breathlessly grunting incoherent words of appreciation and encouragement.

Had it *ever* felt like this with Lenny?

He rode her hard and long before he climaxed. Margot was glowing when they eventually rolled apart. She reached out and played lazily with his hair, tracing the line of his smile with her finger. She was drifting towards sleep when he turned her over and slammed unexpectedly back in from behind. Her response was eager, her hands reaching back past both of them to press his own buttocks closer while his own grip crushed her breasts. When he came again she came with him.

As they fell apart she remembered the kettle. 'Later,' he told her. 'I switched it off before I followed you up, Margot.'

Had she told him her name? It didn't matter. Maybe she had. Maybe Lenny had. Christ, what a time to think of Lenny.

'You've followed me up, okay,' she answered, turning back towards him and kissing him.

'Yeah.' The word was more of a sigh than an affirmation. He lay back, all hair and muscle and afterglow. 'Fucking good job ol' Len wasn't here. The secret life of Morley Gardens, eh? Where is he, anyway?'

Margot shook her head and reached for a few strands of her hair to chew, her eyes bright and firmly on his own. 'Last thing I heard he was in some hotel in King's Lynn. The Duke's Head, I think.'

That rang an almost audible bell with Ennio. That was where Andrea Buchanan had her late lunch that day he'd followed her to the churchyard. 'Any idea why?' he asked calmly.

Margot shrugged. 'Checking on some girl called Pauline Stafford who was killed about fifteen years ago. Ever since he did that job for Mrs Buchanan he's had some bee in his bonnet about solving a big case. You know, those murders in Manchester and Bloomsbury.' She wasn't being very discreet, she conceded, but it was hard to be discreet with a man who'd done what Ennio just had. Besides, Lenny was running round with a head full of clouds.

And that was just as well. Otherwise he'd be here and this wouldn't be happening to her. She reached down for Ennio's penis, wondering if there might still be a spark of life in it somewhere. He closed his eyes and let her.

So Gaunt had worked for Andrea Buchanan? And got onto poor dead Pauline? He realised the pun and grinned behind closed eyelids at the vision of the detective trying to screw Pauline's decaying corpse. She'd probably been at her prettiest when Ennio had fathered Pravus on her.

251

Just as well she'd died. That kind of fleshy beauty usually faded pretty fast. In another six years she'd have been a worn-out old slag of twenty-one.

He flicked the speculation away as Margot rekindled a small but willing spark. The butterfly knife was shouting at him from his coat pocket, urging him to give it some exercise. No two ways about it, Gaunt was coming too close to things for him to be allowed to live. And Margot?

'That was the last you heard? Len was in King's Lynn?'

Margot nodded and bent her head closer to her manipulations. 'He was going to talk to some old witch today, but he didn't say what he'd be doing after that. Maybe he'll have another go at the Buchanan woman. Hey,' she added, eyes wide and expression girlish. 'Look at this. You going to have another go at me with that?'

She was glowing all over and, probably, too tired. But you didn't let an experience like this one pass too easily. There might never be another one like it if you lived to be a hundred and fifty.

Ennio forced her face to his, smirking. 'Is that what you want, Mrs Gaunt?' It would be such a shame to have to kill her. She was all woman, this one. She deserved better of him. Well, more of him, anyway. And now there was more of him to give, while he made up his mind.

While the butterfly knife in his pocket made his mind up for him.

40

THE SUN VANISHED for the day behind cloud long before it was due to set. The sandwiches and coffee vanished with remarkable speed, considering Gaunt had indulged in a Duke's Head breakfast. He felt grubby, and that quantity of MacDoughty he'd drunk to keep Dolly Fortress company wasn't sitting very well.

In short, adding the number of times a minute he was now looking at his watch, the whole exercise had begun to strike him as irredeemably futile. Sure, he had plenty to say to Andrea Buchanan. Yes, he knew she was home. But so was her husband, and Gaunt didn't want to have to ask his questions to the both of them. Not husband and wife sticking together to face him out.

Ringley Abbey looked set for a quiet Saturday night at home. Leonard Gaunt, Private Enquiry Agent, found himself beginning to feel desperately in need of the same. He ached. He was cold. He felt slightly nauseous.

He gave up.

Maybe tomorrow would work out better. While Andrea

was home with hubby nothing was going to happen. A night home with Margot would help him feel better and maybe think a bit more clearly. Then he could come back tomorrow better equipped. Fit and ready for battle, ha ha.

The one thing Gaunt really found himself resenting was the drive home to Catford and back out again. One day he'd have a car he could sleep out in, when he had to. And keep a change of clothes in the back for times like this. Trying to sleep in the Allegro was rather like putting an MFI chest of drawers together – more effort than it was ultimately worth.

He made his way back to where he'd left the car, missing the spy in the drive. Okay, Margot might be cross with him for not showing up earlier, but that cheque for £7000 and the wad of bills in his pocket would quieten her soon enough.

The drive home missed the worst bits of town on a Saturday night. He followed the M4 to Chiswick, then cut south through Putney and Clapham. Yeah, the Buchanan woman could wait another day, after all. Margot's chatter and a plateful of her stodgy food, after a long hot bath, would sort him out. And what really was there to say to Andrea Buchanan, once he began to look at it dispassionately? You saw Pauline Stafford having it off with some freak on a tombstone one night? The answer to that could easily boil down to so fucking what?

No, he needed something that was going to take him closer to the heart of the case, instead of leaving him following inconsequential odds and sods from Norfolk to Abbots Ringley and back again. Andrea Buchanan held some kind of key to what was going on, but she didn't have all of it. He needed some kind of link to the killer, or killers. Something positive.

He parked the car and walked along to the house, preoccupied. He hardly noticed the girl in the anorak standing outside. He was too busy surveying the front of the house.

No lights. Not even drawn curtains. Even if Margot went out she'd leave a light on somewhere, and maybe a radio playing loudly as well. That was only common sense.

Gaunt frowned as he fitted his key into the lock and let himself in. He closed the door and stood in his narrow hall, his eyes trying to make sense of the darkness. He reached out for the light and clicked it on, its yellow glare emphasising the silence around him.

'Margot?' he called.

An uneasy nothing echoed back to him.

Gaunt checked out the ground floor, turning on the lights as he went and leaving them on. This total absence of his help and support wasn't on. She should be there to welcome him, feed him, cheer him up.

He looked at the stairs, then at his watch. She didn't normally go to bed this early, but he'd try the bedroom anyway.

A few seconds later he wished he hadn't bothered.

Gaunt was out of breath, as usual, when he reached the top of the stairs. It made him feel more queasy than he'd been before, and he'd been bad enough then. When he switched on the light and saw Margot lying on the bed, turned away from him, he knew immediately that something was very, very wrong. One, she never slept naked like that. Two, they didn't have any red-blotched sheets.

His legs threatened to give up and he sagged against the doorframe for support. 'Mar . . . got?' he asked, much more weakly, peering at her motionless form out of the corners of his eyes.

No answer.

I ... have ... to ... know, he told himself, fighting down his bile. He forced his legs to work again as he walked around the bed, trying not to look at her until he was closer. It didn't work. He couldn't take his gaze off the blood-streaked figure. And he knew long before he saw it that her face would be missing. He'd expected that.

What he hadn't expected was the angular lettering carved and congealing across the surface of her abdomen. The two short words that really churned him up and emptied his stomach in a sudden rush of vomit.

YOU NEXT

Me? *Me*? He stared back at the peeled awfulness which had been so comforting the day before. He thought of the pain that must go with each severed strip of skin, the raw stinging, the bleeding, the terrible knowledge that there was nothing left but this. On and on, and on into death.

No mercy. No relief. Just that two-word promise carved in Margot's flesh.

His legs collapsed and he sat down heavily in his own mess, eyes bulging in a way that Margot's never could again. He nodded when he felt the tears begin to flow, misting the horror. He hugged himself for warmth, for the comfort Margot could no longer give him. Then the world gave up and he pitched over into darkness, his face resting on the edge of the bed mere inches from the wreckage of his wife's.

41

MAN HAD TAKEN the Magister's message and passed it
along to Ennio, who had been still asleep in the circular bed
in the ritual room. Now with Ennio dressed and gone, and
the message burned in the grate downstairs, he made his way
to the black room to talk to Pravus.

She was at its centre when he entered, seemingly taller
than usual. At least, Man thought, her head is higher than
usual towards the ceiling. But her feet . . .

He shook his head. A trick of the strange light in that
room. But then there were so many strange things about
his little girl these days. The words she'd been pulling out of
nowhere. The power she'd appeared to exercise over Ennio
Zabetti on that video. Some great change was taking place
in her, and Man was determined to find out what it was.

'My father has gone out about his work,' she stated.

Nothing supernatural here, Man thought. Just a rather
nasty trait he hadn't noticed before. Pravus was obviously
creeping round the house spying on them. She'd seen him
give her father the message and now she was making it

sound pseudo-mystical.

He'd play the game, though. 'And how do you know that, Pravus?' he asked her.

She smiled like a madonna gazing on her infant. 'I and my father are one,' she said softly.

Man felt the skin at his temples tighten. Like so many Satanists, he'd once been heavily involved with the Christian faith. Heavily enough to know the Bible when he heard it quoted.

Like now. *John* 10 verse 30. *I and my father are one*.

He restrained himself. 'Strange words, Pravus. Tell me, dear, where did you get them from?' Be nice. The beatings can come later.

'Out of the books.' Her smile remained chaste, contrasting oddly with her nakedness.

'Which books?'

'Oh, these.' She went over to the shelf and removed a few hard-core porn magazines, holding them out to him. He took them and looked at the titles. *Color Climax. Blue Climax. Arsch und Fotz. Kinder-Liebe.* Text in English, Dutch and German. He began to open them, to go through the scanty texts.

Schwanzverschlingende Teenys warten auf euch!
Pikverslindede teenies wachten met smart op jullie!
Cock-sucking teenies are waiting for you!

He threw them back at her. They slapped her body with their graphic pages. 'There's nothing like that in any of these,' he snapped. 'Nothing I can see, anyway.'

They settled around her feet. The smile persisted. 'Can a devil open the eyes of the blind?' she asked him.

John again. 10 verse 21. This was intolerable.

'Keep this up and you'll get the thrashing of your life, my girl.'

'Where's Woman?' The question totally ignored his

threat. Man felt an odd tingling, as if the strength was draining from his body.

'She's . . . downstairs.'

'Call her up.' The voice was gentle and child-like, yet it thrilled with undeniable power. Man found himself automatically complying. They waited in silence as the sound of Woman's footfalls grew louder, dull and approaching up the carpeted stairs.

Woman entered the black room. She saw the magazines scattered around Pravus' feet. 'Whatever do you think you're doing?' she demanded. 'Tidy those things up at once.'

Pravus obeyed. Man tried to speak and uttered a faint gurgling sound. Woman looked at him.

'What's the matter?' she asked. 'Aren't you well? You sounded all right when you called me just now.'

'Perhaps he's possessed by the Devil?' Pravus suggested.

His eyes bulged and his limbs began to shake. A sudden thought flashed into his mind and hung there as he fought for breath, gazing at that young body he'd abused so many times, helped others to abuse so many times.

We've taught her too well, screamed through his skull. She doesn't need the words any more.

He felt his heart begin to fibrillate. Woman shook him and, for the first time ever in Pravus' presence, spoke his name.

'Peter? Peter? What's the matter with you? Peter!'

She shook him harder. He couldn't feel it. All he could feel were those unseen fingers of the child's will tearing at his chest, scraping through the flesh to pry the ribs apart, to touch and grasp his wildly-beating heart.

Pravus raised her arm, her hand palm-out towards him. Was she standing on the carpet? Or was she really hovering several inches above it? He couldn't tell reality any more.

The pain had become too intense, too all-consuming for that.

Woman stared at him, her features paling. 'What in the name of Hell is happening?' she whispered. She could see his chest beginning to bulge outwards beneath his shirt, as if something inside it was madly struggling to get out.

He felt the snapping, tearing, bursting open of his body. He glimpsed his heart, still pumping, in her grasp. Then it was gone, together with the pain, and he slumped back against the wall, struggling to stay on his feet. He raised his hands and carefully touched his chest.

It was intact.

He felt numbed, broken. Her voice filtered through his uncertainty with its question.

'Who is one?' she asked him.

'You . . . and your father,' he affirmed.

Pravus nodded. 'Have you seen, Woman?' she enquired.

Woman shook her head to try to clear it, to try to force some understanding. 'I've seen,' she said. 'But I don't understand . . .'

'Then you never will.'

Her voice throughout had remained calm, child-like. Whilst she was obviously in control in a way that neither of them would ever have expected, she was courteous, speaking with a measured politeness which reminded them both of Ennio Zabetti. The icy courteous of the deliberate and bloody killer.

'And now I must be about my father's work,' she announced.

Her wide mouth pouted slightly, as if to blow them a kiss, as she went to the rail and selected a plain dress to put on. Their eyes followed her, Woman supporting the still breathless Man, her words ringing in their ears like the death-knell of a thousand hopes. They'd bought her an anorak for the morning out and Pravus took this as well, together with a pair of plain, serviceable shoes. Nothing else.

She went down the stairs, Man and Woman looking at each other, then after her. Man was clutching his chest and standing slightly hunched over, but he shook off Woman's arm. 'Get after her,' he hissed. 'Stop her going out. The Magister will kill us if she leaves here now!'

Woman followed Pravus down into the main room and went over to the desk. Opening one of the drawers she took out a Sig-Sauer P230 pocket automatic, a modern reworking of the Gestapo-issue Walther PPK. Pulling back the slide she fed a 9mm round into the breech.

'Pravus, dear,' she said with ill-concealed anger in her voice, 'do you know what this is?'

Pravus was at the further door, the one leading out into the entrance hall. She turned slowly and looked at Woman. 'It's a gun,' she answered. 'I've pictures of them upstairs.'

'And do you know what it does?'

'It goes *bang*.'

'That's right, dear.' She aimed the weapon, only slightly conscious of the slight vibration in the magazine which fed up through the handle. But as she sighted along the barrel at Pravus' thighs, determined that her shot, if she had to fire, wouldn't kill her and ruin their years of work, the vibration grew stronger as the spring feeding the rounds struggled to expand.

At the top of the stairs Man started down, grasping the bannister-rail firmly to support himself. His chest ached and he'd begun to wonder if this was what a heart-attack felt like.

Pravus looked at the gun, then turned away and opened the door.

'Pravus! Stop!'

Woman's finger began to depress the trigger. It only took a three pound pull to fire. Not even as hard as squeezing the opener to take the top off a can of beans. The aim, just above the girl's right knee, was faultless.

The spring in the magazine forced its way upwards, distorting the bullets as they pressed against the bottom of the loading-gate, now sealed by the firing mechanism. The rounds became ovals as the brass jackets started to buckle and split and the lead bullets flattened against one another. When the primer in one of them finally detonated the pistol exploded into shards of flying, fractured metal, taking Woman's hand and most of her forearm off in a glistening red mist.

Half-way down the stairs Man heard the explosion. It wasn't a shot. It was *worse* than a shot. He struggled to hurry his pace.

Woman stared at her missing hand until the blood-spray reached her eyes and blinded her. She began to scream. Pravus looked at her dispassionately, then glanced towards the stairwell. With a cry Man stumbled and pitched down the last half-dozen steps head-first. When Pravus looked away, back into the room, her gaze rested on the open fire in the grate. A burning log slipped and rolled forward onto the carpet, setting it alight. Behind the rising flames Woman was still screaming, thrashing about blindly, her ruptured flesh spurting like a crimson laser-show.

The front door closed behind her and she walked out into the street. Robert March, Sales Executive for Trident Communications, was cutting through the back way towards an appointment to discuss new paging equipment for staff at the Edgware General Hospital. He saw the blonde girl, young and undeniably pretty despite a certain sharpness in her features, and stopped. Afterwards he tried to reason it out, but by then he'd missed the appointment and the sale was gone anyway.

Pravus opened the passenger door and sat down, her eyes luminous. March depressed the clutch and slid into first. 'Where to?' he asked her.

'Catford,' Pravus instructed him. March let up the clutch and his Cavalier moved off, back into the traffic. Somewhere behind them smoke was rising and an elderly lady with four cats was dialling 999.

It was shortly after twelve when March dropped her off at the end of Stanstead Road. She walked around for a while, then felt hungry and went along to a snack-bar and read the cellophane-covered Me '-n-' U. It surprised her that it didn't have wine on it, so she had coffee and two bacon sandwiches, picking the meat out and leaving the bread. Nobody asked her to pay, which was just as well as she didn't have any money. Not that she needed any money. There was very little that Pravus actually needed.

She began to understand this herself as she watched people Saturday afternoon shopping, struggling with their boxes and carrier-bags and wire supermarket trolleys. Pravus had learned about money in theory, and actually seen the theory put into practice in the restaurant the day before. Now she saw other people using it, exchanging it for packets and bundles, watching its alchemical trans-mutation into other forms and substances. At one point two men in rough clothes, smelling of beer, came out of a betting-shop with a wad of the stuff, riffling through the notes and handing them to one another as they staggered along the pavement laughing. The one in the donkey-jacket dropped a fiver. Neither of them noticed. Pravus picked it up and looked at it, turning it over to read the writing and look at the pictures on both sides. Then she threw it away.

When the shops closed and there was nothing more to see she walked around some more. It was starting to grow dark when she found Morley Gardens and made her way down past the parked cars. Most of the curtains in the houses were drawn now, with lights shining behind them. Occasionally, if Pravus looked too hard or too long, a bulb would pop and the room would grow dark, then loud with ineffectual curses. One house had left the curtains open and a man and woman sat staring at the flickering light of a TV. Their sofa was back against the opposite wall, but a child sitting nearer was badly cut when its screen exploded.

I used to need the words, she thought to herself. Now that I don't need the words any more I must be careful.

She found the house with death upstairs and knew her father had been there. For a while she stood outside, looking up at the room where the faceless woman lay, feeling the lingering echoes of her pain. When the fat man bumped into her she knew at once who he was, although she'd never seen him before or even heard his name. Man had been so wrong about her spying on Ennio. It simply wasn't necessary.

Pravus watched as he opened the door and went in. Lights came on and fell through the glass, lighting her up as she stood there. She must have been standing there for hours, just watching. That dark-dressed man with the shiny buttons and silly hat, and the crackling radio clipped to his jacket, had passed her twice, though she'd made sure he didn't notice.

The bedroom light came on. She felt the man's pain now. It wasn't the same as the traces of the woman's. It was more poignant, more involved with continuing to live. And there was something else in it as well, something that she'd never really thought about before. This man with his pain was afraid of her father, which was natural. But he hated him as well.

When the impressions stopped Pravus knew that it was time for her to go in. There were things that she had to do with this man, and the time had come for her to do them.

42

SHE FOUND JOSH still in his study, as if he hadn't moved all the time she'd been out. Andrea pecked his cheek and he looked up at her from where he was sitting, holding the hand she'd placed on his shoulder. He looked worried.

'Problems?' she asked, trying to sound really interested. It was too early to tell him about Tim and force a split. That had to wait a while longer.

He shrugged. 'Just business, Andy. Nothing that can't be sorted out.'

It didn't matter to her, whatever it was. JB Enterprises could sink whenever it had to. Her own funds were tied up, protected, and it would bloody well serve Josh right if he went broke. That'd teach him to fuck around when he was supposed to be working.

Andrea left him to it and made herself some coffee. There was so much she'd meant to say to Tim that she hadn't got round to, and it had left her a little cross with herself. Suddenly her life had so much going on in it, so different from a few days before when there had only been wine and videos and . . . yes, more than a trace of self-pity, if she was really honest. What with Tim, and Josh's adultery, and that trunk full of stuff she'd found in the outhouse.

And her grandfather's razor.

She vaguely remembered him losing it, or saying that he'd lost it, anyway. His stubbled face had come round the kitchen door (he always stropped and shaved in the kitchen – there was a hook screwed into the door-frame for him to hang his mirror on) and peered at her. He had other razors, though none of them had his initials on the handle, and he settled for one of those to scrape the bristles off that scraggy turkey-neck with the protruding adam's-apple he never sliced off.

'Yhu seen my razor, Andy?'

No, she hadn't seen his razor. What did he want to worry about his razor for anyway? There were more important things in the world right then. Like poor Pauline's death, or the finding of her dead at least.

Well, she'd seen his razor now. She'd found it in the box with the skull-mask. In the trunk with the robe and the rest of that horror-film junk out of her nightmares.

She didn't realise how firmly her fingers were twisted together until she reached for the coffee cup. When she'd drunk her coffee she'd go down to the vault and see if the razor had anything to say to her. It'd talked readily enough last night, so maybe today it would tell her how it came to be with the rubber mask.

Don't let Josh see it.

The thought hit her like a bullet. Christ, she'd been out all day with it lying around down there. And Josh here, knowing how to get into the vault. He did, sometimes. He'd leave her another video as a surprise. Something the shops didn't come up with, like *Snuff*. That one hadn't been the real thing, though. Just a lot of hoo-hah. A whole lot of fake hackings-up with the cast and credits edited out to make it look real.

She left the dirty cup where it was and went down to the cellar. The entrance to her hidden vault didn't look disturbed, but she went in to check anyway. Everything was exactly where she'd left it. Nothing had moved an inch. Not even grandfather's razor.

Have you come to see me, Andy? it asked her.

She stared at it, her mouth open and working. Not even her bedroom had gone so far as to call her Andy. The house was always more formal, sticking to Andrea or, if it was cross with her, Mrs Buchanan. But this strip of honed steel was different, addressing her intimately like a husband or a lover, as if it had known her for years.

Upstairs a phone rang briefly before Josh picked it up. It might be for me, Andrea thought. It might be Tim. Or that slob Gaunt.

'Stay there,' she told the razor firmly.

She closed the vault and hurried upstairs again. Josh was still in his study, sitting at his desk. The phone was back on the hook and his hand lay beside it, the fingers shaking slightly.

His face was ashen.

Andrea made her features a picture of concern. 'What's the matter?' she asked him.

He stared at her, his eyes slowly returning to focus, then forced a smile. It looked ghastly, painted on like Ronald McDonald's. She wondered if his nose was going to light up.

'Oh, an accident to a friend of mine. Nothing that you have to worry about.' The phrasing was stilted, clumsy. As artificial as the statement itself.

He stood up. 'I'm sorry,' he began. 'I know we were going to have a quiet evening, Andy. The two of us. But I have to go out for a while. Just a few hours . . .'

He kissed her like a man with his mind somewhere else, which he was at that moment. Then he went out through the kitchen towards the garage, only pausing to pick up a coat on the way. Within minutes Andrea heard the BMW take off down the gravel drive.

She made herself a risotto out of odd items in the fridge and settled down in front of the TV with a bottle of Vranac. The light outside the tall windows faded away as she toyed with the plate, picking out favoured morsels and ignoring the rest. Her limbs felt heavy and she wanted to go to sleep and wake up in a different world. Instead hooded figures marched in torchlit procession and cut-throat razors danced above unwilling flesh to the sound of an incomprehensible chant.

Ave Andrea, gratia plena, Dominus Inferi tecum . . .

A bell tolled in the background somewhere, gradually becoming louder and more insistent.

Like the one on the front door.

She was only half-awake when she shuffled off to answer it. Josh back? Forgot his keys? Uhh-oh, they were on the BMW's keyring. Then not Josh. Maybe a creature out of her dream come to bring her nightmares to life?

She opened the door and peered out into the porch. It was dark out there because she hadn't remembered to turn the light on before she'd settled down. Yet some of the light from the hall spilled out past her, touching the figures standing hand in hand.

Andrea knew both of them, though she was more than a little surprised at first to find them standing there together. The surprise passed quickly enough, and she stood back to let them enter.

Behind her the TV turned into snowstorm as BBC1 shut down for the night. She led the way through and switched it off, the perfect hostess. She poured wine and handed it to her visitors, smiling, laughing with delight. Finally unable to restrain herself any longer she wrapped her arms around the girl and hugged her close and tight. May Eve had come at last and for Andrea Buchanan reality had wavered.

'After all these years,' she whispered. Then, standing back but still holding the other's hands in her own: 'You've lost weight. But you don't look a day older . . .

'. . . Pauline . . .'

43

HE'D THOUGHT VERY strongly about waiting, but there was only a limited amount of time, or things to occupy that time, that Ennio was prepared to cope with once Margot was finally dead. And after he read the message in Margot's flesh Gaunt was going to be too scared to do much anyway. It was almost as good as being able to take care of him there and then.

While Pravus examined and discarded a fallen banknote Ennio was driving back to the house at Mill Hill, touching base at his Greek Street flat long enough to pick up a change of clothes. The afternoon was tiring towards evening when he approached the house. Or what remained of it.

For a moment he couldn't believe the smoking shell. A police car and two fire tenders were lingering outside it, and he decided to park further up the road and walk back to find out what had happened in his absence. Smoky black flecks lingered on the air, tainting it as he went up to the nearest fireman.

'Anyone hurt?' Ennio asked, trying to sound casual.

The fireman nodded under his helmet. 'Man and a woman. Both dead.'

'Hell,' Ennio breathed. Then: 'Good job there was no-one else in the house. There wasn't, was there?'

'No. Just those two. Bloody awful mess. Good job a neighbour called it in before it started on the rest of the block.'

'Yeah.'

One of the policemen noticed the conversation and came over. 'Did you know the people here?' he asked.

Ennio shook his head. No, he didn't know them. He was just passing by.

'Like everyone else,' the policeman muttered. 'Nobody seemed to know them. Not even the folks next door.'

Ennio walked back to his car and got in. He started the engine and moved off, parking again round the corner where he'd be less conspicuous to gather his thoughts.

Dead man and woman. No one else. That meant Pravus must still be alive. Only question now was where the fuck was the little cunt?

He found a pub and sat there over several drinks as it filled up with Saturday night revellers. Maybe he ought to get in contact with someone. Carole maybe. There was no way he'd find Pravus in London on his own. She could be anywhere . . .

His eyes narrowed over his gin and tonic. That wasn't strictly true. Whatever else she was, his daughter was a remarkable girl. She knew where she was supposed to be tomorrow night and something told Ennio that she'd be there. Wasn't that what all of her life so far had been about? Closing the blood circle?

Yeah, she'd be at Ringley Abbey okay. She'd be there waiting for him when he got there himself.

271

And the ritual?

He shrugged to himself. She'd taken him back through the years to it the night before. He realised that now. And she needed it to go right as much as he did. She'd help. She'd make sure it went off okay. Her juicy little pink bits were on the line as much as his own if it didn't.

And as for telling anybody about the house, that didn't matter. If they were all that good they'd know anyway by now. And if they weren't it was nothing to do with him.

He wasn't to know that Carole had caught a TV news and identified the smoking property in Mill Hill. Nor was he to know that she'd phoned the Magister Inferi and told him about it.

Yeah, Pravus would be there when he needed her. After what he'd seen, and felt, he was prepared to believe almost anything of her. No problem for someone like that to be in the right place at the right time. She'd already proven that once today by not being in the house when it went up.

It was all going to work out fine, he told himself. No shit. No worry.

Ennio Zabetti walked remarkably steadily, considering the amount of gin he'd taken in, to the blue Fiesta he'd parked away from the pub, and drove himself back to Greek Street for a relaxing night of particularly pleasant dreams.

44

CAROLE VANBRUGH POURED herself another coffee from the *la cafetière* she'd placed beside the bed. This time she decided to light a cigarette to go with it. Her eyes flashed across to the figure still sleeping beside her and she wondered whether or not to wake him up.

She decided to let him sleep on.

The emergency quorum, convened the night before, had made a detailed examination of the options facing the Sons of Samael as a result of the fire in Mill Hill. Personally she had her doubts about the course of action they'd decided on, but the majority, consisting of the Magister Inferi, Madonna and the other High Priest, had overruled them. Things were to stand as they had been previously agreed, with Carole taking charge of the support ritual and the main rite, starring the unknowing Andrea Buchanan, under the control of the Magister himself.

'And what about Ennio Zabetti?' she'd asked. 'Supposing he was the man killed in the fire?'

The Magister, unmasked amongst his trusted subordin-

ates, shook his head. 'Not Ennio,' he told them. 'He's too
. . . dexterous for that.'

'Then why hasn't he made contact?'

'Because he doesn't need to, and he knows it. He and
the girl will be at Ringley Abbey in time for tomorrow
night. He may even be there already. Still,' he considered,
'it won't hurt to ring his flat. Vera?'

The Madonna nodded and stood up. 'Use the phone,
Carole?' she asked.

'Go right ahead.' Then: 'You never did explain the girl,
Magister. It would help us to know what we're supporting.
I take it she's something more than some kid with a dirty
mind that's been pulled off the street?'

'You take it right,' the Magister agreed. 'Pravus is the
result of Ennio Zabetti's union with the granddaughter of
a Norfolk witch, nearly sixteen years ago. The child was
taken from its mother at birth and brought up according
to a strict regime. In total secrecy, I might add. Until a
few days ago she'd hardly been outside that house. And
until she was initiated the other night she didn't even
have a name. She was simply *Girl*, who lived with *Man*
and *Woman*.'

Vera came back from the phone. 'Ennio's back in Greek
Street,' she informed them.

'Did you speak to him?' Carole asked.

'No. I just let it ring and listened when he answered. It
was his voice, all right.'

The Magister patted her hand as she sat down again.
'Then all we have to worry about is Pravus. And we don't
really need to worry about her at all.'

Carole looked puzzled. 'A fifteen-year-old kid who's
hardly been out of the house in her life? She could be
anywhere, doing anything. *Telling* anybody.'

'No, not Pravus. She's been brought up to be dedicated

274

to her purpose. She has no knowledge of law and the only person she can identify by name is Ennio. If she was talking to the police Ennio would be in custody, which thanks to Vera's call we know he isn't. Don't worry about her. She'll be where she's supposed to be when she's supposed to be there. I'm certain of that.'

Paul Haighton-Jones, Carole's male counterpart, slim and fifties with grey flashes at his bushy temples, nodded his agreement. 'I'd be told if either of them had been picked up,' he agreed. 'But I think you're putting a great deal of faith behind the child, Magister.'

'Quite right, Paul. And that's because I've put a lot of work behind her. Pravus was born to be special. Tell me, what is the primary aim of the Sons of Samael?'

'To formulate the overthrow and replacement of the Enemy,' he shrugged. 'That's in the Black catechism. We've all been working towards it. You and I for the better part of twenty years, Magister.'

'Exactly, Superintendent. During that period we've sharpened our ritual skills within the group and our other skills outside it. A little acquisition here, a shade of subversion there and so on. But there is a problem with any group, Satanic, magical or what-have-you. Members are individuals. They come and go. They have differences. Sometimes they even behave like St Judas, though to our detriment. Like Ennio's father did when we wanted to co-opt his son.'

Carole agreed. 'I never did know why you wanted that creep in, Magister.'

'Because he is an unusual and very special person. Ennio Zabetti is completely and utterly without any normal feelings of guilt, remorse or pity. He would have made a magnificent Nazi. He's also as ambitious as he is ruthless, and I admit that it has been difficult keeping him in check over the years. Yet all of this has qualified him for his part in the Pravus project.'

'Which is?' the policeman asked.

The Magister Inferi sighed. 'I was going to announce it once it was successfully completed and under way, but you three might as well know now. Through the years we have welded the Sons of Samael into a sort of family. Now, though, we have the basis of an actual family within the brotherhood. Ennio and his daughter, Pravus. Bear with me for a while as I explore a little redundant mythology.

'Take a husband and wife, the basis of the Enemy's society. Let's say an older husband, called Joseph, and a younger wife, who for the sake of demonstration we'll call Mary. According to the myth Mary is made pregnant by the Enemy's agent. She gives birth to a child, in shitty surroundings, to which Joseph has to be content to be foster-father. The child grows up as the Enemy's representative and shapes the future history of this planet. Any problems so far? No?

'Then to continue. This so-called holy family has formed the basis of the Enemy's stranglehold upon man's natural instincts. It has throttled his development for two thousand years. Now, while this stranglehold has proven impossible to break by normal means, it must be remembered that it sprang from humble beginnings. It took years of work and a coven of disciples to put it on the map.'

'Hey,' Carole remarked, the fingers of one hand twisting in her loose red hair, 'you're putting Ennio up as Joseph in all this? And Pravus as Mary? Where does Andrea Buchanan come into it? Assuming you're going for an *unholy* family, that is.'

'That is. As you say. Joseph was foster-father, but Ennio will be father. Mary was mother, but Pravus will be foster-mother. All she can teach her foster-child will be what she has learned so far. And that is a total commitment to our Infernal Lord. Between that and Ennio's complete lack of morality the child will come closer to the Anti-Christ, with our support, than anyone or anything has done so far. And the family itself will eventually become the core of the brotherhood, collecting anti-disciples from our ranks. You see? We have parody and effect rolled into one devastating package.'

'Shades of *The Omen*,' Paul Haighton-Jones muttered.

'Better than that,' the Magister answered. 'The only supernatural forces are the undiscovered ones within ourselves, the ones repressed by the Enemy's shaping of our lives. Satan is our archetype and our inspiration, but to regard him as an objective reality is ludicrous. Even so, some people need the ludicrous in order to rationalise their behaviour and call it faith, and that's something we can turn to our advantage. With proper manipulation of the media over the next thirty years we can blow Christianity off the face of the earth once and for all.'

'And rule it ourselves,' Carole breathed. 'Jesus fucking Christ didn't have satellite TV behind him, otherwise he'd have been in total control by AD40. I have to admit, Magister, it makes a weird kind of sense . . .'

She crushed out her cigarette and thought back over the remainder of the meeting, which consisted mostly of an examination of the main and support rituals.

It was now almost eleven o'clock the following morning, and Carole decided to make fresh coffee before she woke her sleeping partner.

Her luxury apartment in Regent Villas, Chelsea, was in a modern, climate-controlled building. She didn't bother with even a wrap as she slid her legs off the bed and

277

wandered into the kitchen. Behind her she heard a movement of the sheets as the Magister began to wake up.

The Magister.

Carole smiled to herself. Somehow she never lost sight of his position, even though she called him by name when they were alone together like this. She filled the kettle and swilled the old grounds out of the coffee-maker before returning to see how awake he was. It was a matter of pride that her body would be the first thing he saw on that Sunday morning. Maybe it wasn't as young as it used to be, but it was still in bloody desirable shape. Besides, if her flesh could give her an edge it was worth showing it off.

Yes, he was starting to wake up, but he'd be a few more minutes yet if past experience was anything to go by. Carole padded back to the kitchen and finished making the coffee. Then she made up a tray and carried it through to the bedroom, setting it down on a bedside table.

Leaning over she took the drowsy Magister's face in her hands and slid her tongue into his mouth, feeling the gathering strength and wakefulness of his response. His eyes opened as they parted and he looked up at her, stretching and yawning.

'Unnh,' he grunted. 'What time is it, Carole?'

'Time for coffee, Josh. Oh, and about thirteen hours away from the conception of your pet Anti-Christ,' she added, grinning.

45

GAUNT'S DREAM OF a nightmare drive through the night with a flayed, animate Margot sitting beside him, persisted to the very moment he opened his eyes and sat up, rank with sweat.

In a strange bed.

He glanced wildly around himself, trying to take in both his dream and the new reality of his surroundings. His clothes lay across a chair close by, neatly folded in a way that he never bothered to do for himself. Above him the ceiling was lost in a perplexing arrangement of tangled wooden beams and supports. Of all the places he knew that could house a room like this there was only one that was relevant. He was in Ringley Abbey.

Then . . . the rest of it was real as well. Oh Christ!

Gaunt buried his face in his hands as realisation dawned. It was real, okay. All of it. Finding Margot's bloody corpse. The girl. The drive to Abbots Ringley. Even the way that Andrea Buchanan had greeted his companion like her long-dead schoolfriend.

All terrifyingly real.

He should have been with the police right now, telling them everything he knew. Including the Buchanan woman's connection with Pauline Stafford's death. They could be checking out her movements, seeing if she'd gone anywhere near Catford yesterday. Checking her alibi for a hole she could have killed Margot in. Not sleeping his knowledge away in the possible killer's spare bed.

But somehow it hadn't worked like that. He'd taken the comfort which that strange young girl had held out to him, burying his fury and his grief beneath her need to reach Ringley Abbey. In a way it even, in retrospect, fitted in with his own plans. Now he was here he could have a go at breaking Andrea Buchanan himself. Save the police more time and effort. And as the relict of one of the victims the publicity would be even greater for him.

What the fuck was he thinking? Margot's dead. *Dead.* And I'm sitting here working out everything I wanted while she was still alive. Put up for the night like some pissed guest at a party. I'll give her party. Just as soon as I'm dressed . . .

He ignored the soap and towel put out with his clothes and climbed into them as quickly as he could. Still fastening his belt and zip-fly, jacket hooked under one arm, tie loose at his collar, he burst out of the room and headed for the staircase.

'Mrs Buchanan,' he called, his voice echoing towards forever. 'Where are you? It's about bloody time we did some straight talking.'

Only the echoes came back as his answer. He reached the staircase and began to thud down it, heavy-footed.

'Andrea Buchanan,' he called again.

Still no answer.

He stormed through the great hall, pausing only to push open the doors to the adjoining rooms, slipping on his jacket and abandoning his tie. Outside full daylight showed through the high windows and he rapidly glanced at his watch.

Nearly one. He'd slept the clock round. With Margot dead.

What the hell was the rest of the world playing at?

Nobody around.

In the kitchen he found the back door locked from the inside. He decided to see over the rest of the house. There had to be somebody about somewhere, didn't there? Upstairs, maybe.

Gaunt was heading for the staircase again when he began to wonder about a cellar. Old heaps like this often had extensive crypts or dungeons and things. Maybe he was walking over everybody's heads without knowing it. He found the doorway easily enough and looked down the steps. Soon find out, he thought grimly.

Woman with a razor, maybe?

Gaunt shuddered and told himself to close off from that. There was an electric light burning down there, and he fancied he could hear somebody talking a long way off. Andrea Buchanan and the girl, perhaps. Now what the hell was her name?

Like a lamb to the slaughter, he thought, starting downwards. Or a lamb to do the slaughtering. They've fucked me about just *too* much. It's time for some answers and I'm bloody well going to get them.

He reached the bottom of the steps and looked around. Racks of wine, some odd boxes, and a set of shelves that didn't quite sit flush with the wall. And nothing on them.

That couldn't be right. Nobody left cellar shelves empty. Unless they weren't safe. Come to that these didn't look too good. Loose at one side from the way they're sitting.

He went over and shook them. They swung towards him. Beyond them a light was burning.

He stepped through.

The voices grew louder as he walked along the L-shaped corridor. The door at the other end was ajar, as the shelf door had been, and he paused to listen for a moment.

'. . . be needed to hold the torch. I shall give him the words as he has to say them.' That was the girl talking.

'The robe won't fit him, Pauline,' Mrs Buchanan replied with laughter in her voice. 'It's far too big. It'd look better on my husband.'

'Oh, he'll be here as well, Andy. There's a special place reserved for him.'

She must have gestured at that point because both of them laughed briefly. There was a quality in that laughter Leonard Gaunt didn't feel altogether happy with. It felt pervasive, numbing. He found himself wanting to share it without quite knowing why. Determined to confront them he strode forward, pushing into the vault.

Andrea was sitting in the chair at the centre with Pravus at her feet. Pravus' head was resting in Andrea's lap.

'Well well, look who's woken up at last,' Andrea announced, stroking Pauline's hair.

'Supposing I get some answers?' Gaunt demanded, stepping forward.

Pravus caught his eyes with her own and held them. He felt his anger and determination begin to drain away like used bathwater. 'You don't need any answers,' Pravus told him, her voice gentle and almost deferential.

282

She was right. She'd been right the night before so it was only proper that she should be right today as well. Gaunt's determined stride faltered and he slowed to a halt before them. The set lines of his face relaxed and a familiar relaxed glow spread through his limbs. He wondered briefly if it was okay to give in to it like this, whether he ought to fight it off. But that was nonsense when you were this comfortable. Besides, this gentle little girl could fry your head if you didn't do what she told you to.

'Set the things up, Lenny,' she instructed.

Was that her or Margot speaking? Not that it mattered to him. He'd have obeyed either one as readily when their voice held as much promise as this one did. This carrot had to be worth working for.

'Is there something you wanted to ask me, Mr Gaunt?' Andrea enquired. Pauline looked up at her and they both laughed again.

Gaunt thought for a moment. There had been, but it was gone now. Not that it had been important in the first place. He shook his head and began to arrange the candlesticks around the vault. Once that was finished he pushed the VCR and TV over to a side wall, clearing the centre of everything except the tin trunk and the chair which Andrea was occupying. He was about to close the trunk's open lid when Pravus signed for him to leave it open.

'Just like East Bilney,' Andrea whispered to her.

'It will be, when the time is right,' Pauline whispered back. 'And the time will be right very, very soon.'

'And Ennio will be here again.'

'But you'll be on top of the burial chamber this time.'

Andrea looked puzzled. 'Yes,' she sighed, 'I suppose I will.'

'You know you will. You've been looking forward to it ever since you saw *me* there.'

Andrea nodded. 'But where will you be, Pauline?'

'I'll be in your place,' Pravus answered. 'Sort of. Don't worry, Andy. It'll all come right.'

Of course it would. Nobody could doubt that any longer. It was all going to be just perfect.

Andrea stood up and helped Pauline to her feet. As soon as it had been vacated Gaunt moved the chair over beside the TV and the video. Then he stood back himself and surveyed his handiwork.

A place for everything and everything in its place. How nice.

Andrea took Pauline's hand and squeezed it affectionately. 'I'm so glad we're friends again,' she told her. 'Come on. Let's go back upstairs and wait. You too, Mr Gaunt,' she added, beckoning with her free hand. 'It won't be long now.'

46

TIM GARFIELD'S SATURDAY night had been okayish, no more. He'd spent it at a party at a friend's house, with a woman he liked and who also liked him. The only problem was that she didn't even slightly remind him of Andy, and Andy was the only person he was really thinking about just then.

They'd been back together twice now, and it looked set for a third time pretty soon. Now, with her those few years older, and him heading for success in his own right, they stood the best chance they'd ever have of making it work at last.

Great.

So why am I here with Ginny?

Getting drunk . . . er.

When he finally passed out he did it with style. Cardboard cup clenched in his teeth by the rim, arms outstretched, he managed to occupy most of the centre of a large room. Making *broom*ing noises helped the uneasiness of his stomach, though it did little for the remains of his head.

What the hell are you up to, Timmy?' somebody asked him. Was it Ginny? Might have been. Didn't matter anyway. Wasn't Andy.

'Conn . . . corde . . .' he announced from inside the cardboard. Then he pitched over flat, squashing the cup beneath his nose.

Like a good friend his host picked him up and put him to bed. In the morning he woke early and wished he hadn't. His head was distinctly elsewhere, except when it reminded him of its physical presence by proceeding to split wide open. Black coffee helped, together with the distant background mumblings of LBC, but the hand that held the cup was as unsteady as the ears that tried to listen.

He apologised for his behaviour quite profusely, to his host and especially to his host's lady. Towards mid-morning she sat him down and took his hand for the kind of gentle probing that any man's woman *friend* manages to do so well. Eventually he confessed.

'Andy's back in my life.'

His lips were too large for the words to come out properly, but she heard anyway and held his hand some more. Yes, this time it was the real thing. Oh, it had been before, yes, but it was even more real this time. Just as soon as she left Josh they'd get together, for ever. And ever.

Amen.

He stayed for lunch, which was naturally running late. Someone else had taken Ginny home and he was grateful for that. He didn't want to have to either explain the cause of his behaviour or lie about it to her. It was so much easier to pass out and say nothing.

Roast *pork*?

His stomach threatened to part company with him once and for all, but he struggled manfully through the meal and sat down with more coffee (A brandy? Sorry, Miles, I don't think so) afterwards. As people started to make noises about tea he decided it was time for him to go.

He still felt dreadful, but some people have a knack of pulling themselves together once they get behind the wheel of a car, no matter how bad they thought they were. The drive grew progressively easier, though it rained some of the way. Quite heavily in patches.

No worries there, though. His MGB stuck to the road like fleas to a dog. And with those nine-inch thick doors to either side anything that wanted to take a swipe at him would leave him completely unscathed. Safe as houses.

On the San Andreas fault.

He decided he wasn't going to go back to Kensington. It wasn't his brightest decision, but it was the only one he was capable of making at that time. No, all there was in Kensington was his austere and empty flat. No cheer. No comfort. No Andy.

But there was an Andy at Ringley Abbey. An Andy who probably wanted to see him as much as he wanted to see her. Maybe even more. And husband home or not he was bloody well going to see her. Even declare his love in front of Josh Buchanan if he had to. Sod all this fucking about. Let's get together and take things from there.

He headed west.

When the tanker ahead of him jack-knifed he slammed on the anchors with a force that threatened to send his foot and the pedal through the bulkhead. Everything on the MGB stopped, including the wheels. But the car kept going, skidding in a perfectly straight line towards the centre of the tank. Between the wheels. As the car slid underneath the top peeled off like a sardine can, windows crunching and shattering.

The remains of Tim Garfield's face still looked surprised when the emergency services found it, fifty yards back up the road.

47

ENNIO DIDN'T WORRY too much about finding Ringley Abbey. He looked up Abbots Ringley in a road atlas and decided he'd be there in plenty of time if he left about dusk. As for Pravus, she was probably there ahead of him. Either that or they'd find each other on the way.

Yeah, it didn't make sense to worry too much about it. Worrying didn't help and it could hinder your performance. Ennio didn't want his performance hindering. Not tonight. Not with Andrea Duncan after all these years.

It had to be more than good. It had to be perfect.

He found the village well before ten and stopped off at the Bell and Horns for a few gins. There was no indication of what might be waiting for him at the Abbey but he didn't phone ahead to find out. Besides, he thought, whatever it is it's going to be easy enough to take care of.

The knife in his pocket, still hungry, agreed.

At eight-fifteen Josh said goodbye to Carole Vanbrugh and they wished each other luck. For Carole, who still found herself unable to take the Pravus project seriously, there followed a period of stern self-admonishment. The Magister had placed her in charge of the Sons of Samael for this very important night, and she determined to take that responsibility seriously. There was always the chance that the girl *had* become something rather special, and if that really was the case then it was her duty to see things through to the best of her ability. Fuck things up and you don't win prizes. Not in the Sons of the Poison Angel.

At ten she took a cab across town to Clerkenwell, leaving it outside a publishing house on Clerkenwell Green. Making her way on foot from there she started down an alley beside a grocer's shop and unlocked a door in the wall which led down into the basement underneath. At the bottom of the steps was a small area with a door leading further in. Here she put down the case she'd brought and switched on a dim overhead light before unlocking this next door. Beyond it was a room with a few chairs and several pegs on the wall, some with robes hanging from them. Its overall appearance might have reminded a Christian observer of a church vestry. In the far wall yet another door led through to the ritual chamber of the brotherhood.

In the street above other figures came out of the shadows and the night and came down through the unlocked street entrance. Carole robed and went through to the ritual chamber, where she uncovered the stuffed Alsatian and checked that the censer was clean and prepared with fresh charcoal. The candles too would have to be replaced for this one.

More of the brethren arrived and began to gather in the changing room. Some smoked and chatted, the acrid smells of tobacco and cannabis hanging on the air. Others sat in silence, robed and waiting, the uncomfortable and depersonalising rubber skull-masks in their hands or resting on their laps. Slowly the talk began to fade away, and an expectant silence grew in its place.

Josh Buchanan reached Abbots Ringley shortly after Ennio. Like his subordinate he went into the pub, preferring to wait there until the last minute before driving up to Ringley Abbey. This was going to come as quite a shock to his spying little wife. But at least, after this, he'd have no trouble getting hold of her money as and when he needed it. And with that kind of capital at the service of the Sons of Samael his plans for the future of the order were completely and utterly assured.

He noticed Ennio sitting at a table near the bar, but didn't identify himself. Ennio in turn saw the big man coming in and felt that there was a familiar quality about him, and that he ought to know who he was. When the landlord greeted Josh with a hearty 'Evenin', Mr Buchanan,' Ennio held his glass a little tighter.

So this was Andrea Duncan's husband. Well, he'd cut up the same as all the others, the knife assured him. The bigger they are the more of them there is to stick. Or slash. Or slice.

And that's what he was going to do before the night was out.

Okay, so the Magister had told him not to go after the name Steffi Holt had given him before she died. But when that name belonged to a man who was likely to interfere with the most important ritual of your lifetime, there wasn't really any choice in the matter.

When he explained it like that the Magister would be bound to see that he was right.

Wouldn't he?

He finished his gin and left his future victim at the bar. It would give him a substantial advantage to arrive at Ringley

Abbey before Andrea's husband got back there, and he intended to make full use of that advantage. The gates at the bottom of the drive stood open when he reached them and he drove straight up, tripping the eye alarm. Outside the main entrance somebody had parked a battered Austin Allegro rather badly. Ennio hadn't seen Gaunt's car before, and figured it had to have something to do with Pravus' arrival. There was no way that the Magister would have driven anything like that.

Turning the Fiesta round before he left it, just in case he needed to get out of there in a hurry, he crunched across the gravel towards the double-arched porch and the oriel window rising above it. His eye caught a weathered corbel beneath an arched window to one side. It winked at him.

Ennio stepped into the lighted porch and decided to try the door-handle before he rang the bell. His fingers were reaching out to touch it when the door creaked slowly and invitingly inwards.

All on its own.

While Tim Garfield was being parted from his hangover for ever, Leonard Gaunt was sitting quietly in the great hall at Ringley Abbey, working his way through a bottle of one of Josh's best wines. In actuality it was one of the world's best wines, and the powerful claret was serving to numb his confused senses still further.

He finished the Château Latour and laid the bottle flat on the table in front of him, spinning it to see where it ended up pointing. It pointed at him. Directly at him.

'Fair 'nuff,' he mumbled.

What did you expect? the Abbey asked him.

True, he conceded. There wasn't anyone else in the hall with him for it to point to. The others were upstairs, doing things he'd only seen in dirty postcards. Things that Margot would never have done, anyway.

He leaned forward and placed a hand over his eyes in case he was going to cry. He wanted to cry so badly, to feel his eyes raw and aching with a wet, salt mixture of remorse and self-loathing. There was so much he could have been doing, should have been doing, to bring Margot's murderer to justice. So why the hell was he merely sitting here, waiting for God knows what, getting pissed out of his skull on *premier cru de Medoc*? And not even crying for them both?

Gaunt sighed and looked up towards the minstrel gallery. 'I did love you,' he said aloud. 'I do love you. So why can't I do anything? Why?'

Why does Andrea call the girl Pauline, Leonard? Pauline's dead, the house kept teasing.

Yeah. Pauline's dead. Dead, gone and rotted into nothing by now. Probably her baby is as well. Throat cut in some ghastly bloody ceremony . . .

He sat up. That could be the answer. If Mrs Buchanan called the girl Pauline it must be because she saw something of Pauline in her. And that could only mean that the kid was Pauline's baby, grown up some.

But that didn't get him anywhere either. What he needed was the child's father. Right there. Right then. Then he'd break out of this bloody lethargy and get some straight answers. With the girl and Andrea upstairs he was already beginning to feel more like his old self again.

He struggled to think back to what he'd heard in the vault, those snatches of conversation that had penetrated through his befuddlement. They'd mentioned someone called Ennio, who'd been on top of Pauline. And on top of the burial chamber.

That table-tomb at East Bilney.

Gaunt felt a new determination surging through him. It was all coming together. This Ennio character must be the man who'd got Pauline Stafford pregnant.

Coming here. Tonight. For some other unholy ritual.

That meant the black magic group that had killed Pauline was still active. It *had* to be connected to the murders. The coincidence was too strong, too damning to be ignored. If this Ennio wasn't doing the killing himself he'd most likely know who was. And to find Margot's killer Gaunt would chop his fingers off, joint by joint until he talked.

Nobody fucks with Sam Spade and gets away with it.

He stood up, rather unsteadily. What he needed now was some sharp instrument, to put it in copspeak, that he could do the chopping with. Kitchen. Always knives in a kitchen. Try the kitchen.

He tried the kitchen, and found a drawer-full of lethal-looking Sabatiers. Yippee. He could do the full *Psycho* number with any one of these.

Taking off his jacket he rolled up his left shirt-sleeve and tried shaving the hairs off his arm with two or three of them. Once he found the sharpest he rolled the sleeve back down and slipped it into his inside jacket pocket, puncturing the lining so that the blade passed down inside, leaving only the handle in the pocket proper.

Where he could grab it easily when he needed it.

Andrea stretched languidly on her bed and looked at Pauline, not a day older, her figure even younger than before she'd conceived her baby, and smiled, archly. If she'd been a cat she would have purred at that particular moment.

Pauline looked back through Pravus' eyes. Outside night had gathered its darkness around them. Some miles

294

distant Ennio Zabetti was through Slough and heading for Gerrards Cross and the Abbots Ringley turning. Andrea's husband, the Magister Inferi, was still working his way into Slough.

Downstairs the fat man sat waiting with a knife in his pocket. Pravus knew all about the knife. She'd been in its blade as his hairs clung to the metal, just as she was going to be in the door when Ennio arrived and reached for the handle.

She could be further away as well. As far as Clerkenwell. In a taxi on the Farringdon Road with Carole Vanbrugh.

'C'mon, Andy,' she prompted. 'Let's take a shower.'

Andrea sat up, then knelt on the bed. In the soft bedside light she looked almost as young as the girl who still lay there, looking up at her. The girl that Pauline Stafford had never grown past birthing.

'Great,' she replied, her voice girlish. 'A shower. Together.'

'Of course. Then you can find me a night-dress. Like the one you wore at East Bilney . . .'

'. . . And a carrier-bag. I mustn't forget the carrier-bag. You'll need it if you're going to pick herbs.' Her face suddenly fell. 'What are we going to do for herbs?' she asked, perplexed. 'There aren't any down here.'

'It doesn't matter. We can pretend there are. We'll have the table-tomb, and that's all we really need.'

They took their shower together, exploring one another beneath the raining water with that flagrant abuse of innocence which only the possession of innocence can bring. Andrea Buchanan wasn't Andrea Buchanan any more. She wasn't even the Andrea Duncan that the late Tim Garfield had known. She was the Andrea Duncan who picked herbs to make up the formulae in her grandmother's old book, the Andrea who lived on her grandfather Ted's farm at East Bilney. The only thing that mattered to her now was that she and Pauline were going to change places on top of the grave of Joshua Samson, deceased. That it was going to be her, not Pauline, that the fair young man with the handsome, wicked face was going to *do it* with.

Andy and Pauline dried one another off and went back into the bedroom to hunt out a suitable night-dress for Pauline to wear. Beneath them Leonard Gaunt brooded and waited, his heart sharp with the flint of vengeance. A few miles away Ennio was ordering a gin and tonic in the Bell and Horns.

'Come on,' Andrea said, taking Pauline's hand. 'Let's go down and find that carrier-bag. There's bound to be one in the kitchen.'

They came down the wide oak staircase together, Pravus floating in long flannelette, Andrea still quite naked. Gaunt looked up from his brooding in astonishment as they passed through the great hall, his mouth dropping in sheer amazement at the youth and beauty which had overtaken Mrs Buchanan. Why, she'd lost . . . fifteen years or so.

His eyes followed them into the kitchen and a pang clutched at his heart as he wondered if they'd gone there to count the knives. If they found one missing they'd immediately realise that he'd taken it, and they'd probably guess why as well. He was reassured when they came almost straight back, the girl in the night-dress now holding a plastic carrier-bag.

This was ridiculous, like something out of a surrealist painting. Let's get these two under control before this Ennio character arrives, he told himself.

He tried to stand up, but Pravus looked at him and he felt his mind changing. He tried to pull out the knife, but his hand wouldn't reach that far and he gave up.

'You can keep the knife if it makes you feel better,' Pravus told him. 'Shall we go down, now?'

Gaunt discovered that his legs were working again. Only problem was they were doing what they were told, not what he told them to. He stood up and followed the two girls down into the cellar.

Two girls? Both of them. Not a day over sixteen, either one.

Andrea left the vault entrance wide open as she went through. Pravus stopped at the shelves and turned to Gaunt. 'Take your clothes off,' she told him. 'There's a robe for you to wear inside. And bring the knife with you. You'll find it helpful, later on.'

He did as he was commanded. Stark naked, feeling old and fat and ridiculous in the presence of these tasty, deadly little morsels, with the Sabatier eight inch utility knife clutched in his right hand, he flopped along the L-shaped corridor into the vault.

Ennio peered around the door, one hand on the knife in his pocket. It could be out and open in a flick of the wrist if he needed it.

There was no one behind the door, and that made him feel uneasy. Doors shouldn't open by themselves like that. No sound of anyone running away after playing the joke. Nowhere for anyone to hide, either.

He shook his head to clear it of the tendrils burrowing into his brain, tendrils of doubt and uncertainty. And something else. Something he refused to admit might be fear.

He stepped wearily into the hall, suddenly drained and tired and old. He'd have to shake that off before he slid into Andrea Duncan. He'd never give her his best if he continued to feel like this.

No one in sight. No sound from anywhere. 'Pravus?' he called.

The door slammed shut behind him and he jumped and turned at the sound. 'Down here,' said his daughter's voice from somewhere beneath him. 'Come down, Ennio Zabetti.'

He thought for a moment. Yeah, that was Pravus all right. Funny how she wasn't calling him *father* any more.

'Which way's down?' he called back. The question struck him as ridiculous. Down was down. Where the fuck else was it likely to be?

'This way.'

He found the cellar entrance and went down the steps. Pravus stood waiting at the bottom. Except that she didn't look like Pravus any more. She looked more like the Andrea Duncan he remembered. How many sodding gins had he had?

She gave him his instructions and he obeyed them. With his clothes off and his knife in his right hand he entered the vault and looked around him.

Pauline. Andrea. Robed figure, though the robes didn't fit. Too short to be the Magister.

Ennio gestured with his knife. 'Who's this?' he demanded.

Pravus took his left hand and led him over towards Gaunt. She placed their left hands together as if they were shaking, and introduced them.

'Ennio Zabetti, this is Leonard Gaunt. The man the Magister told you to kill. Leonard Gaunt, this is Ennio Zabetti, the man who killed John Howard, Steffi Holt and your wife, Margot.'

They shook hands and smiled at one another, each still holding his knife. Their greeting was as cordial as if each had admired and wanted to meet the other for decades.

298

'Didn't he kill you as well, Pauline?' Gaunt asked Pravus, dispassionately.

They heard the alarm in the drive go off again. Pravus kissed Andrea lightly. 'All is about to become one,' she told her softly. 'The blood circle is closing.'

Josh fitted his key to the front door and opened it. Without bothering to check the ground floor he went upstairs and removed a suit-bag from the back of his wardrobe. Zipping it open he changed into his robe. It would make his entrance so much more tidy than if he went straight down to the vault and they had to hand the stuff from the trunk out to him. Besides, his goat-mask was up here as well.

Once suitably attired he took a can of lighter fuel from the cabinet in his bathroom. Probably everyone else had forgotten that the torch would need something soaking into it before it would burn properly. This might be his show, but he still had a responsibility for the minor details. Best to be prepared.

The entrance to the vault was open when he reached the cellar, as he had expected it would be. He walked along the L-shaped corridor and stood at its further end, surveying the scene before him.

Pravus in night-dress. Andrea naked. Ennio naked. Tin trunk to replace table-tomb. Candles burning. Censer censing. Good.

Now all it needed was himself to hold the torch and direct the ritual drama.

'Well done, Brother Ball-Phegor, Sister Pravus,' he congratulated them. Yes, well and bravely done. You've worked my little puzzle out to perfection, haven't you?

'And you, my dearest Andrea. Are you ready to take that role you've wanted for the past fifteen years at last?'

Andrea wiggled her hips and smiled at him invitingly. 'Not quite,' she answered.

That was his cue. Behind the Magister Gaunt raised the unlit torch and smashed it hard down onto Josh's goat-masked head.

Sister Hagiel led them into the ritual chamber below the grocer's shop in Clerkenwell. They followed her, masked, robed and hooded and took up the places assigned to them, waiting for the moment when their working was to begin.

Carole had timed it almost to perfection. Counting inwardly she had been measuring out the last two minutes between eleven o'clock and midnight, waiting for the exact time when May Eve would become the first of May. Her count had already topped the first sixty seconds and was now only a few digits from completing the second.

The only problem was that she didn't feel entirely herself.

The ritual chamber could do that to her, to all of them. No one was ever the person inside it that they were in the world outside. It both closed them in and opened them up, concentrating and expanding them at the same time. And rituals such as this one, based on the effects of sound vibrations on the psyche, were known to have quite dramatic effects upon the participants.

That wasn't it, though. Carole felt she was standing outside herself, watching herself obey the dictates of another. Dictates that were both unsensed and unknown to her conscious persona.

She began the chant.

Quautem, virius, ad in hastibus homec.

Vestis, qualibus, et ab horridus graumec . . .

The others took it up. The Madonna placed incense in the glowing depths of the thurible.

Maugam, tassigus, os har demandius mordec . . .

The walls began to hum with the sounds. They echoed back to the chanting brethren, joining with them and reaching out into the night beyond.

'A little more,' Andrea instructed. 'He's not fitting in there properly yet. Cut some more off.'

They'd already broken one of Josh's legs in an effort to get the lid of the trunk down on top of him. He was a big man and he wasn't fitting its confines particularly well. The pain had brought him back to consciousness and his screams were echoing off the vaulting while Pravus chanted.

Maugam, tassigus, os har demandius mordec . . .

'In Satan's Name!' he howled. 'Ennio. Ennio!'

'Ennio was prying at the ankle-bones of the protruding leg. With the foot off it should go in more easily.

'*I'm the Magister!*'

Blood was painting Ennio's nakedness a glistening brown. Gaunt held the torch, still unlit, across Josh's throat, choking him back whenever he attempted to rise.

His eyes sought Andrea's, imploring through their agony.

She smiled back at her husband. 'We can't get the lid on 'til you fit,' she comforted.

His arms reached up, fingers hooked, clawing at Gaunt's ample robe. His leg thrashed wildly in Ennio's grasp, the foot hanging loosely from an unsevered tendon, spurting and reeking. Gaunt smashed one arm just above the elbow with the stock-end of the torch but the other hand persisted, working desperately for his throat.

Ennio finished cutting the foot off and dropped it into the trunk with the other pieces. He grasped the leg and forced it in, bare bone scraping on the rusty metal. Josh began to spasm violently, twitching and shaking until the trunk vibrated and Gaunt's jowls shook above his failing clutch.

'*Andreaaa*. . .'

'You see, Pauline remembered the detail that all of us had forgotten,' she began to explain to him. 'That small thing which we had to get right before we could start the ritual . . .'

The broken arm wasn't going to give him any more trouble, so Gaunt took hold of the clutching hand and began to double the fingers over, breaking them one by one.

'Andy . . .' Josh called, his voice failing, his throat scraped sore by the screams they'd already ignored. 'Andeee . . .'

Faugas, massius, in vos cavaribus laudec . . . ¬

Like the clacking of a bone-bag on a string.

Next Gaunt broke the wrist. Josh howled again.

'Better have his tongue out,' Ennio grunted, more to himself than anyone else. 'He's disturbing the vibrations of the chant.' He used the point of his knife against the palate to force Josh's mouth open and hold it until he could seize the tongue. The muscle was tough and the knife was starting to blunt by then. It took three hard cuts before it came away. Josh coughed and gurgled. His chest heaved and his torso forced up out of the trunk. Gaunt placed the remains of the arm, wrist and fingers stuck in painful and unnatural attitudes, against the edge of the trunk and smashed down on it with the torch.

Josh shrieked and twisted. Ennio stood clear as Gaunt took hold of the lid and slammed it down. It smashed Josh's nose before it bounced back up again.

'It was the inscription on the tombstone,' Andrea continued to explain. 'Your name, Josh. Joshua Samson. Joshua, Son of Sam. Or Son of Samael . . .'

Ennio shook his head and looked at the skull-masked Gaunt. 'We'll have to have his head off,' he said, wearily. 'We'll never get him in while he's still got his head on.'

Ennio stepped around the trunk and reached down for Josh's hair. Pushing Josh's head forward, forcing the bloody mouth and chin down onto the chest, he began sawing at the back of the neck. Very little blood flowed and, after a few seconds, the head went limply to one side with a sharp crack.

Gaunt's skull-mask nodded. His robe was blood-splashed, hanging damply. As he lit the torch he said: 'That'll do it.'

Josh wasn't dead. He was dying and parts of him were still conscious enough to know it. The damage to his spinal column was making him twitch and flop uncontrollably, a thousand raw nerves shrieking in complaint with every involuntary spasm. When they put the lid of the tin trunk down on top of him he contined to bump around in the metallic darkness.

Pravus had stopped chanting at Ringley Abbey, though she contined as Carole in the basement in Clerkenwell. Andrea wiped splashes of Josh's blood away with her hands and looked at her dead school-friend. Pauline stood there in her night-dress, plastic carrier in hand.

Andrea Buchanan mounted the burial-chamber of Joshua Samson and felt its metal hard and cold, and moist in places, against her bare back. Beyond her Leonard Gaunt took up the chanting Pravus had relinquished and held the burning torch up to the vaulting.

Ennio Zabetti threw away his knife and approached her as she lay there, waiting for him. His body was wet with her husband's blood. More than that, it was wet with the blood of the Magister Inferi, the life-force of the coven-head. His eyes glistened in the torchlight as he surveyed Andrea's unnaturally young body, lingering on her breasts before progressing down to the mons veneris, where a trickle of red clung in droplets to the tangled hair.

As he moved towards her he felt his body thrill in a way that was more than purely sexual. It was as if the Devil himself had stepped into his physical frame for these precious, long-awaited moments that were to come. Far from being tired by his exertions with the struggling Josh he was tingling with energy, his limbs more powerful, his stand much harder, than he could ever recall before. He wanted her, needed her, had to have her.

'Are you there, Pauline?' Andrea whispered.

'I'm here, Andy,' Pravus assured her. 'I shall always be here, I and my father.'

Ennio wasn't listening. He was stepping forward, parting Andrea's thighs for the first of several ecstatic thrusts.

'Yessss,' Carole hissed.

Paul Haighton-Jones, Brother Asmodeus, echoed her. 'Yes.'

The brethren took it up, their chant unknowingly timed to Ennio Zabetti's thrusts.

'Yes!'

He fell back, exhausted, spent. His buttocks thudded down onto the bloodstained carpet beside the trunk. Atop its lid Andrea Buchanan was moaning with delight at the life he had pumped into her womb. She had no doubt in her mind. No doubt at all.

She was pregnant.

Ennio looked around through weary eyes. Leonard Gaunt had slipped back the cowl on his robe and pulled off the sweaty rubber mask. Inside the trunk the last of the thumping had coincided with his climax. If Josh Buchanan wasn't dead he was at least immobile.

Ennio turned his head to look at his daughter. Pravus was smiling sadly at him, her eyes almost pitying. He followed her gaze as it moved towards Gaunt, who still held the torch in one hand but had replaced the skull mask in the other with the gleaming length of the Sabatier.

'My Father rewards his servants, Lenny,' Pravus said. 'This man killed your Margot. Now, by my Father's grace, he is here before you. He is naked, exhausted and unarmed.

'The rest is up to you.'

Ennio heard the words as they were spoken, but only began to understand them once they had ended. He scrambled to his feet, his eyes looking wildly across the carpet for his butterfly knife.

It had disappeared.

He glared at Pravus as Gaunt started mechanically towards him. 'You stupid little cunt!' he yelled. 'I'm your father! Me!'

He raised his arm to fend off the first slash. Gaunt followed through with his other hand and the torch struck the side of Ennio's head, setting his long hair afire. As he screamed and started beating wildly at his head the knife came down again, skewering his right thigh. Gaunt pulled it free and jammed the torch into Ennio's stomach, holding it there as he forced the killer back against the wall of the vault. Ennio felt himself begin to gag on the smoke and smell of his own flesh burning.

Not for long.

Gaunt stood there, pressing him squirming against the stonework. With both arms outstretched like a demented and murderous crucifix. The hand holding the torch was at arm's length. So was the other one, still holding the kitchen knife. In one continous arc, turning on his own axis, howling wildly with delight, Leonard Gaunt spun the torch away and replaced it with the knife, slashing across the charred and blistered stomach, severing the muscles that held the entrails in place.

Ennio's hands sprung pressing to the wound. For a moment they held there, blood rilling through the clutching fingers. As the first pinkish-grey loop pushed outwards his eyes sought Pravus, asking the question he was too shocked by the nearness of his death to speak.

'The Father of Lies,' she whispered, pouting at him.

He dropped to his knees as the intestines erupted outwards. His eyes glazed and his vision went before his brain stopped working. With every laboured, desperate breath more of his entrails pushed out through his fingers.

Ennio Zabetti was still trying to understand her when the demonic mouth opened, and her father welcomed him to Hell.

Time will be

48

LENNY AND PAULINE came to see her regularly through the next few months. Gaunt had a few difficulties explaining Margot's death away to the police, but eventually they were forced to concede that he *had* been in Norfolk at the time of her death. Even if he hadn't been, Brother Asmodeus would have found a way to pull him out of the sticky.

Carole Vanbrugh was a regular visitor to Ringley Abbey as well. It was she who arranged the private facilities for the last few days of Andrea's pregnancy, including the consultant gynaecologist who eventually delivered the baby.

On January 16th following that May Eve a boy, Samuel Joshua Buchanan, was born to Andrea Buchanan, nee Duncan, of Ringley Abbey, Buckinghamshire. The child was premature but very strong, and arrangements were immediately made for its education. It had fair hair and the bluest eyes that the nursing staff had ever seen. And three teeth, all of them canines.

Andrea returned home with her son three days later. Her husband's disappearance was still a talking point in some circles, but JB Enterprises had gone into voluntary liquidation shortly afterwards and it was assumed that he'd anticipated its failure and made off with what he could.

Carole Vanbrugh took over as Magister Inferi of the Porta Inferi coven of the Sons of Samael, though she never felt she was more than nominally in charge of its workings. Though she had tried to resist, Pravus had made a meteoric rise through its ranks to take over her place as High Priestess, and all quorums somehow fell under the teenager's influence.

Leonard Gaunt and some carefully chosen help cleaned out and refurbished the vault at Ringley Abbey. It was refitted and the basement in Clerkenwell abandoned. That had been Josh's eventual intention all along, and it was a good thing to do in his memory. It was also practical, as house-parties at the Abbey aroused much less attention than might have been the case if the brotherhood's base had remained in Clerkenwell.

Ennio Zabetti wasn't missed, and the *face-murders*, as the press came to call them, remain as unsolved as the activities of Jack the Ripper. Another of the brethren took over the lease of his flat in Greek Street and is there still.

Sister Melek-Taus was installed at Ringley as little Samuel's nanny. She was a qualified midwife and the ideal person for the job. She'd already been moved in when Andrea returned from hospital with the boy.

Andrea's commitment to her son, and to the circumstances surrounding his conception, was total. Before her confinement she made a new will naming Carole Vanbrugh and Paul Haighton-Jones as joint guardians, and leaving

310

her entire estate to the child. It was a comparatively small detail, but it saved the Sons of Samael a possible legal wrangle later.

With Margot dead Gaunt liquidated Factfinders and became chauffeur/handyman to the Buchanan estate. His initiation into the Sons of Samael was encouraged and passed through unopposed. Carole found him 'sort of cuddly', much to everyone's surprise, and quickly succeeded in transmuting Margot into a dim and unpleasant memory of a former lifetime. Today he is one of the brotherhood's most active members.

It fell to him to drive Andrea and baby Samuel back to Ringley Abbey. Unlike many children of the brotherhood his birth was legally registered, though the exact spelling of his name on the birth certificate is *Samael*. Registrars sometimes make mistakes like that, and at least one Brian is still alive whose name is actually *Brain*. Mother and son arrived home on January 20th. Son was immediately whisked off by Melek-Taus to the nursery, and his mother put to bed in her old room, the corbel on the wall outside being left to keep an eye on her.

The following morning Pravus called to see her dead mother's old schoolfriend. She brought two things with her. One was a bouquet of imported roses that the nanny arranged in a cut-glass vase beside Andrea's bed. The other was an old-fashioned cut-throat razor with the initials E.J.P. on the handle.

Andrea was drowsy, only half-awake, when Pravus came into her room. She opened her eyes and smiled at Pauline, reaching out a languid hand to hold her friend's.

'Have you seen my lovely son?' she asked, the words almost a sigh.

The medication was working. She wouldn't feel too much. Just enough.

'He's beautiful, Andy,' Pauline told her. 'Everything he should be and more. We're very lucky.'

'Mmm,' Andrea agreed. She didn't dispute the *we*. She was so lucky to have Pauline back with her. And such a wonderful and important baby as well. At times she regretted that it hadn't been Tim Garfield's. He'd been really inconsiderate, getting himself killed like that just when they were about to come back together. It didn't matter, though. Not with friends like Pauline all around her.

'Pauline?'

'Yes, Andy?'

'Are you going to stay with me?'

'Yes, Andy.'

'No, I mean, for ever? Are you always going to be with me now?'

'Is that what you want?'

Andrea nodded drowsily. 'Oh yes,' she answered.

'Then I'll be with you for the rest of your life.'

A kiss floated up from the pillows towards Pravus. 'Then you've forgiven me?' Andrea asked her.

Pravus nodded. 'I've forgiven you, Andy. You shouldn't have done it, but it *was* a long time ago.'

Andrea felt the tears begin to gather at the corners of her eyes. 'It was,' she said. 'Oh yes, it was. But you *have* forgiven me, haven't you, Pauline?'

'Yes. You're forgiven. There's just one thing, though, Andy.'

The tears were flowing now, tears of friendship and relief. Andrea struggled to look at her friend through them.

'Anything,' she said. 'Anything you want.'

'I want my face back, Andy,' Pravus told her.

That was when grandfather's razor went *snick-snack*.

312